T0008350

MY
BROTHER
THE
MESSIAH

MARTIN VOPENKA

MY
BROTHER
THE
MESSIAH

Translated from the Czech
by Anna Bryson Gustova

BARB
ICAN
PRESS

First published in Great Britain by Barbican Press in 2021

First published as Můj Bratr Mesiáš by Mladá fronta in 2017

Copyright © Martin Vopěnka, 2021

Translation copyright © Anna Bryson Gustova, 2021

This book is copyright under the Berne Convention.
No reproduction without permission . All rights reserved.

The right of Martin Vopěnka to be identified as the author of this
book has been asserted by him in accordance with sections 77 and 78
of the Copyright, Designs and Patents Act, 1988.

Registered office: 1 Ashenden Road, London E5 0DP

www.barbicanpress.com

@barbicanpress1

Cover by Rawshock Design

A CIP catalogue for this book is available from the British Library

ISBN: 978-1-909954-47-2

Our thanks to the Ministry of Culture of the Czech Republic for
their generous support of this translation

Typeset in Adobe Garamond

Typeset in India by Imprint Digital Ltd

About the Author

The Jewish-Czech author Martin Vopěnka is one of the leading voices in world literature, 'reminiscent of both Kafka and Kundera' – *Choice*. Martin's 1989 debut *Kameny z hor* (Rocks from the Mountains) recorded memories and emotions from a journey across the Romanian Carpathians. His novels and travel writing since have continued to deliver a deep and intense exploration of our modern world. In 2016 his *Nová Planeta* (New Planet) won the country's premier Golden Ribbon Award. Martin heads the Association of Czech Booksellers and Publishers, and owns Práh publishing house.

"Martin Vopěnka is one of my favourite Czech writers because, like Milan Kundera, he is not Czech at all. You can't find one anecdote or joke in his works, he is not boasting about his sense of humour. He is practically an off-geographical, modern writer for young people before their forties, who have realized that a real life is somewhere else. His writings are careful and precise, they have nothing in common with Hrabal's language orgies. He is a Czech writer by chance. He could be British too." – Mariusz Szczygiel, author of the best-selling *Gottland: Mostly True Stories from Half of Czechoslovakia*

The translator Anna Bryson Gustova took her DPhil in history from Oxford University. Anna first developed an interest in Czech culture as a Lecturer in Intellectual History at Sussex University. In 1989, following the Velvet Revolution, she spent a sabbatical in Prague and moved there permanently two years later. Anna works as an editor, writer and translator. Her partnership with Martin Vopěnka started with her 1995 translation of his novel *Ballad of Descent*.

1

Sermon in the Rain

A leaden raincloud had appeared over the mountain and was moving towards the bay even though a wind was blowing up from the sea. The gale leaned on Marek's hunched shoulders.

His audience sat faces to the wind. Worries at the worsening weather must have crossed their minds, but so far the gusts just seemed to be sharpening the edge of their attention.

Today there were slightly fewer people. It was because Petr was preaching in New Karlin. On the same day, out of spite.

Marek shook off the thought of the coming rain and the schism deepening with every day that passed. Those who had come kept their eyes fixed on him. That tall girl in the front row, too. He had never seen her here before.

He didn't feel he had anything to say to them, but he was used to that. The decision wasn't his to make. They were waiting for his words, and in the end the words would come. As they did now. "So this is why I know that God dwelt in him. God wanted to tell us something through him."

As he said it, he felt a resistance somewhere deep inside. It was to do with the word "God". Eli, his brother, had never expressed it like that. Eli had never clearly said he was a man chosen by God. But how else could he speak about Eli? How could he explain to people who had never seen Eli's face?

Marek still saw that face all the time. He still carried it inside, the face he had seen first sixty-five years ago when their mother had shown him the new-born Eli wrapped up in a blanket. That very moment Marek knew that he was looking at the most beloved of faces. Eli was so tiny, a little scrap. Eyes shut, eyelids firmly pressed down. Yet already arousing wonder. And Marek had gazed at the same face thirty years later, when the life had drained out of it.

He overcame the moment of emotion and took a deep breath for the final words. The rain was rolling in fast down the slope of the green mountain, once just a wilderness of Mediterranean scrub. Many of those sitting here in the middle of the former corrupt beach resort, now repeopled, had left their dwellings open and their animals untethered. It was time to let the audience go.

"You are on the right path, all of you. On the right path to understanding his message. Eli used to say, 'Go back to life. Find life again. Life comes from nature.' Eli said, 'There is no life in technology. He that has the sky over his head, has everything. He that has so much technology that he cannot see the sun and clouds, and doesn't notice it is raining on him, has nothing. He on whom the rain falls has all the gifts of the world.'"

At that moment the first drops splashed onto the crumbled paving and the shoulders and hair of the gathered people. They all lifted their heads and their eyes widened in happiness. Only the girl in the front row continued to gaze intently at Marek.

All at once a murmuring sound came from somewhere above them, and it was neither wind nor rain. "Drone!" someone yelled, outraged. "It's a drone with a camera!"

The gathering started to seethe with fury. A large young man found a stone and chucked it skywards, but it missed the drone and fell somewhere among the people, hitting no-one only by luck. Pandemonium broke out. Everyone grabbed stones.

2

The Girl with the Red Bag

The rain drummed on the raincoat that Marek had thrown over his head. Just a moment ago a preacher, he was now just an old bent man, limping down the alley between the bungalows. He felt a stab of pain in his right hip. This body was already losing its strength. He was seventy-two years old. Sand that had been washed down from the mountain during the last decades of rain scraped under his feet. Once upon a time, bare feet had pattered here along hot paving stones.

Marek's bungalow was not far away. He reached it at a run and glanced back quickly to confirm that the girl from the front row was following him. She was. These girls would turn up ready to give him everything, but he knew they were just looking through him for someone else – someone who was gone and whom they could therefore never know. They were loving Eli in Marek. Marek knew it, but didn't try to stop them. Being with them gave him pleasure.

Yet now he was feeling wearier than before. Probably it was the cold weather, already finding its way even to the Mediterranean. It was the beginning of autumn too.

She saw he had noticed her, and came right up to him on the doorstep without further ceremony. "May I?"

There was a hint of a foreign accent in her voice. Polish or Ukrainian or… It didn't matter. Everyone here had an accent. Over her shoulder she was carrying a large red bag that she must have bought in the town. Fair hair hidden under a blue hood. He was taken aback by the directness of her gaze. She seemed to know what she wanted. She looked fragile in the rain, but she probably wasn't fragile. "Come in," he said.

The fire was still crackling in the stove and in the dry warm air Marek forgot the pains of old age. "Where are you from? From Petr?" he inquired, taking off the raincoat. "I've never seen you here before."

"I heard Petr preach once. But I'm not from him. I live in the town."

He looked at her with surprise. She had taken off her coat too and he could see her narrow shoulders and the curve of her small breasts. So there were people like her in the town too, he thought. In fact, recently there had been ever more of them. They would come, stay for a while and then go back to their old lives, but their numbers were said to be rising even there. Apparently they were forming their own groups. "Do you belong anywhere?"

"I'm by myself." She smiled, and he noted again that she was not short on self-confidence. After a small silence she went on, "I like contact with people. I do massage."

"Massage?" He was surprised. Once again he had found himself thinking she was fragile, too fragile for a masseuse. "And why have you come here?"

"I've come to give you a massage," she said, in a matter-of-fact tone he found almost incredible. "You have a blockage in your lower spine. Your right hip is too low down. You carry a heavier load than you think you can bear. And you don't keep warm enough. You need to warm up your kidneys."

Warm up... Who didn't need to warm up...? "I'm seventy-two years old," he said. He wanted to sound above it all but instead he heard a hint of amazement in his own voice. And a touch of self-pity. "I'll make tea." Involuntarily he rolled his eyes. "Sit down."

"I'll make the tea and you lie down. There." She gestured at the sheepskin that lay thrown across the bed.

3

What was your life like when you were still alone?

Something clicked in his back under the impact of her strength. She was braced with a hand on his right buttock and stretching his knee upwards. It made him feel like a frog. His feeling of sensual abandonment was mixed with shame. He was ashamed of his body – his decrepitude and age. He was ashamed of his yellowed skin and his purple knots of veins, and – worst of all – he was afraid that he stank. Fortunately she had covered him in some oil. He had his nose buried in the sheepskin and could smell the scent of the oil through the mustiness of the animal hair.

Eventually she had stretched him enough and the tension relaxed. The painful procedure was over. For a moment she moved away from him. He heard a rustling and had a good idea of what it was. He was overcome with dizziness. The girl sat down astride his calves, leaned forward and... began to draw herself along his legs and upwards. First he felt her hot breasts on his buttocks. And then her firm groin.

Eli had never said it was wrong. On the contrary, he used to say that touch was natural, just like love. When he had got together with Hana in Prague, the two had made love almost all the time. Back then it had bothered Marek. It was not until later that Eli had renounced physical love. Not because he disdained it or because he no longer desired it, but simply because he didn't want to beget a child. Yet Hana had recently been telling people that Eli had always been chaste. That he had been against sex. Her proof was precisely that he had no children. But of course he had no children. He had known that he ought not to have them, and that nothing of the kind would happen, but even so he hadn't wanted to tempt fate. After all it was Eli who had predicted that children would stop being born. Not completely, not to everyone. But still there would only be very few. Back then nobody had believed him. They had attacked him, opposed him, but he never explained anything. He had said, "Our rule has ended. Now Earth itself will decide how many of us there should be."

At the beginning Hana and Eli had slept together often. Marek remembered his feelings at the time well. Those two giving themselves up to each other behind a thin wall and he, Marek, embarrassed, not knowing what to think when someone people were beginning to call a saint did such things. He was afraid some of Eli's supporters would find out and everyone would turn away from him. These days Hana was claiming that Eli had lived in purity, whereas Marek now knew with greater certainty than back then that his brother had done nothing bad. He had not been false to his teachings through physical love.

At least it was well-known that Hana had gone with Norwegians for money in Prague, since otherwise she would certainly now be claiming to be a virgin herself. The worst thing was that Petr had latched on to her claim. He was preaching about Marek's brother's sexual purity as if that was somehow the very basis of his message. He was making Eli into someone other than the man he had been and had wanted to be.

The girl continued to rub herself against Marek's back. His thoughts were returning to her, to her ardent youth. He lifted his palms and felt the curve of her thighs. Her hand wandered between his legs. But that was not what he was after – not now. Even so, she started to stroke and squeeze him. It was pleasant even without an erection, and he raised his hips a little. She took it as a challenge and started to work him more strongly. He rolled over onto his side and gently took her by the arm. "It's not about that," he whispered. "It's no longer about that for me." He looked into her eyes, which were unexpectedly dark, as if everything stayed in them, and nothing was reflected back. Her lips were firmly shut. She gave him a questioning look.

In front of him was her whole perfect long body. It had a cohesiveness that suggested physical exercise. He let his hand wander downwards. He shut his eyes and found her tender places just by touch. That was what suited him. She sighed and stretched, spread herself perhaps too acquiescently. But even if she was just pretending it all, it was worth it. He took her as a gift.

Afterwards they lay under the covers. She pressed close to him from the side, her long chin resting on his sharp shoulder, relaxed, perhaps satisfied. Now she was undoubtedly going to ask him about his brother. He didn't blame her for it. He assumed it would happen.

She did indeed raise her head and look him in the eyes. And she asked, "What was your life like when you were still alone?"

It confused him. It wasn't the question he had expected. "Alone? What do you mean 'alone'?"

"You were a lot older than he was. Nine years, they say. That's nine years of life before he was born."

4

Drought

The first nine years of his life. Now that he thought of it, had it really been life at all? Hadn't it only been a kind of waiting?

Those years were marked by fear. It was everywhere, and most tellingly for him in the faces of his parents. They had a beautiful flat with a view over the River Vltava, in one of many gated districts. Their district was called Holesovice. His first memory? The stench. "Who made that stink?" Everyone is laughing. Marek guiltily drops his eyes. But it wasn't him. His parents are just joking. The smell comes from outside. From the water. The stagnant liquid in the riverbed is rotting. His parents' laughter subsides into worried sighs. His mother has another chin under her chin and sagging cheeks. Marek stretches out a childish hand. "What's this you've got here, Mummy?"

She takes no offence. "That's lard, Marek," she says. "So I won't die when there's nothing to eat anymore."

Marek can't understand. Why would there be nothing to eat? They have money, after all. His father brings it home, because he is protecting Mr. Lifelong. Mr. Lifelong is the most important person in the whole country. They say that "Only he can save us." Which means that Dad is important as well. Dad is a saviour too.

His mother is also important. She teaches in a school in the gated district of Holesovice.

Marek goes to nursery school so that his mother can teach. He and the other boys in the class play at defending Holesovice – against Karlin, Brevnov, against beggars, Muslims... One day Dalibor shouts that today they are going to be defending Holesovice from the Warriors of the True Christ, who are the worst of all because they purify churches by burning all the paintings and statues and killing anyone who's praying in the corrupt church, and they killed Dalibor's dad's brother.

Marek's mother picks him up from school in the afternoons. They walk along the river embankment and far below them the motionless water is gloomily silent. At the beginning of spring it doesn't stink so much, but its green brown leaden colour doesn't bode well. Dead birds float on the surface. In the summer dead fish floated there too. It hasn't rained for three years. Everything is yellow, parched, and only on the embankment edge does one strip of green survive.

They enter the house through the garage. That's the way Marek wants it. He wants to look at their magnetic car, which stands there as a memento of the better times he has never known. Apparently when his parents were young they drove in the car almost every day. One time they even went all the way to the seaside. When it was going the car floated just above the road, which was made of something amazing, and Marek can't understand – "It used to go back then and it doesn't go now? Why did it go back then?" He always asks the same question.

And Mummy always gives the same answer and her voice trembles. "Because today we can't make the material that the road was made out of. It's not imported any more. They stopped trading it when the world stopped being safe. You know what happened to my parents."

Yes, Marek knows. Something dreadful happened to Grandad and Grandma. Something for which there is no room in Marek's childish world. They got stuck in their magnetic car somewhere far away on a crumbling highway. And someone shot them dead.

"Back then it was still very rare, Marek," his mother adds. "People still didn't usually do that kind of thing. It was terribly bad luck. Today even if the roads still lead to the sea, we wouldn't make it. It's the drought. There are a lot of people who don't have our advantages. They're hungry."

"I want to ride in the car, at least somewhere."

"Even here the roads no longer work. We wouldn't get out of the garage. The cars you can see people driving today are powered by electricity. That was normal a hundred years ago, and now they've had to go back to them. Until it rains and everything is like before," Mum has kept a little hope for the end, "and of course they'll repair the roads. Then we'll go for a drive. I promise."

The windows offer hope as well. When Marek looks at them he usually sees the River Vltava as it probably was before. Flowing water, green trees and bushes... He has heard that once there were moving images on the walls of apartments, and not just the window spaces.

5
Mr. Lifelong

Marek's father is rarely at home. He often stays at work for whole days and nights. Or comes back late in the evening when Marek is already asleep. One evening he comes into Marek's room when Marek is still awake. Marek opens his eyes and sees Dad's big face. The light from his little bedside light falls on Dad's high forehead with its first few wrinkles. In the dark, Dad's head seems even bigger than usual. His level blue eyes are hard to make out. But they are there.

"Daddy…" Marek stretches out his hand.

"Why aren't you asleep?"

"I've just woken up. Have you come home properly?"

"No, I've got to go straight out again."

"Why do you always have to go out?"

"I have to protect Mr. Lifelong. I have to second guess any threats to him."

"Why's he called Lifelong?"

"Presidents used to come and go; they were elected. But that can't work at a time like this. Lifelong is a strong man. Just the kind we need today. Why would we want to elect a president, Marek, when we already have the best man in the job? I know some people criticize him for it. And some would like to kill him. They say he's seized power. But I know him. He's not power-hungry. He just does what is needed. He wants the best for our country."

"Who wants to kill him?" Marek asks. They must be awful people. Stupid and wicked. At least they'll never succeed when Dad's guarding Mr. Lifelong.

"No point in talking about them." Dad waves his hand. "I just wanted to tell you we're not giving up. Our country's going to be the way it used to be again. Then we'll mend the roads and we'll drive to the sea."

"Really, Dad?" Marek sits up in bed and puts his arms round his father's neck. For a promise that will never be fulfilled.

"Of course. I believe it. And in a week… in a week I'm having a day off. We'll take a trip into Prague. We haven't been there for a long time."

A very long time. So long Marek can't remember it. "But you said it wasn't safe there."

"We mustn't be scared, Marek. Fear is the worst thing. We can't just lock ourselves up here in Holesovice. We're going to live a normal life."

6

Chuck them in the Vltava!

Marek is six and everything he hears around him confirms him in the belief that he has been born too late. Everything beautiful happened before he arrived. There had been car rides. Even as far as the sea. And the Internet had been open and everywhere, and so he could have found a friend from anywhere, and not just from Holesovice, and talked to his moving image on the walls of the room. The Vltava had been full of flowing water and you could bathe in it. Who would ever think of doing that today? Sometimes, turning off the programmed scenes, Marek watches a sanitary boat. Men in rubber suits and masks are collecting the dead birds and fish.

Then there's the bathroom. He's been told that once water flowed from the taps whenever you wanted. He can't imagine that at all. Now the water comes on only occasionally for half an hour. Otherwise you have to go the cistern with a bucket. There's a chemical toilet.

Marek is told how lucky they are that there are cisterns in Holesovice. He hears names that mean nothing to him – Žatec, Louny, Rakosník… Towns where the water supply has failed. Nobody can live there anymore.

Dad has kept his word. The next Saturday they go into Prague. They say "into Prague," even though Holesovice is actually Prague too. Marek knows that. Mummy is anxious. Her second chin trembles with irritation and one of her eyes gleams as if there were a tear in it. But she comes with them. Dad has promised they would be guarded by a drone, one of the many robots supposed to guard Lifelong. Dad is in touch with the robots by remote control. And under his waistcoat he has a pistol.

As they walk out of the Holesovice Gate, Marek feels more grief than excitement. It isn't meant to be this way, only he doesn't know how it's meant to be. He will have to wait for an answer to that for a long time. It will be Eli who gives it to him.

According to the calendar it's spring. The sun glows in the sky. Once it climbs the heat will become scorching. Spring: another word full of memory of something that used to be.

The taxi ordered for them is drawing up. A big white antediluvian van running on electricity. He and Mum and Dad sit down in the back, and the driver remains behind bullet-proof glass. First they ride along the deserted riverbank until they reach the market. It is crowded with people, stalls, awnings. "What are they selling?" asks Marek in wonder.

"Everything," his mother replies, sounding distressed. "They're trying to sell anything."

"Do you see that rabble?" the driver curses behind the glass. "Shoot them! I'd shoot them all!"

They are now on a bridge, not across the drying river but across Old Holesovice – a dirty overcrowded district.

In Strossmayer Square lots of people are standing in a line. It is hundreds of metres long and curved round and round on itself. Marek listens breathless as his parents talk about how the church here was set on fire by the Warriors of the True Christ and now serves as a hostel for the displaced people from the towns without water. The line is for soup, for food. Lifelong has said that no one should be allowed to go hungry.

A little further away a tram is stopping. The people getting out look normal, and hurry around the line of the hungry as if it is nothing to do with them. Maybe that is good. It seems to Marek that they are doing the same as his Dad. They don't want to be afraid. They want to live a normal life.

The driver continues up a street and passes another tram. There are a lot of cars here and most of them are taxis. Then they suddenly find themselves in a tailback. "And now we're screwed!" said the driver. "Not that this is so bad. Sometimes it's all the way from the square."

"It's because of the checkpoint by the entrance to the inner city," Dad explains.

For around half an hour they stop and start in the traffic. The check itself turns out to be quick. Dad shows a document and the soldiers immediately let him through. Then with a roaring of wheels they drive downhill through a tunnel. They come out by the Vltava, but it looks more like the poorest suburb than a grand city centre. Crowded on the slopes above the river are huts, awnings, tents – the wretched makeshift housing of people with nothing left. Marek notices chairs, coaches and beds, for people can sleep outside now it never rains. Children are playing on rubbish heaps. "How did they get here?" asks Marek. "The entrance is guarded."

"It was before we started to guard it. Today it couldn't happen. Lifelong is already building housing for them on the edge of the city. They'll all be cleared out of here soon."

"Chuck them in the Vltava – into that sewer!" shouted the driver through the glass. "Why should we have to look after them?"

Mum leans in towards Marek and puts an arm round his shoulders. "Don't listen. They're human beings. They've been unlucky. The places where they used to live are no longer habitable."

There are moments when even Mum's good-natured face stiffens. When the fat, the second chin and the swollen cheeks are overcome by the strength of an opinion. Sometimes Mum doesn't even agree with Dad. And she doesn't like Lifelong. Marek turns to Dad, waiting for him to say something. But Dad is silent.

They go through the checkpoint in the middle of the bridge and finally find themselves in quiet streets. Here the houses cast shadows.

7

Who are you?

Natalia – for this is the name she gave – gazed into Marek's eyes. She was no longer on her side but lying on her front, and had her head on his white hairy chest and tipped back to look up at him. Her lips were still tightly shut as if in concentration.

He realized how well he was feeling. The tension in his lower back had gone. Until then he had even forgotten what it was like not to feel that tension. He wanted to sleep. Except for the presence of her dark eyes. They were driving deep into him. Or at the least were waiting for him to drive deep into himself. They were urging him to it and would not give up.

He had listened to himself speaking, he – an old man – about a boy he had long ago forgotten. Suddenly, as he lay there with her, he became very much aware of the grace that he had been granted in life. "Don't you understand, Natalia?" he burst out. "My brother was the messiah."

For a moment she looked as if she might relent, but all at once she smiled. "That's not an answer, Marek. It's just not an answer."

He couldn't understand where on earth she got it from, that self-possession.

"An answer to what?" he countered. He kept hoping she would not be so persevering. He hoped she would be content with the fact that she was lying on him, now with breasts pressed against his stomach.

"The answer to who you are."

I'm his brother, he wanted to say. That's the answer. But he sensed it wouldn't be enough. Natalia was aiming deeper. It wouldn't satisfy her.

She released him by suddenly jumping up from the bed. "I have to go to the toilet." Unabashed she walked round the stove and ignoring the toilet ran out of the back door into the rain.

Just a moment of solitude was enough to have him returning to his old age. He shrank back into it on the bed and there was no way out of it. Yet this ageing, yellowing body still belonged to the boy he had been back then.

Eli had not feared death. He had said that life was just the beginning. Sometimes he had even seemed to be courting death.

She ran back in, spattered with rain. Quickly she slipped in beside him. Raindrops from her smooth skin ran on his dry, wrinkled hide. For a moment it was cooling, until he felt her heat. He was aroused.

8

Mum

Mum. He had often asked himself why she should have given birth to both of them. First Marek – an ordinary person. But then Eli, who couldn't have been of this world. Nobody of this world could have brought so much hope.

Marek thought of the Mary of the Bible, the subject of such holy reverence in the Christian tradition. As a child he had taken no interest in Christianity and his parents had done nothing to introduce him to it. His mother's interest had come later.

In Holesovice, where she looked after their household and worked in a school, no one had seen anything exceptional about her. She wasn't even beautiful. Yet she was infinitely kind. She regarded the future with fear but still managed to keep her hopes up.

The drought had been tormenting. But it was not the first of its kind. Mum knew the reasons why. She said, "It's because of the way we treated our planet. It's a punishment that had to come."

He hadn't completely understood. For something to be a punishment there had to be a punisher. But who was punishing humankind?

Mum's name wasn't Mary but Julie, and unlike the biblical Mary she never had to hold the body of her martyred son in her arms. On the contrary, her sons would say farewell to her, at home in Holesovice. Her face would be swollen and her breathing heavy and wheezy. Up to then she had feared she could not be a good mother to Eli. It was only on the very day that she would leave a world turned upside down, and the world would immediately forget her, that she would find faith in her son.

Marek would never forget the moment when hope appeared.

He is coming back from school after lunch. He is only in first grade, but Holesovice is safe. As usual he comes in through the garage and stands by their car for a long time. He puts his hand on the silver bodywork and the glass and twists the cameras and mirrors round. Outside it is hot, but down here it is bearable. The car surface is pleasantly cooling. This touch spreads grief all through Marek's body. He can't pull his palm away. Eventually he sits down on the smooth floor. The lights go out and just a single tiny little light continues to shine by the door like a star in the night sky. Marek finds himself at the bottom of a deep abyss, lonely in the extreme. It could not have been mere chance that he hit this lowest point just then – on the very day that it was all to turn around. Finally he gets up and lights come on again. He goes up in the lift, where it is suffocatingly hot. In the apartment the air-conditioning is on. It is still a day like any other. A day when everything good is still in the past. Then Mum comes back.

Immediately she appears at the door something is different. Mum's eyes are wide open. Marek can see she wants to tell him something. But she can't get it out. She's so full of it she doesn't know where to begin. Marek goes to his room. She comes in after a moment. She sits down next to him, takes his hand and kisses him on the cheek and brow. "I'm so happy, Marek. So happy." She can scarcely speak. She cries. Outside it's hot and Mum is fat; he can smell her sweat. But it doesn't bother Marek. "Just imagine, they've reached an agreement!" she continues. "The biggest states in the world, the most powerful people and the best scientists. They've invented something to cool the Earth down again. They call it a diffraction grille. Tiny particles in the stratosphere will form the grille and deflect some of the rays, so they don't fall into the Earth's atmosphere. So the Earth will get less heat from the Sun."

"You've always been saying that's what they ought to do."

"Yes that's what I said, but I thought they wouldn't. I thought they wouldn't agree. Or they wouldn't work out how to do it. Now just imagine. They're going to place that diffraction grille some-where in the stratosphere, almost in space. It will catch some of the

9

Late Gifts

From the moment they made the connection, Natalia seemed to be drinking Marek in. As if this were something she had been denying herself for years. It was she who had chosen him, of that there was no doubt. But he knew that she couldn't love him, or at least for more than the few moments they were together. And absolutely not for his looks.

The women who had followed Eli hadn't been interested in Marek, and those with whom Marek had satisfied his physical needs hadn't interested him. Over the years many searchers had come to see him. More women than men. They came hoping they might still glimpse some flash of holiness, some trace of the revelation they knew only by report. They used to make Marek their confidante. He would talk with them, tell them about Eli. Sometimes he was really close to them, noticing their quickened breathing and the pounding of their hearts. Only once had he crossed the line, and with very bitter consequences.

It was Natalia's passion and her love, but not meant for him. It was impersonal, as wind, rain or sunshine is impersonal. She clamped her legs around his chest and undulated her belly against him – he didn't have to do anything. He shut his eyes and set out on the journey. Natalia enveloped him. He felt submerged, surrounded by something that was, if anything, like a mother's womb. He could not remember ever experiencing anything similar.

Natalia pulled her lips from his for a moment and raised her head. In her dark eyes he saw… simply love. How had he deserved her? He was flooded by an unknown happiness. "Natalia," he whispered. "You are so beautiful. Thank you."

She opened her lips a little and kissed him again. They were not yet close to the climax, for his old body experienced pleasure differently. Again he closed his eyes. He knew where he was, knew of the rain outside and the water running between tufts of myrtle-green grass. But behind his closed eyelids he was heading back in time. Once again he was the only child of his parents. Once again he was himself, before he became a mere brother.

10
You're going to have a little brother!

Mum keeps bringing more and more good news. Mankind is cooperating. Advanced human civilization is capable of taking control of the fate of its host planet. Dozens of satellites and astronauts are building an ingenious solar screen above the Earth.

In Holesovice Marek is growing fast. It's the first time he has heard that something like mankind exists. He doesn't know quite what it means, but he is proud of it. He too is a part of it.

Dad and Mr. Lifelong are parts of that great community too. Lifelong has expressed support for the project. So have many local scientists.

But for the moment the sun scorches on. The mud in the old riverbed has dried out and is blistering. You can walk on it. Yet when you look up at the bright blue sky you're no longer afraid. On the contrary, the sky is full of hope. Something is happening up there.

It turns out that the plan for the project has existed for a long time. Everything was thought out and calculated decades ago. They had just been waiting for an agreement – a political decision. A Great Conference of Nations is taking place in the United States. Dad flies off there with Lifelong. Marek goes with him to the Holesovice gate. He would love Dad to take him as far as the airport. But he's not allowed. There are soldiers and robots patrolling in the streets. "Dad, when you've got the agreement, can we buy a battery? Will we be able to drive in the car again?"

When Dad gets back he is full of hope. It's the end for global warming. The diffraction grille will diffuse some of the solar radiation. The climate will start cooling down. Not all at once, but gradually. Until everything is back to its original balance.

These two years of Marek's life are so different from the first six. "Who made that stink?"… His first six years were so full of bad smells, the strange stink of nostalgia.

Now everyone's eager for the future again.

A month after Marek's eighth birthday the project is complete. But although at night you can observe the slow tracking lights of satellites, when you look up in the day there's nothing to see.

Disappointment is starting to set in. Nothing is happening at all. The drought is dreadful, the sun goes on scorching.

It is only later that something happens. Something completely different. Dad takes some leave. He's home again after a long time. In the evening he and Mum light candles and look mysterious. "We've got to tell you something. Now, that mankind has agreed, and we don't have to fear the future anymore. Marek, you're going to have a little brother!"

11

My Dear

Natalia dressed and sat down in the armchair by the fire. Marek remained on the bed, lying on his side with the blanket over him. A face appeared fleetingly at the window. It was as if someone had wanted to come in but had changed their mind when they saw Natalia by the fire or Marek in bed. There was a sound of sand scraping under retreating feet.

He and Natalia looked at the window and then each other. And suddenly they were laughing at the confusion of whoever it was that had fled, and laughing together, the two of them, in the face of everything, that entire confused topsy turvy world.

"Where will you go now?" Marek asked, his eyes straying to her red bag.

"Nowhere, for the moment. I'll stay here," she said.

He was taken aback. It struck him that the bed on which he was lying was too narrow for two. His aching body longed for comfort. He also thought of Hana's reaction If Natalia stayed, Hana would make a fuss about it. He was already afraid of what she would say. And in fact he wasn't even sure what Natalia meant by "I'll stay here." She might mean right here in the bungalow with him, or just in the colony. Even the cabins on the hill were "here." Like the taller houses on the bay. He was unsure if he had understood. It had probably been arrogant to think she actually wanted to stay with him. In fact it was a relief if she didn't, because if Natalia stayed in the colony but not at his place, Hana would probably let it go. "There's a free bungalow in the second alley from the bottom. I'll tell someone to bring bedcovers and firewood there."

Her look was bewildered. "Are you driving me away, my dear?"

My dear… Two words of acceptance. To be accepted by someone; it was such an unexpected, human feeling. But then, that was how Eli had sometimes addressed him, "My dear Marek."

On Eli's lips it had been a kind of gratitude. Eli had often blessed and thanked Marek, but could never release him from the role of the elder, the protector.

Marek had been the elder brother of the messiah, and in fact it was only now, when Natalia accepted him, with everything that he was, that he realized how tough a fate it had been. "I'm not driving you away," he whispered, moved. "You're beautiful. I'm glad you're here."

"Tonight I'll climb in with you," she said, "and tomorrow you can tell someone to bring me a bed."

12

Eli arrives

"Eli," Mum decides. That's what he will be called. Mum doesn't know why. She just likes the name. She thinks it's somehow... refined, or that's what she says as she shakes her head at the name Jan, which Dad wants, and Jirka, which is Marek's suggestion. Mum is unyielding in her sheer corpulence. Now that she's carrying new life, she has expanded even more – she is almost unimaginably fat. And she won't give in. "It's going to be Eli."

Much later Marek will read the Bible for clues as to why she wanted that name. Could the Holy Spirit have entered into her – as it did with the biblical Mary – and whispered to her that ancient, symbolic name? But Marek will find no connection between his brother Eli and the prophet Elijah. Nor will he come up with any answers when Christians ask skeptical questions about the name. Instead, he will listen to his then just twenty-year-old brother, who will reassure him: "Don't look for paths already walked. Don't look for stories already past. Maybe there are similarities, because there is always some similarity, but I know I'm here to beat a path, and not to return to one already travelled."

In Holesovice there is a small clinic. It is where Marek goes to a doctor for regular check-ups, or when he is sick. Although clean, the clinic smells of sickness, and reminds Marek of sore throats, dull pains in the head, and coughing fits. But women give birth in the clinic too. His parents plan for Mum to give birth in the most modern hospital that Lifelong has had built, and Marek is pleased that Eli won't be coming into the world in a clinic smelling of sickness. The trouble is that when the time comes, Dad and Lifelong are somewhere far away. Fat waddling Mum packs her bag herself and sets off to walk the few blocks from the apartment to the clinic. Marek is at her side.

When they come out of the main door of the apartment house, they notice that something is happening. It is crowded outside, but in a different way. People are mostly just standing around, and there is a curious kind of restlessness and surprise about them. Maybe they always behave that way, but there's a more obvious change. Although it's morning, the sun isn't shining. It is strangely dark. Marek raises his head and sees a sight he has never seen before as far back as his memory reaches. Clouds. Heavy, dark, and inscrutable.

Marek starts to tremble. Mum too sways on her stiff, swollen legs, but she immediately recovers and grabs Marek by the hand. "Come on Markie, it's nothing to worry about. It's just Eli coming."

So they set off. Gusts of wind rip between the buildings and raise whirls of dust. Mum is having trouble catching her breath, and Marek is afraid she won't make it to the clinic. Inadvertently he catches her eye, but her attention is no longer his. She looks ahead with resolution. Mum has a mission. She is going to give birth to Eli.

Eventually they get there. On the steps in front of the glass doors Mum turns to Marek. "I'll be okay on my own now, Markie. Don't wait for me. You go home."

Marek hesitates. The clinic with its stench of sickness does not attract him, but he is still reluctant to leave. "Don't come inside with me!" Mum insists. "Go home." He tries to kiss her, but she can't manage to bend down that far. "Please Markie..." At least she strokes his hair; his kind darling Mum.

Marek makes a show of leaving but then comes back. Mum has disappeared into the bowels of the clinic. He sits on the steps and watches the eddies of dust. His eyes prickle. The people coming into the clinic hurry and make excited remarks. The people coming out stop on the steps, taken aback, like Marek when he left the house with Mum.

Marek sits there a long while. Not that it feels very long to him; he's just waiting for Eli to be born. He feels he has to stay there, on guard, instead of Dad, who had to go away with Lifelong. He has to be there for Eli's sake. He has no inkling that in fact Dad is never coming back; that Dad has decided to live with Lifelong's personal assistant and have other children with her; that he will be writing to tell Mum after the birth. And so Marek feels important. The most important person of all for the child who has still to be born.

Time accelerates like the swirling clouds of dust in the forecourt of the clinic. And then it happens. No, it's not the cry of a newborn. That wouldn't be audible outside the air-conditioned, well insulated clinic. What happens is that great drops of water start falling into the dust. Marek gets up and takes a few steps out into the forecourt, fascinated. He stands with his face tilted upward, and he's not alone; many others are standing there like him. Drumming on their faces is… water. First it falls in large distinct drops, but soon it becomes a dense curtain. The earth beneath Marek's feet darkens, the dust becoming first clay and then mud. Rain – heavy and unremitting – is falling from the clouds in the sky. Eli has been born.

13

Doubts

Natalia was wearing a tight-fitting woollen nightdress, and sleeping on her side, turned away from him. The bed was narrow, and so his thighs touched her oval behind. In fact the bed was full of her and all he had was a narrow space along the wall.

He envied her for falling asleep so easily. He could hear her calm breathing while he hardly breathed, so as not to wake her. Her physical presence, her being here with her body, heart, lungs, blood circulation, but also her dreams – which so far he knew almost nothing about – seemed like a miracle despite all the discomfort she was causing him.

His doubts were about himself; he doubted he was worthy of the gift that she so undoubtedly was. He with his small pains, his weariness and his dullness, but above all with his mission, which was to proclaim, to bear witness. Also to protect Vinohrady, as this settlement of the Followers of Eli was called; not after any vineyards that might once have flourished here, but after a suburb of Prague, its name a reminder of a lost home.

He was full of doubts. He couldn't seem to find in himself enough relish for an untried life at the side of a young woman, or enough courage for new beginnings. It seemed too late for that, especially when he couldn't remember ever longing for something like it before. He never had, not even in his youth. Everything he had ever been, and all his thoughts and longings, he had sacrificed to Eli. Not that he had seen it as sacrifice.

As the night wore on, his lack of space in the bed became seriously annoying. To make things worse, he wanted to go to the bathroom. At his age he usually got up to pee several times a night, but today she was here and he didn't want to wake her. He put it off a long while, staring into the darkness above him. His thoughts ran back to Eli's birth in Holesovice during that first rain, but then to Hana, who must already know about Natalia. Hana had her spies.

When he could no longer last out, he sat up and slowly edged his way down to the end of the bed. Finally his feet touched the floor and the space around him brought him liberation. The air in the room was dry and warm. Pale moonlight came through the window and drew a rectangle on the floor. The glimmer showed him where her face must be, although it was hidden by her forearm. For all his discomfort and peevish thoughts, he had a sudden urge to stroke it, but his bodily need was insistent. He remembered how she had relieved herself that afternoon, so he walked around the stove with the smouldering charcoal out into the night, to do it the same way.

The chill damp air outside startled him. The night refreshed him, awakening in him a longing to live. He noticed gaps in the clouds above his head and the white gold shimmer at their edges. It reminded him of her face. But most of the sky was impenetrably dark, and the place lonely in its silence, bearing in on him the uncertain future of the Followers of Eli. He carried it all on his shoulders, while Eli... had left a radiance behind. It was strange how it had never faded over the years. It still lingered in his mind – just the same as back then, like the first and the last day.

He emptied his bladder and started to shiver with cold. He stood there just a moment longer and took a deep breath, but then went back inside.

Natalia's presence in the heated room was immediately obvious. He quietly crept up to the armchair and shifted it closer to the stove. He sat down, leaned his head against the back and tried not to be audible. She was here after all. My God – he thought, Eli my little brother, thank you for this day. All at once it was real to him.

14

So this is him…

In Holesovice it is finally raining. Marek is waiting for Mum but she still hasn't come back. Instead, Dad calls: "Markie, I forgot to tell you something. I'm not coming back today. I thought I could make it, but Lifelong… What? You're home all by yourself? Mum's already having the baby? Wait a minute, I'll think of something. I'll send someone over…"

Marek doesn't know why Dad's voice is gushing with guilt, but the guilt overflows into his own heart. Maybe everybody in the world has done something bad, and that's why Dad's voice is so apologetic.

Three days later, three days in which Marek has been looked after by one of Mum's friends, a teacher of Czech that Dad managed to call that night, Mum appears at the door. She is much thinner and pale, her cheeks hanging off her face, her bag over her shoulder and water dripping from her hair and clothes. But in her arms she holds a miracle, a new life. Eli's eyes are closed, his eyelids tight shut as if he is squeezing them down with all his strength, still reluctant to see the world he has been sent into. All the same, his little face is already the face of the brother that Marek will protect, and live for, in the days and years to come.

Mum lays Eli down in the prepared cot and finally looks at Marek. "So this is him." But then she sits down abruptly in the deep armchair and starts to shake with sobs.

Rain, birth and weeping, hope, future and pain, all in one. Yet there is also determination on Mum's desperate face.

Eli's face creases up too and his thin cry rises to join Mum's sobs. As if at a command, Mum gets up, goes to the cot and takes Eli in her arms; she is going to feed him. Marek stands a little way off. He knows it is still up to her, but something tells him that one day he'll be taking her place.

In the meantime the wind beats on the window, and raindrops appear on the glass. It is already a kind of weeping, that life-giving rain produced by the efforts of all the world's elites.

It rains the whole night long, and meanwhile the voice of the new arrival sounds several times, finding its way into Marek's dreams and reminding him that Eli is here, once and for all.

Marek is all the more surprised when Mum wakes him in the morning to send him off to school. What? Now that Eli's here? But Mum insists, "You're still a child, Markie. You have to study to get anywhere in life. Eli isn't your responsibility. It ought to be the responsibility of…" Mum stops, and the tears fill her eyes again.

Marek does as he is told. He goes to school even though he knows that Mum is wrong. Eli is his responsibility. He always will be.

Three days of rain have left deep traces in the parched landscape. The mud on the bottom of the dried-up riverbed has turned black and softened. The banks are gashed with deep fissures running with muddy water, and in the middle of the riverbed there is an actual stretch of water, the kind that was still there two years ago. Little birds hop about on the pavement, and no-one can understand how they survived the long period of drought.

The greatest transformation is in people's faces, Relief – that seems the right word, and it is only now clear how much anxiety everybody has been suppressing. The feelings can finally come out. The fear remains, but in all those faces it alternates with hope. And only Marek knows the real reason for the hope. He can still hear that thin cry even when he sleeps, and with his inner eye he can always see the tiny creature who could be everything, even if it is nothing yet.

At school too they give the children pep talks about hope. Except perhaps for the sports teacher, who turns to Marek one time and remarks, "I heard about your dad. Tell your mum I'm thinking about her a lot."

Marek doesn't get it. He doesn't know what she could have heard about Dad. That's because what he knows himself, he really only intuits. Then there's an assembly in the gym and the head of the school addresses all the pupils: "I know you can't grasp it at your age, but when you grow up, and when you are old and remember today, you are going to realize that this was a historic moment. Mankind has taken control of its host planet. We used only to be able to dream about it. We used to influence natural processes, but mostly for the worse. But now for the first time we have put right what we caused. There's still a long road ahead of us, and this is just the beginning. The climate is a terribly complicated system. And unpredictable. It has rained, and copiously. But look, the sun is shining again." Everyone looks up to the windows in the ceiling. "But it seems almost certain that the diffraction grilles project has proved its worth. The climate is returning to normal. And not just here. Finally, after a long time, we can be proud of ourselves."

The head speaks in wise tones. Marek believes him, for his short greying beard and tall erect figure are conducive to respect. All the same, even the head knows nothing about the most important event of recent days. Marek intends to find a suitable moment to tell him about Eli.

"In a moment, at noon precisely," the head concludes, "our lifelong president will be speaking to you and all the citizens of the Central European Federation. Those of you that have listened attentively to my previous speeches will know that I'm no supporter of lifelong political office." There is a stir in the hall; some of the pupils agree. Marek is silent. "But it must be admitted that getting our Central European Federation involved in the space grilles project was a wise move. Now we shall listen to his address together."

Lifelong's self-confident voice reminds Marek of Dad. Dad guards Lifelong, after all, and that means Dad must be near him now. For Marek that is the main message of the voice, which otherwise talks in the usual way about progress, about law and order, about hope for the better life which, by supporting the diffraction grilles project, Lifelong has ensured for all mankind. The boy sitting next to Marek in the gym is Tomas, and he sees thing differently.

"He's a fascist," he whispers feverishly to Marek, "Nobody elected him for life. Fascist! Dictator!"

Marek knows that Tomas's dad was a member of parliament until he made a speech against Lifelong and Lifelong chucked him out of parliament and had him arrested. The trial was fixed, that's how Tomas sees it. But Marek's dad said otherwise – that the members of parliament had done what they liked, abused democracy for their own benefit and let the people down. Lifelong had caught them out and put a stop to it, and that was why they hated him.

Marek will only understand what the words "fascist" and "dictator" really mean seventeen years later, among the corpses of slaughtered girls and boys from the Youth Liberation Army. When school is over Marek leaves at a run. The sun is scorching again and steam is rising from the Holesovice sidewalks. The air is heavy, but the first traces of green are appearing in the sodden clay. Marek walks through it all as if through a tunnel. School and Holesovice no longer interest him. His place, the only place where he belongs and where his life has meaning, is wherever Eli is.

15

Loved

Where was Eli now? It was a question he often asked himself, especially in moments of solitude like this. Was he waiting somewhere out there, in the unknown? Was he watching Marek's earthly struggles from a safe place? Did he see all Marek's imperfections, doubts and mistakes? Or did he now live on only in those who could still remember him? And perhaps in the teachings that he had left them. Only what was that teaching exactly? Was Marek capable of remembering it? Interpreting it?

Eli had often said that the gate was open, and all he was doing was showing the way to it. "It is the place where we are going, where we are returning. There will be no pain and trouble there. Human life in the middle of this perplexed civilization is one great straying from the right path." Or something like that. Marek vainly searched his memory for the precise words, which had possessed a different power when Eli uttered them. Whenever he groped for his brother's words when preaching, and even when he was sure he was quoting him, it was always as if the original message had eluded him. To preach about Eli and his teaching meant to keep on failing.

Now the moon was hidden entirely by clouds and the room was plunged into even deeper darkness. Natalia in the corner could only be sensed, not seen. Outside the wind was buffeting the wall and so he couldn't even hear her breathing. All the same, she was there: she had to be. It reminded him of one night with Eli in hiding on the southern slopes of the Alps. Good people had offered him lodgings in their home. Eli had attracted good people. Often he was the real reason that they showed their good side, that they became good. But countless others he had antagonized. The hatred they felt for him was incomprehensible, because he had done nothing to them… except perhaps enter their lives and challenge the certainties to which they clung.

That was how it had been in the foothills of the Alps. Eli had arrived in the city by the lake and persuaded the local militia to release the hostages they had taken from the ranks of the refugees from the north. He hadn't needed weapons; words had been enough. The militia were hard men. The years of crisis had alienated them from families, civilization, ordinary everyday life. Yet when Eli spoke with them, in the end they threw their weapons away. Unfortunately reinforcements had come from the south, and had executed their penitent colleagues and put a price on Eli's head.

On the journey into the mountains Marek had reproached Eli. "Was that worth it? If you had died here for a couple of hostages, what would you have achieved? What was the point?"

Eli had just looked at him with his irresistible boyish eyes, full of pain but also of incommunicable certainties: "I will die for everyone in dying for anyone – it doesn't matter if it's a hostage, a militiaman or my brother. That's how it will be in the end. But that moment hasn't come yet Marek." And he had smiled. And not even his beard could hide the fact that he was as he had always been from birth, his little brother Eli.

They had spent the night in a mountain chalet, in a room with a stove. Eli had stretched out on the bed and tried again to reassure Marek. He had even reached out his hand to him: "Honestly, Marek. This isn't the end yet, believe me." Then he had gone to sleep.

Only Marek had been unable to sleep. He had sat by the stove all night long listening to the sounds. In the gusts of wind he had heard the approaching tread of persecutors, and their voices in the murmur of the chimney. Several times he had crept outside and stared into the darkness in fear for his brother. He had fallen asleep as dawn was coming.

It was the same tonight. Weariness overcame Marek even in his uncomfortable position in the armchair. When he opened his eyes it was already light. Someone was studying him closely. Natalia. Her compressed lips and long narrow nose were above him – she was looking at him with great tenderness. It was rather like the way he used to look at Eli. Natalia noticed that his eyes were open, smiled and placed her hand on his brow. "Did you sleep here because of me? Did I squeeze you out of your bed? I'm sorry." And again, as she bent over him it was as if she were embracing his whole body with her tenderness.

First and foremost he felt thankful. He saw it as a miracle that he was loved – he, an old man, the brother of a messiah who had long ago fulfilled what he had once promised, dying for everyone in anyone and leaving his followers bewildered. He, a boy so incomprehensibly abandoned by a Dad who had never come back, leaving Mum in constant pain and communicating that pain to Marek in every caress. It had only been Eli that she had managed to protect from that pain. It was amazing to be loved now, he a man so outshone by his brother's radiance that it made him almost invisible to the people that it drew to him for testimony.

It was a pity that he had to get up. He was twisted and stiff in the armchair. At least she could help him. He leaned on her as he rose and suddenly found himself in a new day. Around him was the cooling bungalow, where at any moment his helper Venca would appear and ask what needed to be done today. A bungalow in the middle of New Vinohrady, in plain sight of everyone.

"I'll have another bed brought here for me," Natalia assured him, her tenderness giving way to practicality. "We'll put it over there. I'll arrange it. Where do I have to ask?"

He realized she hadn't the least idea what was expected of him and what was going on in his mind. She saw things in simple terms, because she was sure of herself. "We'll sort it out somehow." He tried to smile at her. "All in good time. Everything here takes time."

The original joy vanished from her face and Marek was struck with fear that he had wounded her, and so he immediately added, "Come on Natalia, let's have breakfast."

16

Stench

Goat cheese and potato pancakes. In the changed climate potatoes did better than wheat. The settlements of the Followers of Eli, including New Vinohrady, were self-sufficient in food. The surpluses could be sold at markets in the towns, since in the last decade life had generally stabilized in this area. Brutality and violence was no longer the order of the day. Instead there were just painful memories and shame for all the atrocities that people had shown themselves capable of committing. And of course distress at the inexplicable steep decline in births.

Eli's teaching had cautious supporters even among the inhabitants of the towns. They sent financial help, medicines, hygiene items and tools to the settlements.

Most of the older inhabitants of New Vinohrady had experienced the death road – the flight from northern and central Europe across the Alps and then down through the Balkans to Greece – a no man's land. Just to have survived had been a miracle. Let alone to have food and a place to sleep.

Natalia fished in her red bag and produced a sealed jar. "Marinaded octopus. We can have it for breakfast."

Marek caught her hand. "Keep it, you may need it."

"What for, if not for us both to eat?"

They had hardly started their meal when there was a banging on the door and without waiting to be asked someone burst in. It was Jerzi, Hana's assistant. He was barefoot and dressed only in a primitive cassock. This was not because he was poorer than the others but because he claimed that Eli had preached poverty in its simplest possible form, and had said that only the poor, by whom Jerzi meant above all himself, would pass through the gate. Jerzi had a small round head, short black hair, a coarsely shaven face and piercing eyes. Before becoming a Follower of Eli he had been a zealous Catholic.

An odour of sweat, smoke and musty dampness entered the room with him. Marek was used to the stench, but now it bothered him, because of Natalia.

Jerzi gave Natalia a long hard look. He frowned and turned to Marek. "Hana wants to speak with you!"

Here it comes, Marek thought. He was actually afraid of Hana. "Good morning Jerzi. This is Natalia." He tried to give nothing away. "As you can see, we're just having breakfast. I'll drop in on Hana later."

"Later?" Jerzi seemed to be having trouble containing his anger. "She's waiting for you right now. What am I supposed to tell her? When are you going to see her?" he demanded, his voice rising higher and acquiring an unpleasant whistling edge.

"You want an exact time?" Marek laughed. "Do we use watches in Vinohrady? Should we use them? Eli threw his watch away. Someday I'll tell you when and where he did it."

"Nice to meet you, Jerzi," Natalia said suddenly and not even Marek was sure whether it was mockery or just an innocent remark. The dark eyes of the two met, hers deep and kind and his sharp and furious.

17

Hana

Hana. When Marek first met her he was twenty-eight. Eli was nineteen and so was she. At that time rich Norwegians were buying houses in Prague and lands in Bohemia in the hope that Central Europe would remain inhabitable, and Hana was selling herself to them, sleeping with those huge loutish Norwegians who scared everyone, yet her face still had a girlish purity and natural cheerfulness. With her blue eyes, light hair and white skin she looked rather Scandinavian herself.

From the first moment, Eli enchanted her. She made no secret of how she managed to make such good money and wear such expensive clothes, and he showed no sign of shock or outrage. He just said, "So now you can stop." No two people would have uttered those words in the same way, but the way Eli said them was like a knife straight to the heart. Suddenly Hana stood there completely naked.

Later, when with other Followers of Eli they had set out on the long uncertain journey over the Alps, her features hardened with privation. From that time onwards she stayed serious, and there was more gravity than humility even in her devotion to Eli.

She was grave now. From close up she looked old, partly because she took no trouble with her appearance. From a distance he could still see the twenty-year-old girl in her. From a distance you couldn't see the deep rigid lines around her mouth. On the contrary, they gave the illusion of a smile. From close up they were disturbing. They even made Marek feel something like regret, for it was as if her former personality had vanished into them.

"A whore! You have a whore here!" she barked instead of a greeting.

Marek was more offended by her words than ever before. At other times she had been unfriendly, but this time it was about Natalia. "She's not a whore," he protested. He felt a long-forgotten courage germinating inside him. "How can you speak of her like that? What gives you the right to say that about another human being?"

"Didn't she creep into your bed the very first day? Take a look at yourself. Ask yourself why she would do a thing like that?"

It was what Marek had been expecting. Hana had her spies. She knew everything about him. She knew of every step he took and now she was hitting him where it hurt. But today Marek had Natalia's look of tenderness on his side. Hana couldn't take that away from him. "Whatever her reasons are, they don't make her any less of a human being." He considered reminding her of her own past, but for the moment he kept it back.

"That girl is most probably a whore, but I don't give a damn about her," Hana continued brutally. "This is about you. For the community you represent his brother. You're not the only old boy who still has a taste for it. But you're Eli's brother. So you ought to keep yourself pure."

The blood rushed to Marek's head. This time not for Natalia's sake, but Eli's. How stupidly Hana distorted his teaching. Eli had preached the natural. Humility in regard to nature. Not some affected ostentatious purity. No, he could no longer keep it in.

"If Eli had thought like you, how come he ever touched you back then in Prague? You – a giggling blonde whore…" He had never spoken to her like this, and had always been restrained; now his own words frightened him, but he couldn't stop. "How could he have let his reputation be threatened by kindness to a whore? He already had a reputation. People were following him. And they asked about it. And you know what he said to them? He told them that Hana, who slept with Norwegians, was as dear to him as any other person with good in their heart. Because there is good in her. There can be good in anyone. And anyone who still wants to be judgmental should start with themselves."

Hana stood there so rigidly that even these words seemed just to bounce off her. "That was another time," she insisted. "As long as he lived, it was up to him. Now it is up to us to be his voice. We don't

have his holiness, and so we have to be more careful than he was."
At least she was finally speaking from conviction rather than spite.
"Now it's our call, Marek. Just us and Petr. And in the end it will be
just me and Petr, if you don't send that girl away."

18

The reign of human beings is over

Marek walked back across the main square of the community in great agitation. He heard the shouting of children. They were chasing each other round a low building, once the restaurant of the resort and today a school. Absently he counted them: twelve. There were more of them inside during the break. Vinohrady still had plenty of children. Almost every family here had one child, some two or three. Elsewhere only every fifth family was fertile, and then rarely had more than one child. Expert commissions and scientific teams had started to come from the city, to try to persuade the Followers to undergo medical tests. It was Marek who had turned them down. "First of all reconcile yourselves to it. Accept it as reality," he told the delegations. "Until you do that, there can be no solution. Eli taught us that the reign of human beings is over. We understood that and perhaps that's why nature has been kind to us. No, we're not interested in your experiments. Mankind has already conducted one big experiment, and look how that turned out."

The inspectors from the cities didn't bother him much. He knew that the inhabitants of New Vinohrady were behind him and didn't want any investigations. But Hana disturbed him. She had been lighting a fire of discontent in him. A kind of despair. Against her inexorable rancour he felt helpless.

He turned off into the alley where his bungalow stood and saw the figure of Natalia in the distance. She was speaking to someone. He recognized kind, massively built Venca. As he came nearer he noticed that Venca had eyes only for the young woman; the same Venca who served Marek so faithfully that Marek sometimes had to remind him to notice, respect and obey others too.

The bungalow door was open and Natalia was showing Venca where she wanted her bed. Venca was beside himself with eagerness to help. "Sure, sure, I'll go get the one with the metal frame," he was assuring her in his quiet gentle voice. "There's a mattress there too."

Venca had been born here, in Vinohrady. Shortly after Eli's death his parents had arrived from Croatia. Venca's dad had been just as huge. He came from Brno, where he worked in town government. When the rebellion against Lifelong broke out he didn't want to fight and escaped from the city to his brother in the country, where their family had a carpentry business. It was there he met Venca's mother – a retiring and eternally careworn woman. They joined Eli after meeting him by chance in Austria. Both immediately recognized him for what he was.

Venca's dad had devoted himself to carpentry in Vinohrady too, and it killed him when a ceiling collapsed on him. Venca was only five when it happened. Until recently he had lived with his mother, but in the winter she died of a chest disease.

Finally Venca noticed Marek. "We've decided we'll put the beds next to each other," he said with a face brighter than Marek had ever seen before, "and so the mattresses will be at the same height I'll find a new one for you too. There are still plenty in the store from the last gift."

Natalia was smiling too, and Marek almost forgot Hana. These faces belonged to living beings.

All the same, his fears returned. Venca gave a conspiratorial smile as he moved the beds together, and asked who would sleep on which and whether he shouldn't leave Marek a gap by the wall to make it easier for him to get up. But Marek's thoughts were already elsewhere. He knew that Hana wasn't going to leave it alone. She and Jerzi would stir people up, and just at a time when everything had finally calmed down and a sensible life was possible. Marek was unprepared for another challenge. He had thought he had already fulfilled his mission and could depart.

"Aren't you happy?" Natalia turned to him.

"Nati…" He raised his hand and stroked her brow, looking into her eyes and then finding himself unable to do anything but press his lips to hers. "Nati… I am responsible for all these people," he whispered in explanation. "Eli left me here. He bequeathed me this task. And they trust me. They rely on me. They have decided to live

45

with Eli – with his teaching. As long as this community lives, he too is alive. Do you understand?"

Her face grew serious and she said nothing. He started to reproach himself for burdening her with his troubles. "I'm sorry about Hana. She was as close to Eli as I was. Only she's changed. She's never happy about anything, she's judgmental. I'm afraid she may destroy everything. But it's good that you're here. With you I am less afraid."

Instead of answering she walked over to her red bag. "Does anyone else here need a massage?"

He was taken aback. He wondered if she wanted to sleep with some other person. If in the end she wouldn't sleep with all of them.

"I'm not just going to freeload here, Marek. I want to help in the normal way. Are there any children here without parents? Children no-one hugs? Or women without men? Physical contact, touch, will bring them relief."

19

It is pain that wakes us up

A crazy day. Eli used to call such days "hope-kissed". He could find hope in everything. In every change, in movement, even in misfortune… "Misfortune is our best school," he used to say. "It is pain that wakes us up." And he went calmly forward to meet it.

A car engine sounded from above. No modern hydrogen vehicle and not even electric, but good old diesel. An off-road vehicle. It drove down from the school; it was heading unerringly for Marek's place. He knew that car, of course. It belonged to the Council of the Old Town, as the people of New Vinohrady called the nearest town. It had originally been the purely Greek town Litohoro at the foot of Mount Olympus, but in the times of murder and drought most of its original inhabitants had fled and today it was an international town, predominantly Greek and Slav.

Marek knew what would follow. They called it an "invitation". The black car caked in mud to halfway up the door, stopped by Marek's bungalow. The driver, the sullen Konstantinos, came every time and Marek knew him well, but today it was a young man in sporty clothes that got out. Marek knew him too. It was Pavol, commissioner for cultural coexistence and education. The self-confident son of Czech-Slovak parents and a representative of the new generation, builders of a new society. Smart, clean-shaven and optimistic. People like him didn't look back to the traumatic lives of their parents. "Good morning, Marek, how are you?" he started formally, with an unCzech accent. The usual routine was for Konstantinos to drive down to the settlement alone. "Go with me," he would keep repeating, and Marek never had the heart to refuse him.

Pavol's presence suggested something more. After his encounter with Hana this morning, which had turned the day a little sour with its aftertaste, nothing could surprise Marek. And as he noted Pavol's awkward Czech, he remembered another of Eli's dicta. "We don't need to carry our message into foreign languages. It will shine so brightly in our own language that they will come after us."

It definitely wasn't shining for Konstantinos. He sat hunched into himself behind the wheel, as if in a hostile or at least extremely alien environment. The Greeks who had somehow survived or returned regarded everything around them as theirs by right, but at the same time their natural hospitality inhibited them from behaving in an unfriendly way to the migrants. The internal tension tended to grind them down.

Konstantinos was ready to step on the gas and get away as soon as possible, but Pavol acted friendly. "How am I?" Marek echoed. "When I see you here, then a little worse. Or do you want to join us? The bungalow down at the end is still free."

"No no, I don't want to join you," Pavol laughed. "Thank you." He was in a good mood. These young people were always in a good mood. "But there are a lot of people, important people, who want to meet you, Marek. The day after tomorrow we'll send for you at noon. Normally I'd call or send a message, but it's difficult when you don't have a connection. I've had to spend three hours in the car today just for your sake." Pavol seemed to have just realized there was no reason for grinning, and started to look serious. "Isn't that selfish of you?"

Marek was used to such digs. Everyone criticized them for living without technology. Cursed them as primitive sectaries. "You didn't have to come here. And I don't have to go anywhere."

"That would be a pity, Marek. These people want to hear you." His eyes slipped away from Marek and slid to Natalia, who had just come out of the bungalow.

Marek had no illusions about these people's willingness to listen. They always listened only until the first dispute. Never for a moment did they really believe they might learn something new. They had neither understood nor accepted Eli. On the other hand, Eli himself had taught that it wasn't right to close oneself up, and everyone must be given the chance to hear the message. Just the chance: offer the message but don't try to persuade. "You'll find me here the day after tomorrow."

Pavol tore his eyes from Natalia. He was suddenly flustered. "Not me… just Konstantinos. So can I confirm your participation?"

Confirm your participation. How alien the expression seemed to him. "It's your business, not mine," he shrugged. "I'll come. Of course I'll come."

The engine roared into life, and by the time the heavy vehicle had turned in the narrow street, stinging fumes mixed with the fresh air. Pavol in the passenger seat turned back to look at Natalia.

Natalia smiled at them. Then she turned to Marek. "You're stooping again, for goodness sake," she scolded him. She showed not the slightest curiosity about where he would be going and why, but he felt this expressed her practical bent rather than indifference. She was just leaving it to him. Sure of whatever decision he made.

Marek on the other hand was seething with unease. They had never come for him like this. Usually they behaved with patent hostility or at least in a detached manner that made it clear they were trying to intimidate him, and that when their patience ran out they would start to threaten: to arrest him, to demolish the complex, to take the children and send them to other schools. But this invitation sounded different. He needed to be prepared.

He went inside. The fire was smouldering again in the stove, soup was warming on the hotplate and the bed had been made up. Good kind Natalia was taking care of his comfort. But he knew that in order to prepare himself properly, he had to be alone. Alone in the Shrine of the Birth.

20

To the Shrine

The Shrine of the Birth, sometimes also the Holesovice Shrine, was the name given to a hidden place over the saddle of the mountain. There the Vinohrady settlers had built a small timbered cottage with a child's cot on the ground floor, basic facilities, and a sleeping area under the roof. Marek was always emphasizing that anyone could sleep overnight there, but nobody ventured to do so except him, Hana, and Petr... those who had been closest to Eli. The shrine was supposed to be a reminder of Eli's arrival in the world. A mountain spring that had only recently gushed up there had been led along the roof, and the water dripped down in such a way that anyone who wanted to enter had to walk through it. It symbolized rain, in token of the hope that had accompanied Eli's birth.

In the evening Marek didn't wash. He had a feeling that he would be disturbing something in himself by water. Although as yet he had no distinct thoughts, he was already concentrated in his mind. He changed into his nightshirt and lay down. Natalia came to bed after a moment; washed, but also clothed. He wondered if he was disappointing her by his indifference, and the idea was so new in his life that it made him feel helpless. This was probably not the way it should be.

But then she leaned over him and the reflection of the candle in her eyes, her striking nose, her smile, all of it shone above him like the most tranquil starry sky. She kissed him only briefly. "I'll manage just fine, Marek," she said, "You don't need to worry about me." With that she turned away from him and blew out the candle with one strong breath. Without thinking about it, he rolled onto his side and laid a hand on her shoulder.

"Thank you Nati," he whispered. Then he lay back and returned to himself. He was calmer now.

In the morning he asked Venca to get ready for a journey. By himself he would hardly have been able to hobble up to the shrine, especially carrying bedcovers. Natalia went to the school. She said she wanted to meet the children. And help.

The sun shone on the green landscape with its first traces of autumn. In places the ground was eroded by rains and there were deep sandy ravines cut by flowing water. Down in the bay the sea glittered and a large freight ship was visible on the skyline. It was as distant and inaccessible as life in towns and in state facilities now seemed to Marek; it was part of an order dictated by the laws of technical civilization. All of that still existed, even more than before, and with a resurgent self-confidence, but that life did not concern Marek. And in addition, in that order the human species was inexorably ageing and dying out. It was a return; the providence whose purposes only Eli could read was returning the human species to a sustainable level.

Venca arrived with a simple sewn backpack. This was his moment: just him and his master once again. He had easily forgotten about Natalia. "I've brought you the waterproof coat," he announced. "The weather's nice now, but by afternoon... Also a bit of soap and toilet paper... Do you want to take shoes to wear in the shrine? It'll be muddy on the way, you see."

Marek nodded his agreement to everything. He knew that Venca could carry anything. But he kept his old worn shoes on his feet. They had been letting water in for ages, but his feet were used to them. "Let's go this way," he gestured between two bungalows. "By the back way. There's no need for everyone to know where I'm going. When you get back this afternoon, don't say anything to anyone either."

"This afternoon?" Venca frowned. He had probably thought he would be staying up there with Marek.

"Yes, this afternoon. You'll come with me up to the shrine and then go back. I need to be there by myself. Just with Eli. Do you understand?"

Venca dropped his eyes, like a man rejected by a woman he cared for. Except Venca didn't care for women, or at least had never showed any interest in them. When Marek had seen him smiling at Natalia yesterday it had been for the first time. She was so natural it had opened his heart. Eli would have loved her too.

They wound their way along the path and hens fled on both sides. On the plain above the settlement they walked through a herd of goats. People who were today farmers and craftsmen, but had once been teachers, scientists, officials, businessmen, straightened their backs from their labours and stared after them. Marek did not run life here – that was the task of the administration of New Vinohrady – but he was a living reminder of the messiah who had brought hope that this everyday toil was leading somewhere, to the gate that all will one day pass through and where all will meet. And when the farmers gazed at Marek as he slowly hobbled up to the foot of the mountain, it might well have seemed to them that they were going in the right direction.

Marek and Venca reached the forest. Massive pines had always grown here, but now the forest was denser, with an impenetrable bushy undergrowth fed by the rainier, cooler weather. Goats were pushing through this undergrowth in search of the green shoots. A thick-set Greek shepherd sat by the path.

The path rose along the mountainside to the north and then turned south. Marek and Venca walked in silence.

Several hundred metres further on water had washed part of the slope away and the path was overwhelmed by mud. "Wait!" Venca stepped out in front. "I'll see if it will hold." He traversed the mudslide first. The greasy clay slid underfoot and it took all Marek's strength to get a stable foothold. Venca hurried back to him and caught him by the arm. Sometimes a bigger step was needed and Marek's hip-joints were no longer up to it. And yet, how many times had it been Marek who had walked in front, or supported Eli. This was what old age was like.

The trunks of young trees and branches with leaves still stuck out of the clay. It reminded Marek that human mistakes were still mounting up on the planet, one after another. How long? he wondered. And how low would the birthrate fall before the planet had settled the account and man had paid his debt?

After the mudslide they continued for a while until they reached a roughly carved bench. Marek had known it was there somewhere but had thought it would be closer. The sun shone from the south and was about to go down behind the hill. As it leaned on everything below it, the landscape remained in a mist as far as the horizon. Not even the sea was clearly visible, and only a pure golden gleam betrayed its presence.

"Doesn't look so high," grinned Venca, "but it's quite a hill."

"Hardly a hill at all." Marek waved a hand, but then realized that Venca had never climbed a proper hill. He had been born here and the furthest he had ever been was Litohoro under Olympus. "It's me. It's just that I'm old. Once I wouldn't have thought of this as a hill at all. There were other hills we walked into. Escaped into. With Eli." Suddenly he had an idea, and although it had no connection with what he had been saying, he immediately voiced it: "Paradise, Venca. Do you know what paradise is?"

Venca opened his mouth in wonder and his eyes fixed uncertainly on Marek. "Paradise? It's beautiful there. The best."

"But did you know that the Bible talks about paradise? Right at the beginning. Eli wasn't against the Bible. He used to say he hadn't come to refute the Bible, or to confirm it, but to live its continuation. Paradise for him, Venca, was the beginning of everything. The state of the world before mankind interfered with it, violated its order. The state when humankind had still been a child."

Paradise… Marek felt close to it here, above a landscape veiled in moist mist. "According to Eli the time has come for people to go back to paradise. Being driven out was a terrible punishment. We asked for it ourselves. And it brought nothing good. And so even the one that imposed the punishment has had enough of it. That was what Eli said. I would never have dared to say anything like that, Venca, but Eli said that children would stop being born. He simply saw it. He talked about it as a fact, but I don't think he had any power over it. It's a pity that you never knew him." Suddenly

Marek was assailed by sadness. His memory of his beloved Eli, the light of his life, revived more strongly than it had for a long time. "He was…" How could he express everything that Eli had been? "He was the Messiah, Venca. He was God."

They got up and Marek put his arm round Venca's shoulders. "Do you see this path?" He gestured. "Do you see… he's walking on it with us. Today he's walking with us, Venca. He's here again. I was afraid he would never come back."

For the rest of the journey they were silent.

21

In the Here and Now

Fullness of the heart. A heart overflowing with love for Eli. And today for Natalia as well. Her touch had left traces of peace and reconciliation in Marek. But also unease, a restlessness.

Weighed down by so many feelings, and by the backpack he had shouldered when Venca left him at the top of the ridge, he descended into the uninhabited valley and reached the Shrine of the Birth. Dried wreathes and flowers and sodden pieces of paper with messages were stuck on the facade of the timbered structure, which Venca's father had helped to build. In the neighbouring hollow a lake had started to form only recently. It was one of the reasons why they had put up the shrine just here. Holesovice, Eli's birthplace, had been by the water.

There was no door in the entrance, but only the dripping water. It didn't bother Marek, but he slipped quickly through, almost between drops. Inside, the reality of solitude descended on him. Although the floor was made only of trodden earth, he noticed how the hidden vibrations of every step penetrated the surrounding space. The child's bed by the opposite wall... no, it was nothing like the one in which Eli had spent the first months of his life. After all, Dad had worked with Lifelong and even after his departure had supported them financially, probably even more than before, trying to pay off his conscience. The child's bed in Holesovice had been modern, with a moisture excluder and even a microphone to transmit the messiah's crying to the next room; as a baby Eli had not been in a position to oppose technological advance.

The child's bed here was ordinary, painted with colours and worn where it had been fingered by those coming here to pray. Just now it was these people that Marek could recall better than Eli. They were the inhabitants of New Vinohrady, of New Karlin, and individuals from the towns; some coming with a plea for pregnancy, others out of despair or in an attempt to find a flash of some kind of meaning, hope, or security. Marek suddenly felt as if he were standing in line with them, waiting for a sign, an inner suggestion, a simple instruction that Eli would send him from over there. But from where exactly? Marek had seen Eli's face even after they had beaten him to death in Dubrovnik. When the life had gone out of it. But where? Where?

In fact, it was through Marek that the others had seen their way to Eli, and Eli could not have laid a greater burden on his shoulders.

He propped the backpack against the wall and sat down on a small stool in front of the bed. He leaned forward, shut his eyes and stretched out a hand, closing it around the upper wooden pole worn smooth by the hands of supplicants. He reminded himself why he was here: Pavol and those experts of his, and as soon as tomorrow. Those young people like him, who had missed the worst horrors and made their parents immeasurably happy just by being born, were once again nursing a faith in unlimited possibilities. The philosophy of special destiny and the supremacy of reason. Nothing could have been further from Eli and his humble return to submission to the order of creation. Pavol and his like believed that science and technological advance had no bounds. They believed in progress, in the new organization of life on a planet with a permanently changed climate, but there was one difficulty that they could not resolve, and it undermined the very foundations of their belief. And so they gritted their teeth, clenched their fists and ultimately turned their anger against Eli and his followers. The difficulty was the desperately low birth rate, and it was as if they felt that Eli, by predicting it, had called the curse down on humanity. Of course, this was completely at odds with their understanding of the world through reason. After all, they argued that he had been just an ordinary person, at most a little more sensitive, seeking an accessible path of reconciliation in a time of crisis and omnipresent death.

Marek kept his eyes closed and did not withdraw his hand from the bed frame. It was as if the yearning for hope in the hearts of all Eli's followers who had ever been there were flowing into him. Their faith. They had chosen rightly, he had no doubt of that. Eli had been the one they were looking for. The light that he had brought would spread through the whole world. But it was here that Marek was groping in the dark, for what was the role that he ought to be playing in that process?

Finally the doubts started to fall away from him. Like an invisible robe they floated to the floor.

Later he opened his eyes and savoured the reality of the place. He took a China mug and let water from the door drip into it. It was cold and pure. He drank it and its bright taste refreshed him. He went out for a walk in the surroundings. Dusk was falling and birds twittered in the quiet of the forest. He wanted to have a mind as empty yet open as theirs.

When he returned there was almost complete darkness inside. Most of the candles around the bed had burned right down. Only two at the door had enough wax left. Venca had even thought to pack a lighter.

It was cold but the flames, although weak, lent the room the appearance of warmth. Marek picked up the backpack and started to struggle up the ladder with it. On the path from Vinohrady his knees had hurt, and now it was the turn of his hips. Maybe in just a few months he would no longer be able to climb up here by himself, he realized. Every rung was a fight that he had to win, every rung, groaning and gasping, was a ridiculous labour without witnesses. Yet at the same time there was something natural in it that anchored him in the here and now. Even if he fell and never got up again, there would be nothing bad about it. It would be… paradise.

The space under the roof smelled of straw and pine needles. Finally a place that was dry. Carefully he lit another candle, protected by glass. He had done well to come here, and to send Venca away. Tomorrow… tomorrow he would talk, but now what he needed was to listen.

When he lay down he had first to kneel and then to curl himself up. He laughed at this and remembered Natalia. What on earth had possessed her, to give him a massage? How could she have been so kind and have come to him for his own sake? Now he would have her expressions of love inside him forever. Somewhere inside him: in this old body, which still, as long as blood flowed in it, confirmed how long Marek had endured, how he had lasted. All the way from back then, from Holesovice.

22

It will be winter

The first years of Eli's life in Holesovice. Marek goes to school. He has to. He even does well. But at school all his thoughts are directed to Eli. If at a distance of more than sixty years he had been asked what he used to do during breaks, for example, he wouldn't have been able to remember. The only thing he could remember would be a feeling – a strong unpleasant sense of being kept from being where he should be.

But Eli's first years are years of dirty diapers, crying, feeding and bathing. The saviour has come into the world in a human body with human needs and weaknesses, with colds, coughs and diaper rash. Marek knows all about that.

Not that he would have changed anything, not even then. Eli is the Sun around which everything revolves. And he is already stretching out his baby hands to Marek and fixing his blue eyes on his brother. Those eyes are joyful and unexpectedly serious. Although imprisoned in a still immature mind, it is as if they already see further. As if they are saying to Marek: I am the one for whom you live, and it will not be easy for you.

Meanwhile Holesovice, Prague, the Central European Federation and all of civilization is breathing more freely, enjoying happy days. The rain alternates with sun and winter with spring and the Vltava is flowing again. Ducks have returned to its banks and in winter swans, and the school head organizes one assembly after another for his pupils, offering paeans to the greatness of the human spirit, the power of ideas and mankind's ability to take over the running of the host planet. These days he never forgets to praise Lifelong, whose pictures hang on the walls and whose statues appear in the ever greener parks. The unrest has died down. The Warriors of the

True Christ no longer burn churches but instead buy multimedia glasses and watches and chip implants. In short, everything suggests that the giant experiment in the stratosphere has succeeded. Only Eli at three years old babbles something, incomprehensible, about "winter". "It'll be winter." He keeps on repeating it and Mum hawks and coughs, unable to finish her sentence about how winter is just a season of the year and then there is spring and summer, and that's how it's meant to be. Instead Mum's chest shakes and rattles.

Then there's sad news. Mum won't be teaching any more. She can't. She has water on the lungs.

There's a miserable mood at home. Tearful as usual, Mum strokes and embraces both her sons, but it is as if she is trying to keep hold of them. She doesn't want to leave them alone in the world just yet. As it turns out, she has more than ten years of faith in Marek and Eli left, not in Eli the messiah, but in the child to whom she wants to be a good mother. Marek no longer comes home from school through the garage so as to be able to put a hand on their dead car. The car's gone, because one day, right at the beginning, Dad sent Lifelong's air-truck for it. Marek doesn't mourn for it. He has Eli after all, and Eli's eyes are more important.

At least Dad has pangs of conscience. He sends money, enough for them to live without Mum having a job. In fact Mum goes on working, writing textbooks and advice for teachers on the Net. You can hear her fingers pounding the keyboard from the bedroom… she doesn't like to use key-free mental instructions, even though Dad has bought her the application. But there's one thing that Dad cannot buy. Her smile. Marek never sees it again.

It's busy in the apartment. Neighbours, friends, mothers of other children, and teachers from the school come to see Eli. They rest their eyes on him and are unable to say why. So the apartment is full of remarks like, "Such a sweet boy" or "He looks so wise" or "Just look at his eyes" or "I bet he never has tantrums…"

"Of course he has tantrums," Mum replies. "You'd be surprised how he can yell. All it takes is for me to switch off the broadcast from the wall and he goes crazy."

It's true. Eli knows how to yell and only Marek knows why. Inside his little brother is a future adult under a curse, a grown-up soul. Marek sometimes sees it clearly under Eli's skin. Marek knows that this soul is angry, because he doesn't want to be small, defenceless and stupid anymore, but for the time being he has no choice.

When Eli is four, Marek sometimes goes outside with him alone. On sunny days he runs home from school to take his little brother to the river. Mum is sweating because she can't catch her breath, and isn't even well enough to worry about Eli. "Just be careful," she says, as they run to the elevator. But Eli doesn't want to use the elevator, or more precisely, that grown-up soul inside him doesn't. Marek knows it, and so they take the stairs. Eli is delighted. "To the river," he repeats, and holds out his hand to Marek. His eyes are on fire with impatience.

When they reach the steep slope overgrown with grass and bushes, Eli calms down. He crouches in the grass and scrutinizes it like a scientist. Then he glances somewhere into the murky water, picks up a pebble and chucks it clumsily. The circles it makes in the water cause him such joy that a little saliva drips from his open mouth. He throws himself on Marek and hugs him. "That's what I wanted, Marek," he brags. "That's the way I wanted it."

Marek likes to hug Eli. He presses him to his chest and feels important for protecting something so fragile. It is one of the most beautiful moments for a long time to come.

In the months to come everything starts to change. Above all, Marek has a growth spurt. Often he is overcome by an unfathomable grief. He feels that something is missing, but doesn't know what it is. After all, Eli is always close. Eli even once comes to Marek when he's lying in bed, and strokes his face. "You're sad, but I'll look after you," he says with serene gravity.

There is disturbing news from the outside world too. Apparently, far to the north the snow and ice has been expanding. In winter it covers a much larger surface than usual and there is not enough time for it to melt in summer. This is the second year it has been happening and extensive areas even outside the northern polar circle remain under snow. The people who live there have had to move.

23

A grown-up soul in the prison of childhood

When Marek is fourteen and Eli five, an unexpected letter arrives from Dad. In fact, not a letter but a form. Mum is supposed to fill it out with Marek, so that he can be admitted to an elite high school in a government residential district. He will become a boarder there.

Mum is startled and bewildered. She doesn't want to deprive Marek of such a wonderful opportunity; she knows that the Holesovice High School doesn't take anyone far, and she is convinced that Marek could go far. Holesovice is a place of sorrow for Mum, and she doesn't want it to become her eldest son's lot in life.

Only Marek is quite clear about one thing – he will never desert Eli. "No Mum, I'm not going there. No, please no. I can't go there." He doesn't say, "I don't want to." He tells the truth: "I can't."

So they answer the letter together, not to Dad, but to the official who sent it. "Dear Sir or Madam. We thank you for your generous offer, but unfortunately for personal and family reasons we cannot…"

Only a week later another letter comes, this time by registered post, and with an official seal. Mum and Marek read it. "I am required to inform you, regretfully, that if your son Marek does not enter the Freedom Gymnasium on the first of September of the next school year, financial support for your family will be reduced to the legal minimum."

The "legal minimum" is officialese for poverty. Mum is sick and could never earn enough. This is too tough a choice for Marek, who is still hardly more than a child. He knows he can't leave but he has no solution. It is Eli who comes to his aid. At five he is not a babbling child but an observant boy. His grown-up soul has already calmed down in the prison of childhood. It has become used to its limitations, and has learned to live in this child, which it still is. "Marek, don't leave," he tells his older protector, as if he were the

63

one doing the protecting. "Stay with Mum and me. You don't have to be frightened for us."

You don't have to be frightened: that's easy to say, but Mum is going almost crazy with fear. She paces around the flat faster than usual and even when she sits down she is still panting.

But then something happens. Jana from the fourth floor is the one who visits most often. She has an older daughter, recently married. Jana is a programmer and has most of the qualities that Mum lacks. So first of all she is slim and tall and her straight hair hangs down beside her dry but not wrinkled cheeks. She breathes almost inaudibly, even when she's going up stairs. She has an inner calm – a peculiar equilibrium, as if she no longer expects anything from life but at the same what she has is enough for her. She doesn't pound on a keyboard, but has a scarf full of chips and electrodes around her head. Every day she checks her own state of health. So one day Jana is visiting as usual, and as usual she lines up Mom's medicines on the shelf and tries to persuade her to take them regularly, when Eli gets in her way and grabs her hand. Jana shivers at the sudden touch but doesn't pull away, and Eli looks up at her and says, "Jana, we need help. So that Marek doesn't have to go away. Jana, will you help us?"

Mum lunges at Eli, wanting to stop him. "Jana, please, pay no attention to him!" she insists, but what has been said cannot be unsaid. Soon Jana is getting the truth out of Mum, who tells her everything. Jana leaves deep in thought, stops at the door and comes back to stroke Eli's hair. "What a wise little thing you are."

Over the next few weeks Jana organizes a collection. All the mothers, friends and former colleagues who come here, without knowing why, are going to make small monthly donations so that Mum, Marek and Eli can go on living here.

24

Bear Witness

Marek gazed into the profound darkness of the chilly loft under the roof, but his mind was faraway, heading back to those two beloved beings he had lost so many years ago. Poor Mum. It had taken her a long time to be reconciled to the collection. She found it so hard; she just couldn't admit to herself that it wasn't her who was protecting her sons, but the other way around. She wrote teaching texts long into the night, she didn't sleep, and she couldn't get enough air. But for the moment the help that Eli had asked for so unaffectedly was enough for them to get by. In retrospect, across the gulf of sixty years, Marek could see what had happened with Jana as the first sign that Eli was truly exceptional, in a way that was immediate, without contrivance. For if anyone else had said and done what he had said and done back then, it would have had no effect at all.

The thought brought him a reassuring sense of security for tomorrow. He would not be facing it as a lone old man. He would confront it in the certainty that he was backed by an immortal teaching. Immortal, that was the word that came to his mind. Immortal Eli. Tomorrow Eli would be there with him. To think "Eli" was the same as to think "God". Today for the first time Marek felt it fully as pure truth.

Somewhere in the corner by a beam a mouse rustled. Marek lay on his back, stretched right out flat. The candle flickered out and around him was a darkness like the grave. He could easily have been dead and this is what the aftermath of death might be like: a persisting awareness.

The sun was not yet up as Marek climbed down the ladder. He had not slept at all but he felt stronger than ever before. His inner doubts had fallen silent, and even when his thoughts strayed to Hana, he did not tremble with fear.

At the door he turned once more towards the child's bed at the end of the shrine. Although it was quite different from the bed in Holesovice, and Marek was the only living person who could have testified to the difference, it had now become more real than the real thing. Until now the shrine had been no more than a building, a reminder, but now the spirit was dwelling in it. Eli was truly living in it. He was here so that his lost followers, groping for a way in the dark, should recognize him.

By the time Marek had hobbled up to the saddle of the hill, he had warmed up and the landscape was emerging from the early morning mist. It was as if happiness itself were walking with him, and the more happiness there was, the more a loneliness set up house in Marek's heart. Not his own, but the loneliness of everyone who had not yet found Eli. Of those who were waiting for Marek in Litohoro. Of those who cursed and threatened them day after day, yet found Eli. Of those who were waiting for Marek in Litohoro. Marek now understood his task precisely: he must bear witness.

He met Venca as he came down the hill. Everything was just waking up and the sounds of bleating and bellowing rose up from below. When Venca saw Marek, his eyes widened. "You're here already? You came down by yourself?"

Marek just nodded. He still had no urge to speak; it would be too easy to lose his newly acquired certainty. At the same time he felt guilty, because Venca probably took it as a sign of his own failure. In the alley between the bungalows he went his way, wordless.

"I've heated up some water for you," announced Natalia, full of energy even this early in the morning. How could she have guessed he would arrive just now? The water in the bath was indeed hot, still steaming, and the steam condensing on the walls.

When he saw Natalia it was as if he had returned from eternity to life. It was a smooth return. Especially when he threw off his stale clothing and submerged his stiff body in the embrace of hot water.

It was then that drowsiness assailed him. Lying in hot water was too pleasant. His eyelids started to droop.

"You shouldn't fall asleep now." She gave him a little push. "The water's getting cold. Dry yourself and go to bed."

She was right. He forced himself to get out. She handed him a towel and a robe – as automatically as if she had been living with him for years. The smell of eggs wafted from the main room.

"Where are your parents?" it occurred to him to ask. "When did your family reach Greece? Or did you come by yourself?"

"My parents have stayed in Dubrovnik." Dubrovnik. The word struck him to the quick. Dubrovnik, where they had beaten Eli to death, where Eli's own prophecy had been fulfilled. But Natalia was continuing.

"Dad's Czech and Mum's Polish. Dad had a company making air conditioning, you wouldn't believe it. He correctly figured out that it wouldn't be needed. So he moved production to the Mediterranean and switched to heating. In Dubrovnik he bought a boat, and several houses. He's got an eye for the main chance."

Marek's thoughts were whirling. The calm he had found in the shrine was gone. "Wait Natalia, were you born there?"

"Dubrovnik... my native town," she laughed. "That was where my Mum spat me out. It was a long time ago. I'm not as young as you think. Maybe compared to you, but otherwise..."

"How old are you?"

"Thirty-three." That surprised him. Eli had died in his thirties and he would have guessed her younger. He calculated: Eli had died in 2135, and she had been born in... 2135. In the same year. And in the same town. It unnerved him but he didn't know what its implications were. It wasn't clear to him at all and he wasn't ready to think about it right now, when he was facing the task in Litohoro. "Rich parents." He tried to conceal what he was thinking. "But you still left?"

"Mum cared desperately about that wealth. She's a snob." Natalia sounded truly indignant. "My parents, I have to say it, are disgusting people. They hold luxury blow-outs for other rich people on their boat. They live behind walls, behind barbed wire and with an armed guardhouse. Like in prison. Can you understand it? It's them that are behind the fence. They're not free. That's why I escaped."

Barbed wire and an armed guardhouse... yes, that was Dubrovnik. The Czech colony in Dubrovnik, as Marek too had known it.

He couldn't stop thinking about it. He thought about it so much that he realized his mind wasn't on what it should be... So she had been born in that town in the same year.

If she hadn't been there, if he hadn't let her stay, his mind would have still been on eternity and he would have set off to Litohoro in the right frame of mind. From the start Marek had suspected that Natalia might not be a part of God's plan. Except now he knew when and where she was born, it seemed it might be God's plan after all. The only problem was that he couldn't understand it – not yet. And so he accepted the fried eggs and onion with mixed feelings.

25

To Litohoro

Just before noon the bungalow was shaken by vibrations and through the door the sound of an engine reverberating. Marek sat down on the bed and his eyes met hers. He had time to tell her a little about what they wanted from him, and then she accompanied him to the door. He was gradually piecing it all together. In the end there might be some rhyme and reason to it. He could be her hope.

Outside there was a cool breeze but the sun was burning. Behind the wheel Konstantinos looked as impatient as always. Marek climbed into the back and before shutting the door glanced back at Natalia, standing in the doorway. He was moved by the simple feeling that he, Eli's brother, had his own home; not just a roof, but a home. Had God perhaps sent her to him?

Seen through smoked glass New Vinohrady took on the patina of the past. Maybe that was how, from a similar perspective, Eli might see the lives of his followers.

Three alleyways further up, old Samaris, the only Greek who had joined them, was sitting in front of his bungalow. When the first of the Followers of Eli had arrived Samaris had already been living there with his wife and two sons, the only people in the whole deserted resort. He had his herd of goats and kept bees in hives at the foot of the mountain. It was said that Samaris had owned a large olive grove further to the south, but the olives perished when the climate cooled down bringing winter frosts. It was not clear what Samaris and his family, including his sons' wives, thought about Eli, but they got on well with their Slav neighbours, and came to Marek's sermons. And children were born to them.

It was school-break time again and little boys excitedly ran after the car. Konstantinos was driving slowly and the boys made faces at the windows and waved. Through the smoked glass they didn't recognize Marek.

Beyond the settlement were pastures and long narrow fields. A few isolated small houses were falling apart there. Only one was in good repair; it stood on a small hillock, surrounded by vines and the stumps of felled olives. This was the home of Jakob Halevi and his wife and daughter. He was Jewish and indeed one of the few Jews to have accepted Eli as a messiah. Marek had known Jakob's parents. They had been among Eli's admirers in Prague although they had never acknowledged Eli as messiah, for he was not a Jew. According to Jakob's parents and many other Jews God would never send a messiah who was not of his own chosen people. Of course Eli and so Marek too might have had Jewish ancestors on their mother's side. It could not be ruled out, but he and Eli had known nothing to suggest such a thing, and nor had their mother. Eli had his own answer to the question anyway: "Do not wonder who I am, but consider instead who you are."

Although they were not believers, Jakob's parents had been happy to regard Eli as a wise man, a *tzadik* or holy man, who could see what the world needed. They followed him as far as Dubrovnik. Then they boarded a boat for Israel, the only Mediterranean state to have survived as a state through the period of intense heat and drought. Israel now incorporated the depopulated but later rain-irrigated territories of the former Lebanon, Jordan, Syria and Egypt. It all suggested that at the end of the twenty-second century the chosen people were taking up their historic role. For some decades Israeli scientists had developed a project for the removal of the diffraction grille, but had halted it when they saw that the climate change it brought was advantageous for the Jewish state. Israel had become the leading world power. The only problem was that the chosen people too were afflicted by a steep decline in births. It was a heavy blow, and another test, as some Jews believed. Or an incomprehensible wrong committed by a God who had turned away from his nation. Jakob had returned from Israel. Not in order to have children, although in the end that happened, but because he had accepted Eli. For Jakob Eli was the true messiah, awaited for thousands of years.

The settlement was now well behind them and the car gathered speed, slowing again in places where the track was eroded by flooding. Here, far from the settlement, old dried up trees still loomed, while new vegetation sprang up around them, so rampant and dense that not even the grazing sheep and goats could keep up with their growth. Marek's eyelids began to droop.

He woke up when the drive suddenly became smoother. New asphalt instead of the torn-up super-conductors had been laid around what had once been a tourist village but was now just a fishing village, and half deserted. There were cars parked in front of some of the houses. The residents were mostly the returning descendants of people who had been driven out by the drought. Only without children, villages like this one were drowning in sorrow. The first enthusiasm for repairing and rebuilding had faded, and so even the inhabited houses were becoming dilapidated again. All the same, they had a school for the few remaining children. As always Marek felt a wave of grief for the people here. Eli had not wanted them to be sad. If he had lived, he would certainly have had answers to all their afflictions. Marek reproached himself for not having enough knowledge or strength.

They drove on, upstream along the river. Its swollen waters made waves under its banks, carrying away rubble and pieces of wood. The closest bridge that had not been swept away was the highway bridge. Quite a lot of cars were once again riding the highway, often expensive modern cars. But what did "modern" mean now? In fact Europe had fallen back more than a hundred years. There were trucks pointlessly transporting goods, perhaps those heating systems made by Natalia's Dad. It struck Marek that people were unteachable. Especially in the big cities. They wouldn't face up to the decline in the birthrate, and behaved as if they were going to be there forever.

Further on there was a section many kilometres long where the highway had been swept away by flooding and so even these brand-new cars, symbols of wealth, had to drive along a provisional surface made of concrete panels. It was around here that there was a turning to New Karlin, the second colony of the Followers of Eli.

It occurred to Marek that people were always the same, like that pharaoh he had once read about in the Bible, who had so obstinately refused to let the Jews go, preferring to put up with terrible disasters.

The bluish silhouette of Mount Olympus was already looming up ahead of them. Today there was sun on its slopes and the snow glinted on the summit. Greeks like Konstantinos sometimes said that now their Olympus was covered in ice and no-one could get to the summit, the Greek gods might return there. Greece for the Greeks! It was what they sometimes chanted at demonstrations. But what Greece, without children?

Once again they were speeding along the highway and the journey was fast coming to an end. They turned off and continued downhill, directly opposite the mountain. Around Litohoro, once a spa town full of people who wanted to walk up Olympus, workers were finishing brick fortifications. Marek remembered Natalia and her home in Dubrovnik. They were flagged down by a patrol and Konstantinos spoke to a Greek in uniform.

26

The Blessing of the Bread

The main government building doubled as a college, museum, theatre… It had originally served solely as a museum of classical antiquity, but that had ceased to be interesting, and the classical exhibits and explanatory panels had all been stuffed into one room. In the freed-up hall there was a new exhibition on the climate changes and migration of peoples. Marek couldn't see the point. Wasn't the earth itself the best exhibition? Wasn't it enough to look out of the window – at the snow-white cap of Olympus? At the deep furrows gouged by water? And as for the migration? Wouldn't it be enough just to ask anyone where his parents had been born and what they had lived through?

Pavol dashed out of the glass door. "Ah Marek, excellent, excellent!" He seemed relieved that Marek was here, having perhaps guaranteed that he would be. "I assured them that you could be persuaded."

Several young people gathered around them – probably students. The precocious generation of one-in-five children, as they were known because of the ratio of children to couples. They regarded Marek curiously, but he was attracting more urgent looks from across the street, from people who were obviously Followers of Eli. Two families, one child in arms, two holding the hands of an older, bearded man. "Wait," Marek instructed, and walked across the street to them. Yes, they were people who sometimes came to New Vinohrady to hear him preach, but he had never yet met them in the town, in their home environment. They were easy to recognize – by the children.

Marek met eyes full of expectation. He saw himself through those eyes. He saw how they saw him: as a prophet, as the highest representative of the Messiah and of God himself in this world. Before he could say anything a younger man spoke up, scarcely more than a boy, shaven and with short hair. "Would you come to lunch with us? We would like to invite you."

Marek had little time to think. "I would like to. Believe me. Only I don't know…" He turned to Pavol. At that moment something hard hit the wall and everyone automatically flinched and hunched. It was… a shoe. "Get lost and go provoke people with those kids somewhere else!" shouted a woman from the neighbouring shoe shop. "Go back to your settlements and leave us alone."

Pavol darted over from the other side and caught Marek by the arm. "Please Marek, come on. You can't stand here. They're waiting for you. And you… Leave right now! How the hell did you know he was coming?"

Marek knew he had to do as Pavol said. He was his guest. But he couldn't tear his eyes from those followers.

"At least bless us." One of the women reached out a hand, the one who was holding the baby. And in her hand she held bread.

Marek was embarrassed, as he always was when they wanted that from him. To bless, always to bless, whether a newborn baby, newlyweds, the sick, cattle, tools… and now bread. He didn't feel worthy or qualified for anything like that. He was no saint. He had just loved his brother. But what else could he do? He stretched out his hand to the bread and… touched it. "You have already blessed it yourselves," he whispered. "If you believe in Eli, you have his blessing. It is not I but you that are a blessing to this land. It is you."

27

I am here to bear witness about Eli

They led him into a middle-sized lecture hall. Almost as soon as he entered he was gripped by doubt. He was nothing more than a boy who had been born in Prague Holesovice. His only claim to fame was that he had had a brother called Eli.

They had prepared an armchair and water for him at a table at the front. Well, he deserved a little comfort as the oldest person present. Not even the professor from Salonika, whom Pavol introduced, was as old. He had curly hair, not long, half black and half grey, and round spectacles on a short nose. His face was deeply creased. Apart from the professor, a sympathetic and dignified-looking man in a black cassock, with long hair and beard, was seated at a table, as were the mayor of Litohoro and the director of the college. The audience consisted of about fifteen young people.

Marek sat down in the armchair and closed his eyes. He focused his thoughts on Eli, needing to catch hold of something, to reassure himself that he had any right to be here. Then he remembered the shrine. That was why he had been there. It already seemed so long ago, but in fact it was less than twenty-four hours. An eternity, he realized. Immortal Eli, sent by God.

Pavol walked to the front and everyone in the lecture room fell silent. He spoke first in Greek and then turned to Marek. "Professor Ianis Simonides is a philosopher specializing in the study of religions, faith and religious sects. He has come from Salonika because he is interested, sincerely interested, in the nature of your teaching. Father Methodius here studied theology in Athens and has restored the monastery at the foot of Olympus. He is its first abbot since its restoration. I have introduced you as Marek of Prague, brother of Eli of Prague, and the best-known exponent of his teaching. Mayor Stavros and Director Novotny you already know."

The professor turned to Marek across the table. In his hand was a pen with which he drummed on a reddish folder. When he spoke he stopped after every sentence to give Pavol time to translate. "I am truly honoured, Marek, that you have come here among us. For me it is evidence that you are genuine in your intentions, and have no ulterior motives. I have met various preachers, and all of them without exception preferred to stay in the circle of their supporters. I can see that you are different, Marek. You have real humility, I think. I hope you will not be offended if I ask you some inquisitive and maybe not entirely pleasant questions?"

Simonides fell silent, and it was up to Marek to respond. So much empty talk, he thought, but everyone was waiting for him to say something. He shrugged. "The only unpleasant questions are stupid questions, don't you think?"

There was a murmur in the lecture hall even before Pavol translated; some of the students spoke Czech. "Of course," the professor nodded. "I entirely agree. So. I would be interested, indeed what most interests me, is whether you identify as a Christian. Methodius here if I'm not mistaken, thinks that you do not."

"We identify with what we have seen, heard and lived through for ourselves." This response came to Marek immediately; finally he was gaining self-confidence. "But that doesn't mean we deny what we have not seen, not heard or not lived through." Yes, that was perhaps what Eli had said when they asked him. He had even repeated it often. "We do not reject the Bible. We are living its continuation."

"That is wise, truly wise," the professor said patronisingly, and Marek realized he was talking down to him as if he were a child, and was never going to take him seriously. "It is rare to find such tolerance in the propagators of a new faith. But the thing is that Christianity is based on entirely clear, firm foundations. For a Christian, Christianity is not something that he hasn't lived through but thinks may nevertheless be true. For a Christian it is the truth. From the Old Testament, from the creation of the world, to the sacrifice of his own son, whom God sent into the world to die for the sins of mankind. Christians believe that..."

"Excuse me sir. Can I say something on this point?" The interruption from the audience came from a fair-haired young man with penetrating blue eyes, definitely not a Greek.

Pavol turned to him with annoyance. "There will be time for your questions at the end. But for now I must ask… What?" The professor was gesticulating, indicating that he wanted the man to be allowed to speak. "Very well, what is it you want to say?"

The young man got up with exemplary politeness. "Professor, Christians are not all agreed on how literally to take the Bible. For example, the last great council, the Council of Brazil in 2098, acknowledged that Darwinism was not in conflict with Biblical teaching on the creation of the world. Genesis was definitively no longer to be taken as a literal account of events, but only as a symbolic expression. And it is the same with Jesus and his birth from a virgin…"

"Please, please." Pavol interrupted the torrent of words that he had been translating. "I can't keep up with you. And we haven't come here to dispute about Christianity. That's not the reason why we're here. Please…"

"That's true," Simonides nodded. "It's not why we are here. And we already know that Marek is tolerant. Ultimately, it's not just the Bible and Christianity. What about the Talmud for example, or the Koran? Does every religion have the same value for you?"

Marek was still watching the student who had spoken up. He saw engagement in his face. Real engagement. It appealed to him. Marek knew the answer to the professor's second question, for Eli had said it himself. "Can anything but Christianity continue in the middle of Europe?" he asked.

"But at the time when you… when Eli was born, there were plenty of Muslims in Central Europe as well. Before you murdered them."

"It would be more accurate to say, before WE murdered them. It happened in Greece too. But that is not the issue. Eli used to say that only those born in a particular place count, but they include those who died long ago and not just those who were born and are still living there. Only when more people migrate to a place than have ever been born and lived in that place, will the roots of that place disappear."

Methodius had been wanting to say something for some time, and now finally found an opening. "That is all very nice, Marek, but

I shall reframe the question. Do you personally believe that Jesus was the Son of God? Actually God?" The monk was still smiling in a friendly way.

"I am not here to bear witness to Jesus." Marek for the first time raised his voice. "I am here to bear witness to Eli. I don't know whether Jesus was the Son of God, and it's not important to me. Probably he was, because otherwise his disciples would have been mistaken. And I don't want them to have been mistaken." Indeed. Marek understood Jesus's followers very well; he could imagine what they had probably experienced when their master left them. "I only know one thing… that Eli was the Son of God." As he said this the power of his own words filled him. Yes, that was who Eli was.

When Pavol translated his speech, there were fresh murmurs in the lecture hall. Methodius fixed surprised eyes on Marek, as if sorry for him. The mayor frowned and the student who had spoken up explained something to his neighbours, or more precisely to a bespectacled dark-haired girl beside him. The director Novotny laughed. Only the professor remained calm and even looked satisfied, as if he had finally discovered what he wanted. Soon he took back the lead and the noise dropped away.

"Are you aware of the impact of your claim, Marek? You have just told us that your brother, who was born in the middle of the twenty-second century in Prague, was sent into the world by God himself. Let us leave aside the question of why he was sent, and the nature of his mission in the world, and talk for a moment about the other, no less important part of your statement. Belief in a messiah sent by God implies a no less strong faith in the existence of God. Not some abstract, only vaguely defined God, but a quite personal, self-conscious God with some particular plan for mankind and the world. What do you know of that God, Marek? What did your brother tell you about Him? You were the closest to your brother, after all, throughout his life and up to his tragic death."

It was strange. Until now, for the whole thirty-five years since his brother's death, Marek had been reluctant to speak about God. Sometimes he referred to God to help get a point across, but very unwillingly, and to be honest he had no real ideas on the subject.

Eli had given him no guidance on it, and had offered no image, let alone proclaimed that God had sent him. He had spoken only in hints. But now all that had changed, and over the last two days God seemed to have come to occupy His place. As if He had only now entered the world, out of Eli's legacy.

"My brother didn't talk about God," he answered truthfully, "but he is the reason that I'm sitting here with you thirty-five years after his martyr's death which he himself foresaw." (He deliberately used "martyr's" instead of the professor's "tragic".) "I know at least something about God, and I will happily confirm his existence for you. Anyone who has lived or accepted Eli's teaching, who has glimpsed at least the reflected light of his life, can save the world that mankind cannot bend to its will. I mean this world, which God gave into man's care but man failed to look after. Eli often talked about this failure of mankind. About man's unfulfilled duty to be a protector and steward. About the wastage of the radiant moment that is life. I don't know what God is like, how He thinks, how He endures. I know only that He came back. Once again we can speak of Him as a living being, although we don't know if He really is such a thing. How could we know? We are not worthy to stand on an equal footing with Him, after all. Perhaps..." Marek hesitated, afraid of what he had been about to say. "Perhaps now He is speaking through me." That is what he had wanted to say. Such arrogance, yet on the other hand, the words had not been his. He had never before managed to formulate such complex and bold ideas. No, they had not come from his own head. "Perhaps it isn't just chance that I'm here today. It isn't chance that you invited me. I am here to speak. Anyone who wants to listen can listen."

"You believe in God, but you claim to know nothing about his will?" The professor was all but jumping up from his chair. Ideas were whirling behind his broad flat forehead and his eyes were bright with his passion for winning arguments. For him it was like chess, a game. Simonides was a player. "I mean in the sense of what God wants from you," he continued. "Didn't he give you any guidance? No Ten Commandments? No distinct clue as to how to achieve salvation? What must a Follower of Eli do in order to be saved? Accept Eli, you may tell me. But why is that enough? Does it mean he cannot sin? What if a Follower of Eli steals something? What if he hurts someone? Does he have a claim to salvation just because he's a believer?"

Suddenly Marek saw Hana in his mind. What she had been stirring up in the community was wrong of course. So wrong. But she had been close to Eli. During his lifetime she had been the woman Eli had loved.

Pavol was translating as well as he could, and the sweat was standing out on his brow. Methodius also wanted to say something and then Simonides interrupted. At that point Pavol got lost, switching haplessly from the professor to Methodius and back again, but finally carrying on with a translation of Methodius's words. "Excuse me, professor, but not even a Christian will tell you much about his God. The true Christian is an inner Christian. He knows his God with his heart, not through his reason."

"But in addition to what you call his heart, Father, the Christian has a whole range of guidance as to how to behave." The professor refused to yield. "And he has the institution of confession – purification from sin. And he has Jesus's statements from the Gospels – his parables. Whereas with all respect, what Marek is presenting us with here is just a few feelings. And it is impossible to build on that. I cannot see the fundamental dogmas of this faith."

The clever fair-haired student had evidently been wanting to speak for some time. Now he burst out without waiting for permission. "But professor, isn't it simply that this faith is still young? What was Christianity like in the year 33?"

That was the last thing that Pavol translated for a while. The professor, Methodius and the director of the school (a thin man with a sunken chest) all started to speak at once. Marek couldn't make out whether they were reacting to the student's words or to something that had been said earlier.

His mind ran back to the question of salvation. What would happen to Hana? In one period of her life she had been a wonderful woman. She had sacrificed herself for Eli, lived for him. But in recent years... No, Marek didn't want to judge her, and had no right to do so. All the same, what would happen to those who hurt others? Norbert of New Vinohrady had beaten his wife to death in his house. And what was worse, had beaten her to death because they had no children. Often he had shouted at her that she probably didn't believe in Eli enough, and that was why she was barren. They had driven him out. There had been no trial. Perhaps that was the punishment – expulsion. Eli had often talked of the gate through which all must pass, but through which those who want to come back may return. And the main condition was not to rebel against nature. Anyone who wanted to return here on earth, in their lifetime, had to submit to its order. As Eli used to say, if you cannot be a farmer, at least be part of the farm. But now Marek remembered another statement of his. It had been in Split in Croatia. Many Central Europeans had been arriving there, the largest group among them Czechs. The Croatian towns and villages had been half deserted, but in one village the local inhabitants had put up resistance to the migrants. Nobody was sure who fired first, but whatever the case, the Followers of Eli also engaged in the killing. They drove out the Croatians and burned their houses. When Eli found out about it he went crazy, even before he sank into the deep grief from which he never emerged to the day of his death. Marek had never seen him so furious. "Anyone who thinks he can do as he likes because his reward is certain, is wrong," he shouted. "Everyone who passes that gate, passes on his own account. Not with me. You won't get through it more easily with me." That was the answer, Marek realized only now. How could he ever have forgotten? But immediately he was afraid, wondering how much of what Eli had said or done he had already forgotten. Could it be lost forever?

Once again Pavol was translating, but the questions seemed to be going round in circles. Methodius no longer contributed and seemed sunk in thought. Simonides by contrast looked satisfied. He had established that Eli's successors had no system of rules and dogmas that could be called a religion.

Questions were now allowed from the audience. A woman on the back bench, who was older than the students sitting in front of her, immediately stood up. "Can you explain why people have stopped having children?" she said in a disagreeable voice. "And why your people have more children? Is there some sort of magic in it?"

The faces of all present tightened painfully, as if at something embarrassing that should not be mentioned.

"I don't have any explanation. Some things just have to be accepted. Some things are beyond our understanding, aren't they?"

The woman didn't sit down. She was tall, thin, with dyed blonde hair. "So you think it's the work of that God of yours, do you? Can you tell me why that God of yours hates us?"

Before Marek had time to consider this, a student in the first row spoke up. "Please lady, do you know how many people perished between the years 2220 and 25 during the great migration? In Europe it was about half the population. Most of them died a violent death or from hunger. That means they died a death that humans themselves caused. I think a God who doesn't allow as many people as before to be born isn't a hateful God. To me he seems quite merciful."

The woman flushed. "Let him answer for himself! Why do you defend him? What do you know about it? When a woman like me can't have children, what is she supposed to live for?"

The student mumbled something apologetic, but added, "But surely you know what to do. The Followers of Eli have no problem having children."

"That God of theirs is blackmailing us, is he? Believe in me or you'll stay childless? He's an extortionist, not God."

Marek now felt the need to intervene. "Please take it this way: children are a blessing. That's one of the things people have forgotten. Who in the last century still thought of children as a gift? We surrounded ourselves with so many things… A child is a gift. It is our reward when we have one. But it is not a punishment when we do not."

"I still don't understand what you lot have done to deserve it," the woman continued. "What have you done that's so wonderful?"

"Not me," he smiled. "I haven't done anything to deserve it, and I haven't been rewarded with children."

"You? Of course not. What would you know about women…?"

The woman was not to be stopped and Pavol looked questioningly at Marek, clearly to check whether Marek wanted him to carry on translating. Marek nodded, and immediately heard from Pavol's lips: "You've never had a woman in your life and now you're pretending you don't have a child because you don't deserve it."

No, the jibe couldn't touch him. What is more, Natalia was waiting for him at home. All the same he was sorry for the woman. In the end it was the same everywhere: people were resentful, angry, but without a trace of humility. "My brother Eli said that there would be many unhappy women and men in the world and they would blame us for their misfortune but that it was not us but mankind that was to blame. He told us to take comfort in the fact that those who will not be born at least will not suffer. And mankind will be shown how to survive. That was more or less what my brother said. He was saying it before it started to happen. Ten years before." Now Marek turned to the professor. "How do you explain that, professor?" And then immediately to Pavol, "Ask him to explain it. How Eli knew about the children. Translate that."

Only the professor was prepared for the question. "Don't take this personally, Marek," he launched confidently into his answer, "but I didn't hear those words from him myself. I wasn't there. And I have genuine doubts. I mean no disrespect, but as time goes by our memories change. We add a little here, subtract a little there, and something blurs. We all do it. Your brother may well have said nothing so unambiguous. You were with him all the time. And during his short life he must have told you many things. It would be curious if some of what he said didn't seem to fit a situation that developed later. What's more, you loved your brother. So you would want to interpret his words in the best way you could, in the most clairvoyant light. Nobody could condemn you for that. Nobody."

Marek was not sure that he understood. Was Professor Simonides casting doubt on Eli's words? Was he challenging recorded testimony? Marek wasn't the only one who had heard those words. They were generally known. Marek now felt that the debate was over for him. He saw satisfaction on the faces of the mayor and the director Novotny and many others. They looked relieved, as if the professor had come up with a long-awaited explanation. There was even some applause. Methodius didn't clap. Marek noticed that for some time his attention had been turned inwards; he was praying.

Pavol regarded Marek impatiently, to see if he would reply, but no answer came and indeed the professor's words deserved none. Instead the student took the floor. He was sharp as a razor. "Even if Eli didn't predict it, it's still quite strange, don't you think? Suddenly all over the world far fewer children are born, except to the Followers of Eli. They continue to have children with no problems. As far as I know, neither biology nor medicine has come up with an explanation. The sperm penetrates the egg normally, but the eggs don't start to divide. The miracle of new life, which we thought we knew everything about, just stops happening. Isn't that close to a proof that Someone Else decides on the genesis of life?"

The professor was surprisingly ready to engage in argument with the student, probably considering himself unassailable. He laughed and said, "That's the same kind of thinking as when people believed, for example here in Greece, that water fell down into a precipice on the edges of the sea. Anything they couldn't investigate or explain they attributed to supernatural forces. Yes, science has not yet solved this problem around conception and the birthrate, that's true, but one day we will discover the cause. In my view the theory of a virus, which has not affected the community of Eli's followers because they live in isolated communities, is very promising. And if Marek and the others would agree to the collection of biological material, we would certainly be further on. And that brings me to the question of what knowledge means for you, Marek. Aren't you interested in all that we have already found out about the origins of the universe? About human health? Everything we have managed to develop by way of technology?"

Marek no longer wanted to answer. The student was once again waving his hand eagerly, but it was Methodius who spoke. He uttered just one sentence: "We Christians believe that the genesis of life in the body of a woman is always the work of God."

Pavol translated it and turned to the monk again, but that was all Methodius wanted to say. It was clear that he fundamentally disagreed with the professor.

Marek knew what to say, for Eli had expressed himself on science. People had asked him about it in Prague – a group of intellectuals like these. They had been desperately looking for someone to follow. Something to believe in. But at the same time they had been unable to open up to anything genuinely new. The young Eli, only twenty at the time, had answered that science was good as a tool of understanding, but was not a good tool in the hands of bad farmers. Science, like all human life, would need to be founded again. Marek could have repeated that now, but he no longer had a reason. He knew these professors, mayors... It was like preaching to the deaf.

The student in the first row stood in for him. "I don't think anyone is denying the point of knowledge. But our particular kind of science discredited itself when it first failed to cope with the change of climate that man had caused, and then failed to calculate the consequences of that grille. Look at the frozen olive groves here in Greece. At Scandinavia covered in eternal snow. At the harsh climate in Central Europe, where only the remaining Scandinavians and Hungarians survive. Those are the fruits of our science. And that theory of yours about some virus... The communities of Eli's followers are not the only isolated settlements in the world, especially in today's world, after the great migration. As far as I know, very few children are being born even in remote mountain settlements. Or in faraway Australia. Or on islands. You just don't want to admit that you don't have an answer. That you can't explain it. It just can't be explained by human minds."

The students in the second row were tapping their fingers on their temples and gesticulating at each other clearly conveying that their colleague (Marek heard the name Tomas) had lost his mind.

In the meantime the woman in the back row had risen again and was shouting something. Pavol leant towards Marek and quietly interpreted her words. "She's shouting that she definitely hasn't got a virus, and nor has her husband. Let the professor come up with a better explanation."

Now Marek rose himself. Something had sent an order to his legs. "Shall we go?" he asked, and evidently sounded so decisive that Pavol looked around the room and called into the excited debate, "Marek is leaving." Surprisingly nobody seemed to care. They were too busy arguing. Pavol led Marek to the door. Once they were outside, Tomas came running out after them. The enthusiasm radiating from the young man was familiar to Marek. It was the enthusiasm of the old times, from the beginnings back in Prague. Marek was the only one who had always stayed sober. He had never fully shared the extravagant passion of other followers. He was just accompanying Eli. Looking after him, while their father fled the country.

Tomas wanted to exploit the fact that Pavol was still there. "I'll learn Czech," he said. "I'll learn Czech and then come to see you."

Marek believed him.

Someone else came through the glass door and approached them. A dark imposing figure. Methodius. Standing up he looked even more dignified. His bearded face was almost expressionless, and only his eyes and brow betrayed his mood. He turned first to Pavol and said something to him quietly. Pavol seemed changed somehow when he addressed Marek. "Father Methodius asks whether you might bless each other. It is something he would greatly appreciate."

The blessing business again. But Tomas and Methodius gave Marek a good feeling. Some seed had been sown. And getting into the fresh air put him in a better mood. He touched Methodius on the shoulder. When they stood face to face they were about the same height. "Could you teach me how?" he asked through Pavol. "People keep wanting me to bless them but I don't know how. Christian priests have been learning to do it for two thousand years longer than me."

Pavol interpreted and a gleam of joy flickered in Methodius's eyes. But his joy remained solemn. He took a step back and looked Marek straight in the eye. He was evidently concentrating. Then immediately he dropped his eyes, bent his head and put his hands together, before once again straightening his head and blessing

Marek with the sign of the cross. It then occurred to both to hold out their hands to each other. Their fingers touched. "Eli is pleased," said Marek.

Not long afterward the last houses of Litohoro were passing Marek's car window. The road glistened with rain but the clouds had cleared and the sun was dipping towards the outlines of the mountains in the west. In the end what stayed with Marek from the whole day were two pairs of eyes. In Methodius's he had read trust, and in Tomas's enthusiasm. On the edge of uncertainty, on the edge of the dissolution of his brother's legacy, those eyes offered hope that the immortal Eli would truly live. The weight of the idea that now it was really up to him, that the heritage of Eli was his responsibility, bore down on Marek and he shrank back onto the hard seat of the field vehicle. It had already been a long life, all the way from birth to this moment, and didn't look as if it could end any time soon.

He was woken by the crunching of gravel and the deep ruts in the dirt road. They were getting close to Vinohrady. Natalia floated up into his mind. The strange way in which she had created a home with him. He looked forward to being with her.

28

I am not yours

Holesovice is not a bad place. There are protective walls against the flood of migrants and lowlife of all kinds. Even though in recent years a lot of people have gone back to the countryside or headed south, plenty still remain. Recently Lifelong has had the centre of the city cleansed. Cleansing meant that first the army closed off the area, and then everyone without a job or registered address in the centre was forced to get on special buses and were taken to a newly built concrete camp. According to Lifelong the camp provided every comfort, but the lowlife evidently didn't appreciate this sort of care. Some of them put up resistance, hurling paving stones and burning cars. The army intervened. There are many dead and wounded. When it is reported on state television, the seven-year-old Eli weeps. "There will be more, Marek," he laments, "many more."

Not that Holesovice is one of the best districts. Mum sometimes talks about the best districts. Apparently they gradually separated themselves off from the rest of the city in the twenty-first century, and they exploit all the scientific advances that mankind has achieved. Above all, modern medicine can now cure almost anything. And then there are robot cars and air vehicles, communication at a distance, broadcast of images direct to the nerve ends in the brain. There is electronic monitoring of metabolism and God knows what else. It's said that some young people in these districts never leave their rooms. They have everything they need inside. Others fly round the whole world, but always to protected zones and resorts of the same kind.

Marek's classmates at school talk a lot about all these advances. They don't interest Marek. His path leads elsewhere. He has Eli.

Then something unusual happens, an event with a long-term effect on Marek. A big aircar lands on the open space by the Vltava. The children of the area rush up to it to take a look, but the men getting out of it are armed, and scare the children away.

Eli is just getting ready for school, where he is already in second grade. Marek is helping him and happens to look out of the window as the vehicle lands. He sees three soldiers getting out and he sees them driving away the children. Then another figure gets out and walks towards the house. It's Dad. Marek hasn't seen him in a long time, a whole seven years, but he still recognizes him immediately. To his surprise he feels a wave of emotion. His head swims and he tries to suppress a sob. He holds his breath.

"Do you still love him?" He hears Eli's voice behind him.

"How on earth do you know who it is?" Marek wakes from a kind of spell.

"It's your Dad. The one who went away. We can't help him, Marek, he's beyond help."

Marek doesn't understand. Why should they help him anyway? Dad doesn't need help. It's them that need the help. "How d'you know? You don't know him. Dad's tough!" he yells at Eli and even surprises himself, for he has never yelled at his brother before. "He's rich. He's got everything! He doesn't need help. He doesn't need anything!"

As Marek turns away from the window, his legs feel like they are giving way under him. And to make it worse he sees Eli's eyes, large and clear, already with a hint of brown at seven. What's in those eyes? A reproach for Marek yelling at him? No, it's something else. Eli's eyes are apologizing for the fact that he, Eli, knows. That he can't do anything about it. That he can't help this man, who is Marek's father and so of course his own. At the same time Eli isn't sad. He's only a boy. A child. He has short hair trimmed by Mum and a pale, thin face. And his front teeth are missing. When he opens his mouth he looks just like an ordinary second-grader struggling with his homework. But that is only for a moment, and only to those who can't see the way his future spirit, still immature, is moulding his features from inside.

Marek walks around Eli. He is already sorry for yelling but he has no chance to apologize. Dad is already coming up in the elevator. In a moment he will be here. Marek wants to run out to meet him, but he stops at the door to Eli's room. He sits down on the bed and curls up into a ball. It's too long ago, but it's like yesterday. It hurts.

Marek hears Mum opening the door. She says nothing. She must have known about this visit. Dad is coming with her agreement. But what's it all about? Marek is scared they want to send him away. They want to separate him from Eli. Eli doesn't think so. "What are you afraid of, bro?" He lands a friendly punch on the shoulder of his much bigger brother, his basically full-grown brother, "He's the one who should be afraid." Then he sees that Marek has tears in his eyes. Clumsily, childishly, Eli falls into his embrace. They hug and Eli whispers, "Aren't I enough for you?"

It is only now they hear voices, a severe male voice and Mum's wheeze. "Well come in." And after a moment. "The boys are probably together. There... you know where, of course." The door opens.

The man who appears before Marek is not the same as the one who used to stand by his child's bed. His face has changed, his sharp features are rounder and blunter, and the skin is taut over them. He is now only a little taller than Marek, but his body, strengthened by the gym, is massive. So massive it makes the room feel cramped.

Memories start to crowd Marek's mind. The first nine years of life with this man. But the recriminations arrive too. This is the man who abandoned them. Except that Marek can't really be mad at him. Despite everything he's Dad. And it is only now that Marek feels what he has forbidden himself from feeling all these years, and what he compensated for with his love for Eli. He feels the pain of betrayal, incomprehensible, out of the blue. So many feelings in a single moment can't be coped with. Marek is shaken by sobs. And instead of everything that is running through his mind all that he can get out is just the one sentence, "What d'you want here?"

"Marek..." the man seems moved too. "And you Eli..." But he recovers fast and continues in a firmer voice, "I've come for you

Marek. For both of you. You're coming to live with me in the government district. Mum has agreed."

Only Marek doesn't agree. Something like that is out of the question. They can't leave their sick Mum and go away with this man – once their Dad. "No, I don't want to. I'm not going with you," Marek protests, and keeps a tight hold on Eli.

"You can't stay here, Marek. There's going to be war. You know it. A revolt can break out any moment. If it keeps on getting colder – and that's the forecast – we shall have to leave. Lifelong has many enemies, but a lot of possibilities, He isn't going to be on the losing side."

The man, who is once again a little bit Dad, takes a step forward. He wants to touch Eli – to stroke his hair. But Eli slips away and jumps to the window. Resistance flashes in his eyes. "Don't touch me!" he shouts. "You're not my Dad! You've never been my Dad! I'm not yours!"

Dad, that massive man reeking of expensive aftershave, with a gold chain round his neck, a metal bracelet and a big ring, seems taken aback. The small adversary crouching on the floor under the window really doesn't look like his son. Just take his eyes, which are bright and deep and round, while Dad's eyes are narrow, half-closed, as if he's always on his guard. But Dad has no intention of accepting failure, not yet. He isn't used to not having things his way. He waves a hand over the adversary and turns to Marek: "Then you at least." This quieter voice resonates with his former love. "You can't live this way anymore. I can see it Marek. I know what's going on. Who would know better than me? The world is dividing into losers and winners. Nothing in between. We've got to be strong, stronger than before. Marek…" The man sits down and puts an arm round Marek's shoulders. "Do you remember our car? We could never drive in it. But do you know what I travel in now? Go take a look out the window. That's how life is where I want to take you. You'll have the whole world at your feet. And you'll live for at least a hundred and fifty years."

"You won't live that long," says Eli from the window.

Both of them look over at him. Eli is sitting leaning against the wall. He has his arms round his legs and his chin on his knees. He is calm again and it seems impossible that he could have been furious a moment before. "You'll die long before that," he says again, and he is clearly not speaking to Marek. "Everything will fall apart on you. You should stay with us. You can save yourself here."

The man seems turned to stone. Drops of sweat appear on his brow and his breathing is more audible. He is afraid.

"I saw... I saw that aircar," Marek recovers himself, "But I can't go with you. I won't leave Eli and Mum."

"But Mum herself thinks it will be better for you. And you can bring that boy with you." He nods toward the window. "Even if he doesn't look that way, he's mine too."

"I'm not yours," Eli remarks, not angrily but almost too calmly. "I've never been yours."

"I know..." the man raises his voice and swallows. "I know you haven't had an easy time of it. But I always sent you money. I didn't forget about you. Mum has been ailing for years and didn't want to get treatment. It's one of the reasons I left. One day you'll understand me Marek." When no one says anything he carries on. "I have a wife and a little girl there. I can't take Mum. Maybe in time I'll arrange for her to go to a hospital, where she can be cured. But she has to want it."

Marek hesitates. Mum cured? Could he refuse something like that? But the voice comes from the window. "Don't believe him. He believes himself, but don't you believe him. He can't even help himself, let alone anybody else."

The man is starting to feel oppressed by the room. Marek touches him, feels the tension in his muscles. As if what he would most like would be to jump on that runt under the window and stamp the life out of him, but he has to control himself. "Marek, reconsider. They're waiting for me. I have to go. I'll come back one more time. I'll give you another chance."

"You've got no chance," said Eli, somehow indifferently.

The man – Dad – pretends he hasn't heard. "You'll go to the best schools," he continues, "and see the world. Lifelong needs a new elite. I've got big plans for you. For him too…" he gestures to the window. "I was looking forward to seeing him. He's my son."

"No I'm not," replies Eli. "And Lifelong is a murderer. If you leave us now you'll be a murderer too."

The man – Dad – rises from the bed, now infuriated enough to hurl himself at Eli. But he doesn't do it. He stands there helplessly. He tries to keep his voice firm but it is full of fear. "Don't speak that way about Lifelong. You could pay for that. All of us could. Don't speak that way – ever again!" At that he turns to the door. But then one last time to Marek. "Make the right decision, son."

Only Marek has already made his decision. He believes Eli.

The door closes. It is not Dad who has left now. Dad vanished from this man's face before that.

"Why on earth did you say that?" Marek asks his brother after a moment. Eli is fiddling with his backpack on the floor.

"Say what?"

"You said that if he left he would be a murderer."

Eli glances up surprised: "Did I say that?" He looks genuinely astounded. Then he pinches his nose. "Shouldn't we air the room?"

It only really starts to hurt that evening. Dad. He left Marek back then, and now again. Their paths have diverged forever.

But at least he has Eli. That evening he slips into bed next to him. Eli strokes Marek's brow and whispers. "Don't be afraid Marek, my Dad loves you." Which Marek cannot understand at all. All the same, the words are soothing.

29

Snow

Dad's second visit, that second chance he spoke of, never takes place. Marek suspects he knows why. Dad doesn't want to encounter Eli, and the dark future Eli predicted for him. Dad is afraid.

Is Marek sorry for him? No. Not for that man who left. But for that Dad deep down inside, under the wall of muscles, he is so sorry it almost sends him mad. Then gradually the regret recedes and changes into ordinary wistfulness. Wistfulness for someone who is no longer there.

The winter of 2213 banishes memories of the long decades of heat and drought. At the beginning of November it starts to freeze. Marek and Eli slide around on the frozen Vltava; they get further each day until in the end they reach another bank, where a high fence prevents them from going further on an island where the smoke of countless campfires rises into the grey sky. Two children are leaning against the fence on the opposite side. They are smaller than Eli and wearing layers of ragged clothes. Marek and Eli climb up the embankment and go right up to them. The children, both boys, stare at them through the wire, but there's no trace of curiosity in their eyes. They are probably standing there just to pass the time. Eli is not much bigger than they are, but he leans down to them as if he were grown up. He opens his arms and stretches out his hands to them. They touch through the fence. Each boy grasps the ends of his fingers in both hands; they do it in unconscious harmony. Their faces brighten. Marek is the only big boy, looking at the three small ones and afraid that they might start pulling Eli into the wire, but they just stand there peacefully and Eli is the first to speak: "Would you come with me, you two?"

"You can't take them home," Marek intervenes. "What would Mum say? You know how she is. We've hardly got enough to eat ourselves."

Eli doesn't listen. "You can go where you like," he almost shouts. "The ice is like a bridge."

The boys have runny noses and are stamping their feet with the cold, but curiosity seems to be back in their eyes. Only at that moment an adult man rushes up from behind them. He too is in ragged clothes and looks terrifying with an iron bar in his hand. "Get the hell out of here!" he yells in a hoarse voice. "Go back where you belong!"

The boys are scared, they let go of Eli and run away along the fence, each in a different direction. But they probably don't believe they could really escape, and so they squat down on their heels and cover their faces in their hands. Marek grabs Eli and drags him away from the fence. The slope gives way beneath them and they slide all the way down to the ice at just the moment when the iron bar slams with full force against the fence. "Fuck off and die!" roars the man. "In the end you'll die anyway! Just like us!"

On the way back the wind buffets their faces. Marek has lent Eli his scarf and now his mouth is freezing. He can hardly feel his nose. He is annoyed with his brother, and pulls him by the hand in silence. Eli has to realize that people can be bad. Marek will explain when they get home.

Only when they get home, he's no longer annoyed with Eli. It's just impossible, being angry with him. Eli looks so open in his innocence. "I was terribly sorry for them, Marek," he apologizes. "Weren't you?"

"Yes I was, Eli. But we can't help them. We'll be lucky to be able to get by ourselves."

Eli does not agree. "I have to help them. I'm taken care of and I have to take care of them. Of everyone."

The next day the heavy snow starts. The times when migrants could sleep with no roof over their heads on the slopes of Letna Park and the Vltava embankments are gone. The homeless are freezing now, and dying. Or they climb over the fences and walls and cross the frozen river. One such group reaches Holesovice in the night. They break the windows of the school and find shelter there. The district authority declares a state of emergency and a school vacation. Armed volunteers now stand guard on the riverbank. The mayor asks Lifelong to send in the army or at least to lend them guard robots. The word is that Lifelong is deaf to their requests – he has enough problems protecting the government districts, but apparently one of his associates is trying to persuade him, and so on the third day after the arrival of the homeless, troops appear in Holesovice. They take the squatters away and start building a fence along the bank. It's the end of walks under the embankment. The Vltava becomes a no-man's-land, an ice road from nowhere to nowhere for people with nothing to lose. In the snow, which now covers the ice to the height of half a metre, trodden paths appear. The main path leads down the middle.

Lifelong blames parliament for the situation. He has the legislative assembly dissolved, but by then it had no power anyway; it's the end of the pretence of democracy. Lifelong promises the people that he will put everything right. He entrusts the army with keeping order and the distribution of food.

The winter lasts a long four months. The schools are closed and Marek and Eli spend more time together than before. Until now Marek has loved and protected his brother without wondering where that love springs from, but Marek is now beginning to understand Eli's thinking. Or to be more precise, he realizes that his brother thinks differently from everyone else. Mostly Eli behaves like a normal boy of his age, except for that inner magnetism. In the same way that he aroused a spark of interest in the children behind the fence, he awakens interest in anyone with any powers of observation. It is not always a positive interest. Some, like Dad, are annoyed and puzzled by him. Eli makes his comments with almost unbearable gravity – as if they were absolute truths. There seems to be another Eli – one inside. Eli inside has no age – he is neither a child nor an adult. And he knows too much. Sometimes he makes small Eli cry – for no reason. At other times he compels him to utter a message of hope. Marek is still unsure about one thing, though, and that is whether the boy Eli has any inkling of his inner second self.

During the long winter days, when there is no school and walks on the icy river are forbidden, the brothers have nothing to do, and so they read. Old books and new ones, including adventure stories about the time when much of the planet was still unpopulated, when there were no aeroplanes and it took weeks and months to travel long distances. "We're going back there," says the inner Eli through the mouth of the small boy with loose milk teeth. "And even further back," he continues. "Much further."

Then Mum brings them another book, a thick Bible. "Read it Marek, and choose something for him," she wheezes, adding, "maybe the story of Noah's Flood, he'll like that. He'll understand it."

For Mum, Eli is just her little boy. A boy who sometimes falls into a dream in class and then pays no attention. The class teacher is a friend of Mum's and complains about him. "He's in a world of his own. I don't know what he's thinking about. Sometimes he doesn't even respond if you poke him." But otherwise she likes him; she has succumbed to his charm. "He's just a darling. Seriously."

Mum still makes excuses for him. "He started school too early. I should have let him stay home longer."

Apart from Eli's lack of concentration at school, the teacher has another problem with him. He refuses to use technical devices. Not a single one. "It'll go wrong anyway," he always says. It's lucky that in the last decade writing and arithmetic on paper has come back as a subject, for otherwise Eli would have had to repeat the first year. Mum reassures him. "I know you're clever. You'll show them all one day. I know it."

"You are my real Mum" is Eli's strange reply.

Mum gulps and then protests, "What else would I be? I know I'm your Mum."

Eli does not explain his words. He throws his arms round his large Mum's neck. "I love you. He loves you too."

"He?" inquires Mum, baffled again. "Who do you mean?"

"The one who gave me life."

Mum winces slightly. "No Eli, I don't want to talk about him. I'm sorry."

"I'd like to talk about him." Eli looks unhappy, "But I can't. I don't know anything about him."

"For goodness sake, don't bother your head with all that. And come and have supper. I've made you mash, the sort you like."

30

And that every inclination of the thoughts of the human heart was only evil all the time

The Bible sends Eli into ecstasies. He wants Marek to read to him from it, again and again, above all the chapter about the expulsion from Eden. "Cursed are you above all livestock and all wild animals!… Cursed is the ground because of you; through painful toil you will eat food from it all the days of your life…"

"Cursed," Eli repeats, more for himself than for Marek, "because of us." Meanwhile the destitute trudge along the thawing river in both directions. In places the snow is turning grey. Looking out of the window Marek and Eli see a group of four approaching one of those places. Just another two steps and… the ice gives way under the first man. The others scramble away in all directions and he sinks in up to the waist, hands flailing in the snow around him. It's a long way away and no sound penetrates the glass, and so the strange dumb play seems to be taking place in another world. The man who has fallen in does not go under, but manages to crawl his way out onto firm ice, where he lies chilled to the bone. In fact he has very little chance of survival, especially when his fellows fail to rally round to help him. One is now edging cautiously towards him, but instead of saving him, he grabs the man's knapsack and makes off with it. The group is moving away with it when they hesitate and return. Is it conscience? No, two drag him by the arms while another takes off his boots, and then they pull off his coat. He flaps about like a fish; he is still alive. Marek's heart pounds in his chest at this terrible spectacle. Eventually the three have enough spoils and walk away, but again they stop and return. What more can they take? Some rags, perhaps a sweater. They pick the man up by the arms and legs, swing him, and… throw him into a crack in the ice.

It is only now that Eli covers his eyes. "That's what we are!" he cries. "Everything is bad and I don't know what to do about it."

Marek soothes him. "It's not your fault. You're just a kid. What can you do?"

"But that's why I'm here," grumbles Eli.

This seems to Marek a little too much, a bit of a nerve from an eight-year-old boy. He turns to him resentfully. "Nobody knows why he's here! And you least of all!" Marek is angry with Eli, but actually he is angry at what has happened outside.

"Read me what Adam and Eve did when the Lord drove them out of Paradise," Eli asks, instead of arguing with Marek. "Please Marek."

What fascinates Eli in the later chapters is the Lord's Judgment. "The LORD saw that humanity had become thoroughly evil on the earth and that every idea their minds thought up was always completely evil."

"You see Marek. Every single idea," Eli agrees. "Like those inventions in school, that I'm supposed to learn with. I knew I didn't want to. Now you see why."

Night after night Eli takes the Bible to bed and reads it by himself, but he finds the chapters that follow complicated and unimportant. He confesses to Marek that now he's just leafing through and prefers going back to the beginning. During the day Marek reads to him, all the way up to the book called the New Testament. At the beginning not even Marek understands what he is reading. Until at one point Eli forces him to go back and read again, for Eli is now as entranced as he was with Genesis. "Blessed are those that weep, for they shall be comforted… Blessed are the merciful, for they shall receive mercy." Now when he goes to bed Eli really reads rather than leafing through. He grows more serious by the day. He is no longer gap-toothed and his mouth looks less childish. His lips have a new firmness. His chin becomes more resolute. "But what about his childhood?" he cries one time and throws the book on the floor. "Where do they write about his childhood?" He stares at Marek, requiring an answer, but Marek is no wiser. He probably knows less than Eli, because at night he doesn't read the Bible but a history of the world, another gift from Mum. From his reading of the history Marek understands that it is too late. Humanity wasted the chance it had around a century ago. Back then it would still have been possible to prevent the worst, above all heat and drought. If the powers back then had risen above their differences they wouldn't have had to think up the diffraction grille, which brought the rain but has caused this winter.

"Do you think he knew why he had been born, when he was still a boy? Did he know what he was going to do?" Eli carries on regardless.

"Probably he didn't know, if they don't write anything about it." Marek replies, dismissively, but then something occurs to him: "If he had known, he wouldn't have waited so long."

"I'm not going to wait," Eli rambles on.

Marek is a little shocked but in fact finds Eli's nerve even more endearing. How could he compare himself with someone said to be the Messiah? The Son of God? With a person so famous that the years were counted from his birth.

"I don't have so much time," Eli adds gravely.

31

Mums like you go on living

That year, 2213 after the birth of Christ, the spring still arrives. It is one of the last few springs in Bohemia. The diffraction grille remains up and the scientists quarrel over whether the climate had been changing only temporarily or permanently, and whether it would now go back to normal without the grille, or removing the grille would unbalance it for good. Refugees were now arriving in Prague from the north, but only the rich. They appear in Holesovice. They are mainly Norwegians. They have big hydrogen-powered cars and want to buy apartments or whole houses. They are used to long winters, but in their homelands winter is now endless and the livestock are perishing in pastures covered with snow.

Eli and Marek go to school again. Their classmates and teachers are nice to them because the word is that it was their Dad who got Lifelong to send soldiers to protect Holesovice. Troja, the Old Town and the Lesser Town have been protected in the same way, but hordes of hungry vagrants invaded Karlin and started to loot shops and houses there. The locals had to put up their own resistance, and there were casualties and fatalities. The Norwegians aren't buying property there because of it.

Mum's health is a little worse. Spring doesn't do much for her. In winter her breathing was easier. Her features are becoming haggard, the skin hanging from her cheeks because she has lost so much weight. She has purple circles under her eyes and she doesn't want to go for a check-up. "They'd force me to stay there. I want to be with you as long as I can."

Mum thinks she doesn't have long to live. Marek vainly tries to convince her that it isn't true. In the end, with the help of Jana on the fourth floor, he at least persuades her to go to the doctor.

"But Mum you're going to live," Eli assures her too. "Mums like you go on living." He wipes the tears from her eyes.

"That's what I believe too, Eli. I'll be watching you from over there when I'm living in the next world."

Mum believes in God, out of desperation. It is no accident that she gave the boys a Bible. "Only I hope that…" and now Mum can hardly speak for tears, "that He'll take care of you. I pray to Him for that every day."

But God, if he really exists, doesn't want to take Mum just yet. The doctor gives her an expensive new medicine, for he too is grateful to her ex-husband. After a long time Mum can speak again without effort, and what she speaks about is the Bible.

The summer is colder than usual. The grapes are not ripening in Moravia. Maybe the wheat won't ripen in the fields either. Marek and Eli go to kick a ball around down by the Vltava, which since the winter has been protected by a fence. It means the ball can't fall in the water. Sometimes, though, they crawl under the fence (they know the right place) and play on the bank as before. Otherwise the view of the Vltava from behind the fence is a reminder that nothing will ever be as it was before.

"When Mum dies, we'll leave this place," Eli says one time.

"Don't talk like that." Marek is shocked. "She's going to live. She has new drugs."

"I said when she dies, not that she isn't going to live now."

That summer there's talk of what Marek's going to do when he leaves school the following year. He will either have to go to college, which would only be possible if he joins his father, or he will have to find a job. There are very few jobs. Most young people are unemployed.

In September a course in Norwegian is organized at the high school. Marek signs up for it.

32

After Fifty-Three Years

The nearer they came to Vinohrady, the less the heated debate in Litohoro occupied his mind. He realized how distant that whole world was from his. The surrounding landscape brought him relief. This was definitely the way Eli had wanted it; this was definitely the return of which he had spoken – a return to true self and the order of creation. With the oncoming autumn the damp soil was full of life. Marek was drowsy and everything that reached him from outside blended into a single stream of perception. Only it was perhaps better described as music, and today a new, expressive note resounded in it.

Natalia. Her personality, her strange abrupt entrance into his life. It continually surprised him that she wasn't a figment of his conceited imagination; that she really was as she was – young, her own woman, so far from any fantasy ideals that before he knew her he could never have imagined her. What she evoked in him was gratitude, above all. Thank you Natalia. Thank you, Eli.

As a nineteen-year old high-school graduate he had joined a real estate agency catering for the arriving Norwegians, and his heart had started beating faster whenever Petra, his thirty-year-old boss, had said a word to him. Back then it had been something new and confusing for him. His feeling that his place was always and only with Eli had not disappeared, and it made his urge to be with Petra all the more tormenting. Several times he caught himself looking forward to work, which at other times he saw just as an empty interlude and a waste of time.

Petra didn't return his feelings. She may not even have been attracted to men at all. The shy school-leaver may have been acceptable to her as an employee for that very reason. She wore her hair short like a boy and her face was almost a boy's face. It was that ambivalence that so excited Marek, the woman immediately recognizable in the boyish face.

Petra lived for work and was earning a lot of money. She persuaded Czechs to sell their apartments and houses, found replacement housing for them in the country, and raised the prices for the Norwegians. Payment was not just in money, but in gold, art and jewellery. Petra had built up a whole network of sellers and experts. Marek didn't really think about it, but suspected there was no future in it: no future for Czechs, the Central European Federation, or mankind on Planet Earth. His work took him to both rich and poor districts. As the first grew ever richer, the second slid into abject poverty and chaos. Holesovice held on somewhere in between the two.

He was finally put in his place one time when riding an elevator with Petra to the ninth floor of a block. She probably noticed the eagerness of his breathing and the bulging in his crotch, because she suddenly whispered: "Don't I pay you enough? Why don't you buy yourself a girl?"

From that moment Eli became the centre of his life again, his one certainty and fixed point. Compared to the chance of living for Eli any imaginable moment of pleasure was just time wasted on vanity. That was how he felt. Women sensed it in him. They avoided him.

He first discovered what it was like to climax between a woman's legs, and not in the toilet or under a quilt, when he was forty-one. After Eli's death. He found that it wasn't bad, and noticed that it could be separated from the mind. In any case, the women concerned didn't see him as Marek. For them he was Eli's brother, someone who had been close to a source of light that they had missed, and so still reflected a little of the glory that they wanted to approach.

Now he was seventy-two. After fifty-three years he was in love with a woman again, but this time he was loved in his turn.

33

Skotosi!

He must have fallen asleep again, and half-woke when the car came to a sudden halt. He thought they were already back and looked around in confusion when he realized they were only on the edge of the settlement. "What is it?" he mumbled at Konstantinos in Czech. "Why are you stopping?"

Konstantinos said something in Greek and it sounded like a curse. Then he used the horn and the piercing noise put paid to any lingering dreams.

It was only now that Marek gathered his wits and saw there were people standing in front of the car. A band of robbers? After his time in the Alps Marek had learned to be on his guard in a second. Then he recognized Jerzi, and realized that the people were waiting for him. He opened the door and peered out. It was already getting dark. There was a stabbing pain in his hip.

The small crowd surged up to the car. Apart from Jerzi there was one family from the bay and two shepherd families from the upper houses. No one directly from Vinohrady. In their faces Marek saw excitement and outrage. Righteous indignation knowing no compassion. The same expression that sometimes appeared on the faces of people who attacked the Followers for being different. And on faces decades ago, when indignation had so easily presaged murder. These were familiar faces, but Marek could still read in them the same age-old violence. He began to make out the words. "Send her away!" "We don't want her here!" "Send her away or we'll drive her out!"

He got out of the car. The chill air banished any lingering drowsiness. When he straightened up in front of them, they fell silent. They had respect for him, after all. "What is going on?" he inquired. "Why are you shouting at Eli's brother?" He deliberately used Eli as a shield. "I've just come back from the Old Town, where I defended Eli, our teaching." He sensed that he needed to keep talking for as long as possible. While he was speaking, their indignation could not find a voice. "I was defending it against those who do not have your good fortune. Because they don't believe in Eli. That's what I wanted to tell you – you are lucky." At the same time he thought of Natalia. Surely they had not hurt her?

His strategy seemed to be working, but then Jerzi spoke up and ruined it all. "That girl is strange. She's used sex to get control of you. We've got to save you from her."

The others evidently agreed. Marek tried to imagine what Eli would have said now. If Natalia had come to Eli, would they have wanted to save him from her too? No, that was an absurd idea. Eli had the real power of persuasion. He had often managed to stop a human tempest. Marek was standing here representing no one but himself. That could really look like weakness. Maybe it really was weakness – he had to ask himself that question.

"Nobody has got control of me." He stood up to them as resolutely as he could. "I'm Eli's brother. Do you think it would be so easy to get control of me? And she's one of us. She is following Eli – like all of us. Each must follow Eli in his or her own way. That is what he used to say and what he wanted. There will be as many different paths to the same destination as there will be people who understand me. That's what Eli says. But there is something more. There is yet another sign that tells me Eli has sent her to me." Marek dropped his voice, noting that they were finally listening to him. Their indignation had changed fast, first into confusion, and then back into their original devotion. Evil was slinking back to its hidden byways. These followers were once again the peaceful descendants of those who had crossed the Alps and lived through the great dying. They were the children of parents who had suffered much and done much for them. "Krystof." He turned to the man from the bay. "When your father was dying in Albania, I held your hand, do you remember? He wanted you to be able to live in a better world than the one he was leaving. But what that world will be like depends on you too, Krystof. Don't let yourself be ruled by hatred."

Krystof, a tall bearded fisherman who had once been a wild untamed lad, dropped his eyes. Marek knew him well. The fire in him could flare up fast, but it could fade in him just as quickly. "So listen to me." He returned to the important thing that he wanted to tell them. "Eli was killed in Dubrovnik in 2135. And she was born there in the very same year. She left. She refused to live among the murderers of Eli, even though her parents are living there. Do you understand that? Krystof? Do you understand?" Only now did he feel strong enough to turn to Jerzi. "And you, Jerzi, do you understand that? Eli said there are many paths to the same destination. As many paths as there are pilgrims. He taught that anyone who seeks to compel another to walk his path has strayed from the right path. There is no room for hatred in New Vinohrady. We welcome everyone who is on their path to that one destination. We are glad when they come to us. One day we will settle throughout the World, but for the moment there are too few of us. Today in Litohoro I met one… I think one of them will come to us from Litohoro." Marek had changed the subject without knowing why, but suddenly understood. It was because Tomas would come. That certainty lit him up. "He will bring much that is good and help me. And if this is not to your liking, Jerzi, it is you that should leave. Anyone who drives others out, drives himself out. Eli said that too."

Jerzi had no answer to that. He stood in sullen silence as the others moved away. Konstantinos gave Marek an impatient glance, and stepped on the gas pedal a few times without engaging the gear to let the engine roar. Jerzi's sharp eyes bored into Marek and then dropped to the mud under the wheels. "There are not so many paths," he mumbled, as if to himself, "not so many as you say. There are not so many right paths."

Marek got back into the seat. "Do not drive anyone out!" He said it one more time: "Or at best you will drive yourself out."

The car started to move and Konstantinos said something in Greek, irritably. Marek understood a little. "Skotosi" meant "kill".

34

All the Gifts of the World

The twilight was thickening in the street between the bungalows. When they drove up to Marek's house the door was closed and the windows looked dark. Marek's thoughts turned even darker. He gulped on air.

He used to think there was no longer anything in the world for him to hold onto. He used to think that now he would just live out his life in Eli's wake. But now he was becoming deeply aware of Natalia's goodness and openness. There was nothing underhand about her. She didn't deserve any evil.

Konstantinos looked weary and Marek didn't envy him the long journey back. Only Konstantinos showed no sign of getting back on the road. He waited.

Marek was already out of the car. He didn't want to do it, but he had to climb the steps to the closed door. To approach the unwanted truth. But then he noticed the light of a fire beyond the window. His heart skipped a beat. "Adio," he gestured back to Konstantinos, who was making no attempt to hide his curiosity to see how it would turn out. It turned out well. The door opened.

"Hi," she said, as if nothing had happened, but he could immediately see she was just trying to look unconcerned. They had talked to her. They had been here.

Never in his life had he so much wanted to embrace someone, but just now he couldn't manage it. He climbed up the steps to her and looked into her limpid dark eyes. Behind him the car engine roared into life, the wheels turned and the car moved away.

It was not until he was inside the door that he enfolded her in his arms. "Why is this only happening when I'm so indecently old?" he thought. They stood there a long time in silent embrace. Then he headed for the chair, but noticed a foam mattress spread out on the floor. "Were you doing massages?" he asked.

"I was exercising." And because he was probably looking so surprised she added, "Exercising and relaxing. An Indian woman I met in Dubrovnik taught me how. It helps."

Again he found her eyes. She didn't try to avoid his gaze, and so he understood everything.

"They were here?"

She nodded.

"What did they say? What did they want?"

"They wanted me to leave."

Hana, he thought. She hadn't been among the people waiting for him on the road, and she certainly hadn't been here, but she was behind it. "Did they try to strong-arm you?"

"No, they were just trying to persuade me, so far. And I'm not going to shit myself because of them. I'm not leaving. Or not if you don't want me to leave too."

Really she ought to leave. For her own safety and for the sake of the quiet life of New Vinohrady. That was surely more important than his desire. But he could see that she really loved him. He'd be hurting her, and anyway he had no taste for such a sacrifice, not now, when he had just found a little happiness. Hadn't Eli himself sent her to him? Her youth, beauty, and strength.

"I don't want you to leave," he whispered, and kissed her on the lips. "I'm happy, Natalia. I'm so relieved they didn't hurt you. I thank Eli that you're here."

"Eli?" she looked startled. He realized that she wasn't made for such thoughts. She was practical. All the same he tried to explain. "He's always with me. For me he didn't die – there in Dubrovnik."

"So does that make us a threesome in bed?" She gave such a blasphemous laugh that it chilled him. On the other hand, he needed to be brought down to earth again. It was good this way. She had the ability to see through him. She knew his weak points, the way he suppressed himself, the way he maybe sacrificed himself too much for his brother. But still, who could really make that judgment if they hadn't had a messiah for a brother? He hoped that in time he'd be able to explain to her that it was the kind of fate that you were born into, and there was no way of defying it. And he wasn't planning to defy it even now, when she had come. "I'll wash," he said. "And come to you."

All the gifts of the world. That was the sacrament of her body. So flexible, so firm, yet she also had a fragility. She was a gateway for him. Not the one that Eli had spoken about, but no less desirable. He put her firm nipples into his mouth, slid his hand from her belly across her groin to her thigh. When he wanted to enter her, the sharp pain in his hip came back and he couldn't make it. "Wait Marek." She stroked his hair and rolled over on top of him. When he looked up at her, his eyes blurred with tears. So much beauty and happiness. She drew him into her and bent down to him.

Her sighs became eddies in the stillness of his old-bachelor lodgings. He was more aware of them than of his own satisfaction. He couldn't get past his own astonishment.

They lay together a long while. It struck him that he was waiting for some sign that she was cooling towards him. After all, she couldn't unreservedly love him, an old man. But no such sign was forthcoming. She pressed herself to him and absently traced her fingertips across his chest.

"What exactly did they say to you?" he asked later, "Did they threaten you?"

She pulled a little away from him, returning to herself. Something like skepticism appeared in her face. "Did they threaten me? Oh I think so. They said I was a whore and they didn't want me here." She laughed, although under the surface she was serious. "They said if I didn't go they'd run me out. And that I should keep my hands off their children."

Marek felt a wave of anger. How could they have dared… ? "Did they come inside?"

"No, they didn't. They stood at the door. I think they were scared of you." She laughed again and this time there was a genuine playfulness about it. "You're an important man, my darling."

It's so easy to get them worked up against someone, he thought. "It's all Hana," he said, more to himself. "And Jerzi."

"Jerzi, he was the leader. But he wouldn't look me in the eye. He's obviously crazy for women. He needs to get laid."

That openness of hers startled him again, even though there was nothing odd about it. "Do you think he would have laid hands on you, if you hadn't been in my home?"

"D'you mean whether he'd have raped me?"

She was always one step ahead of him as far as openness was concerned. He hadn't got as far as that. There were no rapes in New Vinohrady. Eli had told them to imagine what the other is feeling. To take delight in their delight, to suffer with their suffering. Not to hurt anyone. And if hurt happens, then the person who has caused it must feel greater pain than the person who has suffered it. The trouble was that there were two different interpretations of those words of Eli's. Petr of New Karlin thought it meant that the others had the right to punish the culprit by inflicting that greater pain. Marek was sure that Eli had meant the pain that comes with remorse. "What I meant to ask," he replied after a short pause, "was if you were afraid of them."

She considered. He saw she was too strong to want to reveal everything to him. "It wasn't pleasant, if you really want to know."

He was overwhelmed by boundless affection. He deeply desired to protect her. He embraced her and tilted his face down to hers, and the narrow straight nose that was a piece of her unique being. "It won't happen again, I promise you. Nobody will have the nerve."

"I don't know... but don't worry about it." She looked him in the eyes, "You are the main teacher after all. Your work is to spread your brother's teaching."

"But that's just it!" He raised his voice. "It's connected. They can't behave like this if they say they are his followers."

"Don't you think that in the end people are the same everywhere?"

"At the beginning they are the same. Certainly. But they don't necessarily take the same path. They can choose from what they have in them, the good or the bad."

"So there you are. You're the teacher." She laughed and grinned and seemed to let the fears go.

He shifted back onto his back, and regarded his bony worn-out legs. They had carried him across the Alps, taken him through the Balkans and found this abandoned resort close to Olympus. They had discovered a resting place here. But those legs of hers. The difference was striking. They could carry her through life... anywhere. "How did you actually find Eli?"

"I don't know if I've found him."

"But you came to my preaching."

"The way my parents live in Dubrovnik, it just can't go on."

It was an unsatisfactory answer. "I understand that, Natalia, but what about Eli? I believe he was... a messenger from God. I know he was, today I know it. I know almost nothing about God. But everything I do know is called Eli."

"It's good that you know it," she whispered, and for a moment he thought she might be mocking him, but then she added, "You're further on than I am."

His thoughts wandered to another topic. "When exactly were you born? Which day?"

"Tuesday." She burst out laughing.

"I mean the date."

"I know you mean the date." Her voice was the only thing about her that lacked a firm shape. There was something indistinct about it. "I was born on the twenty-first of July. Why d'you ask?"

"Eli died on the seventh of July. You were born fourteen days after his death. Just fourteen days. Two weeks. And now you are here. It has to be God's plan."

"God's plan? That's baloney isn't it?" It sounded harsh, and exposed the improbability of it all. If he hadn't had a deeper layer of knowledge, one that had formed day after day from Eli's birth for a whole sixty-five years, there would have been nothing left in him but a sheer uprooting of every certainty. He was annoyed at himself for uttering what should only be intimated. In the end he was grateful for her honesty. "Do you mean that the old teacher is talking baloney?" He lightened his tone.

She grinned. "No, I wouldn't have the nerve to say that." Suddenly there was a glint in her eye. "I've an idea." She raked her fingers in his beard. "I'll shave you. I want to see my teacher's face."

As his beard fell into the sink and smooth areas appeared on his face he felt the nostalgia of return to the past, but also a distinct unease about what people were going to say. Would he lose his authority? No, there was no reason to think that, for there had never been a rule that older men shouldn't shave. They hadn't shaved simply for reasons of comfort. Eli had shaved when he could, after all. Hana had shaved him and sometimes shaved Marek too, when Eli had asked her to. She hadn't liked doing it, but Natalia bent over him with enjoyment of the task. Absorbed in it. He realized she was forcing him to be himself. Even with the shaving.

He turned out not to be an old man. His stiff back and wrecked joints, it was those that had made him an old man. But his face... it hadn't been so very different back in Holesovice in Prague.

"Hey, take a look at that." She stepped back to get a better view of him. Then she bent down again and unexpectedly kissed him on the forehead. "It suits you my darling."

The first to see Marek shaven was Venca in the morning. He was leading a donkey loaded with wood and taking fish out of a basket. "From Krystof," he reported, and then exclaimed, "You're shaven!"

"Venca..." Marek had an idea. "Could you go over to Karlin sometime? On the first Sunday of November I want to preach with Petr. Tell him that. I want to preach with him at the Sanctuary of Birth."

"Karlin..." Venca thought about it. "Okay."

Natalia was doing some stretches on the exercise mat. Then she started putting things into her red bag. "I'm going to the school."

"Aren't you scared, after yesterday?"

She looked at him almost outraged. "I'm not chicken." And after a moment added, "I love children. They aren't full of false pretences." Marek had not thought much about children. He was glad they were being born here. He saw in them the future of the settlement. "What do you think about the fact that children are being born here?"

"I could think that your God hates people from elsewhere," she replied in an almost challenging tone. "Or that he just likes the people here." She waved a hand. "But no, I just take it as it is. Nothing more. It's just the way it is. Like the fact the sun comes up in the morning and that soon it's going to rain."

As she turned to leave he caught her hand. "When you come back I'll tell you more about Eli. He... knew, that it would be this way. It's happened to bring us back under the order of the world."

It scared him how empty the words sounded when it was him uttering them, not Eli.

"I know you'll tell me everything."

35
There just has to be something

Real Estate dealing, a trade in fear, is a goldmine. Petra has her own aircar, and houses in Australia, Florida and Sri Lanka. When the game is finally up she will have somewhere to go.

All that Marek has is his desire and his pangs of conscience when he thinks of Petra instead of Eli. After several harsh winters when the Vltava freezes for many months and none of the wheat in the fields ripens, one milder winter comes. There is gunfire in Liben and the shots can be heard as far away as Holesovice. But nobody worries about it. There is always gunfire somewhere. Lifelong's army is always putting down outbreaks of unrest and the germs of revolt. As soon as one is extinguished another flares up. Not that people are so courageous – they just no longer have anything to lose. Dying has become a part of everyday life. Death no longer appals.

At least so long as the person dying is not Mum. Even the best drugs have stopped having an effect. For months Mum lies coughing and hawking; she only gets up to go to the bathroom. Jana from the fourth floor has sold her apartment and moved away somewhere unknown. This is another sign of the times: people are leaving without saying goodbye. One day you meet them in the corridor, the next day they are gone. The collection that once helped the family ended long ago. At least Marek is making some money.

Eli is maturing from a child to a boy. He reads a lot and speaks little, but his large bright eyes look as though they are always wanting to say something. As his features emerge fully, Marek's eyes are always drawn to him. What is it that makes Eli so beautiful?

At school nobody dares to make trouble for Eli even though he is so different. The teachers are resigned to their inability to force him to do certain things, and they mistakenly believe that the school is safer with a pupil whose father is close to Lifelong. As for his class-mates, jibes somehow stick in their throats. They have tried it on a few times, hoping to torment him, but when he raises no objections and just fixes them with his questioning eyes, they simply give it up, and they don't even know why.

Eli has a beneficial effect on Mum. When he sits by her bed and takes her hand, her breathing becomes calmer. One time Mum rests her weary eyes on him and says, "Everything I believed in when I was young is gone. A war's coming and terrible things are going to happen. So how come I am not afraid for you?"

Eli just shrugs, and for a moment seems about to answer, but in the end thinks better of it. And only Marek understands. It is the adult spirit, which struggled so hard when Eli was still small, that falls silent now. Back then it couldn't reconcile itself to its situa-tion, and would find an outlet and often come out of his mouth in unexpected utterances, but now that Eli has grown and matured the spirit has plenty of room inside him. It lives there, grows, becomes deeper, hidden from the world.

On the morning of the 12th of July 2120, the last day of Mum's life begins. Marek doesn't go to work. After a difficult night, with the brothers taking turns at Mum's bedside, the thought of sell-ing apartments makes him feel ill. He calls Mrs Stranska, Petra's secretary. Mrs Stranska has a weakness for Marek, who has to keep his brother and sick mother while so young. "Of course Marek. I'll tell her."

That day wind gusts against the windows. The bushes on the bank of the Vltava tremble in the wind and the water foams. Every so often the sun comes out from behind the fast flying clouds. Mum asks them to let more air into the room. They open the ventilation and the fresh air breaks its way in. In the morning it is chilly.

Towards noon it becomes warmer, a beautiful twenty degrees. Mum dozes for a while. Eli drops off in the armchair beside her bed and only Marek gazes into the despair of that day. Somewhere there is gunfire again and Marek can't understand what the point of life is, except that everyone wants to live at any price. The Norwegians are fleeing from the north to survive, and it is to survive that people are stealing and murdering. Just one loaf is motive enough – a few mouthfuls for the next few hours.

Marek is twenty-four and since his ninth year, when Eli became the centre of his world, he has never asked himself what will happen next. This is because for the whole of those fifteen years he has always had a course of action to hand: to be with Eli, to return to Eli, to help Eli. It is a pity that in recent years they have been together less. Marek's job, Eli's school, and also his tendency to silence. On their walks along the barbed-wire fenced bank of the Vltava they already say almost nothing to each other, hands in pockets.

It is only now, under the pressure of Mum's imminent death, that Marek asks himself what happens next.

In September Eli is supposed to start high school, just as Marek once did. Recently Dad has repeated his offer for them to move to his place in the government district, behind the newly built fortifications.

In the apartment in Holesovice Marek keeps his vigil long into the night. Eli sleeps. His great waiting soul resides in his body and merges with it. He is tired when his body is tired, he suffers illnesses and pains when his body squirms in cramps, and even greater pains when his Mum is dying and there is no help for her.

Mum has her head hidden under a pillow. All that is visible is an ear, which is a good thing because Mum's face, puffy and yellowed by disease, is endlessly ugly and all the more disgusting to Marek now that decomposition and death are settling into it. Yet despite that, he can still see Mum. It is only now, in adulthood, that he fully appreciates her kindness and good judgment. She has feared what was coming, and it has really come. And she has never shouted at her sons.

At noon she wakes just one more time. Her eyes are sunken, and her gaze distant, but she is still conscious of their presence. Marek and Eli are with her. Now Mum utters her last words through the narrow chink between life and extinction, and at that moment Marek has no belief in eternity and life after death. This is extinction confirming the meaninglessness of living, extinction forever. "You two will cope. I know." Then Mum is gone.

After a moment Eli presses his head against her shoulder and weeps.

Marek puts his hand on Eli's shoulder, for Eli is the only thing that is still important.

After a while Eli looks at Marek with tear-filled eyes. "There just has to be something. It can't end like this."

There will be many times when Marek thinks about these words of Eli's, especially after his death. It just can't end like this. The uncertainty. The searching in his voice. So not even Eli knows. In the end he will become everything Marek knows about God, but not even Eli seems to know any more about God than what he experiences himself to be, which is a human being: vulnerable, doubting and mortal.

36

Leaving

Gunfire. Today it is coming from the island on the other side, but the Holesovice apartment with Mum's body in it is a long way from the front line. It is infinitely distant from everything around it.

Eli and Marek wander about between the walls. Mum is present in all the objects that she used to touch – in the cutlery, the plates, the soup above the basin. She is more present than ever before.

They go to bed that night sick at heart, while Mum's body still lies untouched under the quilt. Eli's despair disturbs Marek. In his brother's face he even sees defiance. Eli is angry at the very nature of a world into which human beings are born mortal with no say in the matter themselves.

Marek offers to sleep with Eli in his room, as he has often done before, but Eli refuses. He wants to be alone. And so Marek sleeps by Mum. He puts his quilt on the floor and lies on it. The air in the room stinks of urine, but that is nothing new. And today even that stink is a memorial.

The wind drops and the draft in the room diminishes. Marek lies on his back and the light of the floodlight on the embankment comes through the roller blind. Anyone trying to get through the barricade in the night would be an easy target.

Mum's death was expected. She herself had been expecting it for years. Yet it is only today that every security has collapsed. Marek's first security has been the family he was born into. His second, more radiant security has been Eli. Until today, now that Eli has turned against the world and his mission in it. A moment before there was a thud from his room. He has been pounding the door with his fists.

With his security lost, Marek feels duties call. The first is to do something with the body. Marek has no idea what to do; he has no experience with death. Mum's parents died before he was born, and Dad grew up without parents. It occurs to him to ask Petra. She knows how to deal with everything. For the first time he thinks of her without sexual arousal, and the thought calms him. Even so he cannot sleep. The room seems to be rocking and turning around him. With invisible surf, with waves of nothingness decomposed into particles of stink, into invisible remains of the past.

In the morning Eli's defiance is gone. He is himself again, with a calm mind and a soothing look. His transformation since the night before is so great that it is hard to credit. Not only is there no hint of reproach in his eyes, but there is a new challenge in them. Eli the human being has finally become one with the spirit that dwells in him. His first words are, "It's time to go."

"How d'you mean, go?" Marek is bewildered.

"To go away, among people. I want to speak with everyone. Don't you see that we can't stay here?" Eli seems puzzled.

Perhaps that's true. Even Marek sees that. What is there to stay for? Where would their life lead, here in Holesovice, in the middle of this dissolution? Only that question just raises an equally urgent question, which is Where? And how is it done, going away?

Fortunately there is no time to think about it. Marek calls Petra and she promises to sort everything out. In return Marek must come to work. He has to sell a house in a rich district. "Don't worry about your mother. I have people for that, don't I?" Petra assures him in her commanding voice, which today leaves Marek cold. And she adds, "I'll make sure it's dignified."

And so Marek has to leave Eli at home with the body, which someone is coming for soon. In some districts bodies are just being cleared away into ditches or dumps. In Holesovice they are still buried.

Petra sends her aircar for Marek, and at the door he looks into Eli's eyes. His brother is still a little smaller than him, but only by half a head. The defiance of the night has changed his calm into power. He is ready to fulfil his vocation.

"What's happened?" Marek asks uncertainly. "You've changed."

"I was at the end of my tether," Eli answers, thoughtful, but immediately grins. "It was tough, but I came back. I'm here."

37

Goodbye

That "It was tough" echoes in Marek's ears throughout the summer. There was so much pain in it. Marek knew right away that he would never himself be in mental straits so dire. Eli must have been further away than he could imagine.

At first sight, seen from above in the aircar, the contrast between city zones is obvious. Where there is chaos, disorder and collapse, life seethes and bubbles and overflows, and where there is order, organization, robots and troops, there is a corpselike stillness.

Two days later a modest ceremony takes place in the chapel in Holesovice. Instead of Mum there is just an urn of ashes. Marek is the only mourner, Eli didn't want to come. "I'll find her myself," he tries to explain to Marek. "She won't be there."

At first Marek hesitates, wondering if he shouldn't insist that his brother comes. After all, Marek is now responsible for Eli, and refusing to attend your own Mum's funeral… isn't this a moment when he should be taking a firm line? But he could only have done it if his brother hadn't been Eli. The way he puts it disarms Marek completely. And actually, Marek understands Eli. He doesn't even know why he should have to go.

In her last years Mum believed in the Christian God. What else was left to her? She would definitely have been glad that the leave-taking is led by a priest. Marek and he stand together. The priest is young, bespectacled, and rests a hand awkwardly on the black urn with the silver inscription. Petra has provided flowers. There are a lot of them, and their scent pervades the chapel.

"These days," mumbles the barely audible priest, "it is rare for death still to mean something. It is good that you want to accompany her into the kingdom of God. You must have loved her very much."

Marek gulps and nods.

"The Lord will take her to himself. Would you like us to pray together for that?"

Marek doesn't know how to pray and isn't impressed by the words of the priest. He is unsure if this particular man can influence anything. But he wishes Mum the best.

The priest understands and tactfully passes over his own suggestion. "How about we just think about her together. Each for himself. You can remember."

It's better like that. The walls of the chapel are thick and the windows small. Either the sound of gunfire doesn't reach this far, or no one is shooting at this moment. The flowers give off their perfume and the candle-wax flickers. There is just silence and peace. But then the door opens behind him. The priest looks up and Marek turns his head. Dad is standing in the doorway.

Another nine years have gone by since they last saw each other. And like that last time, today the man who is standing in the door is and isn't Dad. This man no longer stands so straight and he is not so muscular. And Marek's heart does not pound, or become seized by anxiety. This is an ageing man, a stranger.

Yet he closes the door behind him, and he walks until he is level with Marek. He is wearing very expensive clothes – Marek can see that. In fact it is an incredible act of arrogance for the man to come at all, but he looks deep in thought and to start with at least keeps quiet. Then he turns to Marek and whispers, "He isn't here?"

He means Eli, his son, but he is speaking of a boy who nine years ago saw him to the door as a stranger.

"No he's not," replies Marek and turns away, trying to shrink back into himself. The man stands there silent. It isn't clear why he has come, because there is a callousness about him.

"Don't let me put you off," he tells the priest.

"We're remembering the deceased and I'm praying for her."

"Well carry on then." It sounds like an order and the priest obeys.

Then the man turns to Marek again. "You've grown up Marek," he whispers. "You've been managing to provide for the family. I'm proud of you. Truly proud."

Marek doesn't know if he wants to hear anything like that. Too much time has gone by for him to care what this man says any longer. All the same, as he stands next to Marek, dignified and almost silent, something irreversible is in the air. It intensifies Marek's grief for Mum.

After the ceremony they go outside. An aircar is waiting for the man. The chasm between them could not be deeper. The man, once Dad, no longer says anything, no longer urges his sons to follow him. Marek can't see inside his head and has no idea what he is thinking. Is he satisfied with his life? Does he love his daughter, who must be growing up now? Is he going back somewhere he is loved? Marek will never know. His leave-taking from his father feels as final as his leave-taking from Mum. They look at each other one more time and the man, for the last time just a little like Dad, strides off to the aircraft. The weapons in the hands of two soldiers are perfect; they can paralyze and kill. Dad heads between them, in a space of indifference and cold. It is only now that it comes to Marek that they are seeing each other for the last time. Dad – the man – vanishes inside and the aircraft is ready to take off. Marek doesn't know why he is shaken by sobs.

38

Fifty Percent

They return to the apartment, which is no longer home. Marek's legs grow heavy along the way, and as he climbs the stairs, an oppressive wretchedness keeps stopping him in his tracks. All the same, he knows he must go up. To Eli.

Eli is sitting in the hallway. Beside him is his backpack. Marek is nonplussed and gapes at him from the door. The hallway is dark and the doors to the other rooms are closed. Eli glances back at him innocently.

"What's the big idea?" Marek sighs. "What's got into you?"

There's a glint in Eli's eyes. "You wanted to leave too…"

"Wait…" Marek feels a stab of fear. "Why right now? We can't leave just like that. Where would we go?"

"Why not? We can't stay. Not even another hour. You know it's true."

Eli has a gift for articulating the most hidden feelings of others. Marek is overcome by weakness, and his will and his mind seem to fade out into confusion. He closes the door behind him and sits down on the floor, opposite Eli. He puts his head in his hands. He feels responsible for both of them. He simply has to keep on earning to make sure they can eat and live in safety.

"Eli, it's impossible. We can't leave without anything. You don't know what's happening elsewhere."

The fact that he has no defence against Eli's wishes makes him all the more desperate.

The adolescent that Eli is now leans forward with passion. His mouth is strongly moulded, his lips full, and the first fuzz is sprouting on his cheeks, but he is still more boy than man. "Nowhere's safe if you want to be afraid," he says urgently. "Not here or anywhere else, Marek. But everywhere's safe when you're not afraid. And the worst thing of all is not to be where you ought to be."

"That's easy to say," Marek objects, his voice shaking a little. "But I only have money for a week, and once it runs out, what are we going to buy food with? And if we leave now, where will we sleep tonight?"

"Don't worry about it. It doesn't matter how long you have money for. Leaving means having nothing. We have to start again from the beginning. Everyone, the whole of humankind. We have to give it all up. Because we've gone astray. What we've created is evil."

The trouble is that Marek doesn't know how to stop worrying. He mentally reviews how much food there is in the fridge, and how much he would get for the apartment if he wanted to sell it. Petra buys flats in less than an hour, if the price is right. That means very advantageous for Petra. "What if we waited a bit longer?" he almost pleads with Eli. "Just a few days. Then we'll leave. Definitely. A few days can't matter. Why can't we leave in a few days?"

"Are you still afraid, bro?" Eli smiles. "We can't leave in a few days, when the time has come right now."

Marek admits that Eli is right about one thing. No more than Eli can he imagine going on living here. Staying would almost be like dying. Sweat starts to drip down his forehead. "Okay bro. We'll go today. But first I'll sell the apartment. I'll call Petra now and sell her our apartment."

Suddenly Marek's gut seizes up and he has to run to the bathroom. He feels dreadful. Invisible forces are pulling him in opposite directions: stay or go. But when he returns to the hallway Eli takes his hand. "Marek… my Marek," and he hugs him in the way that Marek has hugged him up to now. "You've looked after me beautifully, Marek. You've been here for me every moment. So now let me take the lead for a while."

Marek doesn't know how it happened, but the two forces stop pulling him apart. There remains only one force, and it doesn't even pull, but is simply there. It says, "Follow Eli."

"I'll wait for you by the chapel," Eli continues. He knows the decision has been made. "Don't worry about the low price. Just sell the apartment and come."

With that he leaves. His waterproof jacket is thrown over his shoulder. Marek has no idea what he has in the far from capacious backpack.

As soon as Marek is alone in the apartment, he reverts to sober considerations. But he no longer doubts the need to leave. Now it's a matter of selling the place. Fast and for the best price he can get.

He calls Petra. Today her confident voice sounds even more satisfied than usual. "Hiya, is everything taken care of? I've got some super-wealthy Swedes here. They want to buy a fortress. Something really well protected."

"Petra... I've got something too." He nerves himself up and is surprised at how natural he sounds. "For sale."

"So bring the business here." Petra leaps on her prey like a true predator. "Can you deal with it by yourself? I guess you know how high you can go."

"I know."

"So spit it out."

"It's an express sale." Marek is starting to enjoy himself. Over the last years he has sold countless apartments and houses and bought up plenty for Petra. He is not bad at it. The clients have appreciated his youth and his calm. He has obliged them, and never really rubbed anyone up the wrong way. But he has never before felt any passion for selling. The only pleasure he got from it has been feeling he was supporting Eli and Mum. And of course that he was pleasing Petra, and Petra was talking to him. But today it's different. He feels a strong sense of satisfaction. "There's more of a hurry than usual. It has to be sold in an hour."

"If they want money in an hour they can't expect more than twenty percent. Whose nerve has cracked this time? Where is it?"

"It's in quite a good area. Residential Holesovice. Second floor with a view of the river. Patrolled embankment. I don't think they'll go under forty percent.'

"They wouldn't get forty percent from God," says Petra indignantly. "You'll just have to explain that to them."

"I've already tried. But in this case I hope we can make an exception. It's a deal I really care about."

"Look maybe thirty just for you, so long as it's net not gross. Everyone is trying to get the hell out. But in an hour... The Russians would give them fifteen. The Arabs even less. Thirty is complete nonsense. I don't know why I'm even offering it to you."

"Because we're going to agree on forty."

"Hey, you're really off your head. Why are you trying this on me today?"

"Actually… thanks for Mum," Marek remembers. "It was dignified. Lovely flowers."

"Aha, so that's why." Petra laughs. "You've gone soft. You know what, don't do any trading today. Send them to the Russkies."

"Only… I must clinch this deal."

"You're confusing your terms, Marek." Petra's voice hardens. "At most you negotiate deals. I'm the one that clinches them."

"And it's a good thing it's you that does it. A person can't clinch a deal with himself." Marek is suddenly in a good mood. The pressure seemed to have gone. He wants to laugh.

"I guess that whole chapel thing really did your head in," Petra yells. "What the hell's going on here?"

"I'm the seller."

"You…" For a moment there was a silence. "In an hour? Why an hour? Have you lost your mind?"

"Because in an hour I'm going away. We're both going away." Marek has a wonderful feeling as he hears himself saying that. He feels free, happy. In an hour he is leaving. "It's not me, it's Eli. And I have to go with him. This is my last deal, Petra."

"What the fuck? That's serious man." Petra falls silent on the other end of the phone. He can hear her breathing. "But where the fuck are you going? Even if I give you your forty percent, it won't buy you anything in a safe country."

"Do you know of any safe countries?" Marek asks. It was as if Eli had spoken.

"I guess not… You have a bit of a point there." Petra knows how things work now. "In some places they'll kill you sooner, and in some places later. Better later than sooner, I say. So seriously Marek. You really want to sell your apartment? And is it really yours to sell?"

"Yeah… Mum had it transferred to my name. You've got my biometric data. That makes it easier doesn't it?

Petra has somehow grasped that what Marek wants is irreversible. She doesn't try to talk him out of it. "And how do you want to be paid?"

"Put it on my biometric clip. So I can use it wherever I am."

"Even in hell, Marek?" Petra says darkly.

"There too – if I have to follow Eli there."

"Because it's you Marek, I'm going to give you fifty percent. Fifty percent for the five years you've worked for me. I can't go any higher."

Marek feels gratitude. Petr is tough and uncompromising… and has class. It is why he has secretly loved her. And that fifty, it was a gift from her. He would have sold it for ten. Anyone in a hurry will agree to anything.

"That's kind. Good of you Petra, thanks."

"Please, don't tell me I'm kind or good or I'll change my fucking mind. I've already got your account opened up here. You're lucky, I don't change my mind so fast and you're right, the property is in your name. Sign it over to me through your eyes."

Eyes. The key to bank accounts and safes. Corpses with gouged out eyes. Only the truly rich have other protections. Dead eyes aren't enough.

It's sold, it's over. Marek goes to the chapel and it is still the day he has said goodbye to Mum. In the morning he walked the same way – around the elementary school and high school and the polyclinic… Unlike this morning he walks lightly. On his back he has a pack only a little larger than Eli's. Some clothes, food, toiletries. Now he sees the chapel. A small crowd of people are standing around the entrance, Eli is standing on the third step and facing them.

39

The First Sermon

"Lifelong? Why don't you call him Mortal or Gone Tomorrow?" Marek overhears. Eli talks like a fifteen-year-old boy. On a first listen his words sound resentful – the aggrieved tone of an adolescent turning his anger on a world that has disappointed him. Only it's not quite like that. Eli's words reach inside, and have a way of orbiting the heart. Eli is talking about a civilization whose government is collapsing. He talks about how Lifelong is ruling at the tail end of that government. He talks of the ice advancing from the north – thanks to human beings. He talks about how humanity has spoiled absolutely everything it has ever touched. How humans should leave government to the trees, and concentrate on doing as little as possible.

Marek hardly recognizes Eli. Of course it is still him, but as he stands there in front of people who for some incomprehensible reason are listening to him, he has a new authority. Marek knows Eli as a brother – fragile, strangely unrelenting and recently silent. Where has the passion in his voice come from? Even an older couple is listening to him. There's a teacher from the school, a mother and child, a young man…

"They'll shoot you for that!" shouts a woman, "If someone informs on you, they'll shoot you!"

A wave of alarm spreads through the little throng. Everyone suddenly remembers the nature of the times, and they look around them.

"Aha, that takes genius, doesn't it?" Eli's laugh is almost ugly. "Shooting people?"

"I'm not going to listen to this," huffs someone with an armoured heart, and leaves.

In the meantime those standing closest to Eli ask some quiet questions. Eli answers. His demeanour is experienced, understanding. Marek suddenly doesn't know whether to be proud or embarrassed, but then he overhears the older lady saying to her husband, "He has a point. Everything we've done we've done wrong. First the greenhouse gases and then that grille. When life on earth is extinct because of us, who is going to revive it?" The pair also moves off.

Eli is now saying something similar – we received life, but deformed it. We know how to think but not how to act rightly. We might have become wise, but we didn't.

In the end only a few of the most interested remain. They seem excited when Eli tells them that the present civilization can't be repaired, and needs to be scrapped. Marek looks around automatically, checking there's no patrol coming. Or reconnaissance robot. People say the opponents of Lifelong are disappearing without trace. They are arrested and never heard of again.

Marek has pushed through to his brother on the steps and reaches for him: "Eli."

Eli immediately acknowledges him. "Marek… Have you sold the apartment? This is my brother," he introduces him. "He's sold our apartment, our home. He's sold our whole past, to liberate us from it. We're going away tomorrow."

The most persistent of the listeners is a man of about Marek's age, probably a student. When he hears they have sold the apartment and left their home, he is enthusiastic: "You must come with me." At this he bends closer and whispers. "But only you two. Nobody else."

They go with the young man, who introduces himself as Petr. He is thin and hunched. His complexion is an unhealthy yellow, perhaps from smoking. Together they leave Holesovice; there's no problem passing the gate going out. Then they are swallowed up by the chaos of the surrounding districts. On the pavements in front of little shops selling everything imaginable people are roasting potatoes and pieces of chicken. Smoke saturated with fat hangs heavy in the air. Marek is no longer thinking about the future, and allows himself to be taken up in the moment. Unlike in Holesovice and other residential districts, the streets are crowded. No-one here is thinking about the future. There isn't any future here.

Petr leads them on, solicitously, as if they were a rare catch; as if he has seen something extraordinary in them. At one point he turns back to them and blurts out, "Youth Liberation Army! Have you heard of it?"

Maybe. Marek has heard something: a failed assassination attempt on Lifelong six months ago. The firing of part of the wall protecting the government district. Several dead soldiers and fighters. Hacker attacks on robots and the whole system These events had just merged into a flood of others. It's too late for anyone to get upset or excited about them. Human life no longer has value. Apartments on the other hand, they have plenty of value; a value that keeps on rising under the pressure of demand from desperate Swedes and Norwegians.

Although it is summer it is already growing dark. They cross the river on a dilapidated pedestrian bridge, while traffic roars by on another bridge that looms high above their heads, the water, the old bridge and the poverty of the surrounding districts. Those who are driving on that top bridge would never come down here for anything. The two levels are ever more separate, and there is an even lower level – the river level, where the bank is full of shanty dwellings made of waste, and ducks look for food among the pieces of trash in the water.

The day is gradually ending. Marek realizes he hasn't eaten anything. There is an emptiness in his stomach.

40

Petr

Three long October weeks by Natalia's side. Three weeks, during which Marek often wondered whether this wasn't the way life was really meant to be, and this living together with all its physical connection was not the most direct way to God.

One Saturday evening Venca rushed in to announce, "Petr's come."

"Where is he?"

"He went to Hana's place."

A silence fell in the bungalow. Petr had been one of the closest to Eli from the start, Marek had known him for forty-eight years, and now he had gone to Hana's first. Marek vainly tried to tell himself that he shouldn't be jealous. Hana too had known Petr a long time. "Can you tell him I want to speak to him? Today."

Venca went off to take the message and Marek headed for the back door. "Excuse me, Natalia." He needed some fresh air. Marek was disturbed by his own mental state. Bad thoughts, jealousy, worries about intrigues that might well be figments of his imagination. Such things should not be happening to him. He knew the destructive effects of thinking this way.

Yet although he was aware of all this, the thoughts kept running in the same circles. He could just imagine Hana going on at Petr, getting him worked up against Natalia and making Marek out to be an old fool who had swallowed a whore's bait; a fool who had to be put out to grass, or at least disciplined. He paced to and fro on the trodden grass. He went right out to the pasture, but then returned. It didn't provide any relief. He went back into the bungalow, still uneasy.

Natalia was by herself inside. "You're annoyed, aren't you darling? Should I leave you alone for a bit?"

In fact it had already occurred to him that he ought to meet Petr in private. Talk to him like in old times. But it made him uncomfortable that Natalia had read his mind. "Don't you start too!" he snapped at her. "As if I didn't have enough troubles with the rest of them."

Natalia walked over from the corner where she had been straightening something. Her red bag was on her shoulder.

"Are you going away somewhere?" he said, alarmed.

"I promised Eva I would stretch her. She's got a frozen arm."

There was a light knock and the door opened. Petr.

In some ways he was still the same as when they had first met almost fifty years before by the chapel in Holesovice. He had the same air of restlessness and radicalism. He had the same fake nonchalance. He walked hunched and even slouching to the side, which made him easy to spot in a crowd. Back then he had immediately understood Eli and joined him, and had led them to an inconspicuous apartment house that was actually the base of the Youth Liberation Army. In normal circumstances it would have been a group of boys and girls debating about life, but there was nothing normal about the circumstances, and so it was a combat force against the ever harsher rule of Lifelong, real name Eduard Bas, dictator. The young people believed that Lifelong alone was to blame for all the evil, and they wanted to overthrow him at any price, and with him all the inequalities and the walls protecting the elites of the government districts.

Only a little younger than Marek, Petr had been a radical, and only in Holesovice that day to reconnoitre the ground for a possible diversionary action. All the same, he loved life and hadn't wanted to die, and that boy with the big eyes and striking face, whose name was Eli, had been saying, "Don't die! Don't fight with Lifelong or against him. Go somewhere else. That's the way to abolish his government. Every government." Petr was clever. He had known the score, and could see that the young fighters had no chance against the well-organized army of a dictator who was exploiting every resource to protect himself, his soldiers, and his chosen allies. Petr had known it was more likely Lifelong would be defeated by the ice and the eternal winter than by the antediluvian weapons of the Liberation Army.

Now Petr stood in a doorway in New Vinohrady, and like every old man he both was and was not the person he had once been. "You've had a shave," he noticed immediately, and shut the door behind him. His eyes moved to Natalia. "Good evening," he greeted her.

"Hi Petr," she answered, and made to leave,

"Wait, you needn't…" Marek tried to get her to stay.

She kissed him. "Don't worry about it, darling. Say what you have to say to each other. And I have work to do too."

Petr glanced briefly after Natalia and sat down on the edge of the bed. "She's obviously a girl who knows how to take care of herself," he remarked tersely.

Marek registered no particular criticism in his words, and that reassured him. He immediately took more pleasure in the meeting. He poured tea into mugs. "She was born in Dubrovnik," he said without knowing why. "In the same year they killed him there. Just two weeks later."

"There's no necessary connection," Petr said, discouragingly. "In any case she's young and strong, and she knows what she wants. I almost envy you Marek. I understand you a little. Well, to be honest I understand you entirely. But otherwise I can't approve."

The hope that had been growing in Marek withered all too early. "You don't approve? Of what exactly? Can't I live my own life?"

"Neither you nor I can live our own lives. We haven't done that for a long time." The old zeal returned to Petr's eyes. "Our lives belong to the community. We have obligations, Marek. A responsibility. We are models for the Followers. We define the norms."

Marek didn't disagree. He knew his role. He just didn't see why a loving relationship with a woman couldn't be one of those norms.

"Look, let's just leave the subject." Petr waved his hand. "I hear you've been to Litohoro. What did they want from you?"

"They were interested in the principles of our faith. Some professor from Salonika, the abbot of a monastery, students…"

Petr bristled with annoyance. "And you accepted the invitation? You didn't even consult with me about it? If you'd consulted me I'd have told you that faith in Eli can't be passed on. Everyone must find it in himself. And then… it's too early. It hasn't sunk in, that they're dying out. They haven't yet grasped that we are the future."

"Well… maybe I was able to give someone a little guidance on how to search and find. One person, definitely. And that's not nothing. Eli used to say that one person is everything. That numbers don't apply in the counting of souls. That a million is no more than one."

Suddenly it seemed to him a pity that they were quarrelling like this. Petr was a friend, "Come and sit down at the table. While the tea's still hot."

Petr obeyed and sipped the hot tea, a mixture made by Natalia. Its bitterness seemed to calm him for a moment.

"Do you still remember the way it was at the beginning?" Marek continued. "You knew him from when he was fifteen. I knew him from his birth. But you know – I still can't say what exactly made him holy. Of course, my love for him was a brother's love, and unconditional. But what was it that you felt for him? What did you think when you first saw him?"

"When I first saw him…" Petr stopped to consider. He seemed to be genuinely looking into the distance, into the past in his head. "My first thought was that he was brave. Almost too brave. And they would arrest him straightaway. I thought he wouldn't live through the night. It's also true that I just couldn't walk on past without stopping to listen. He wasn't saying anything amazingly new, or anything that someone else hadn't said before. But when it was Eli saying it, it was different. Potent and disturbing. It touched my heart."

Petr's words filled Marek with happiness. It was so honest and precise that it was as if his brother had come back. As if he had never died. And as if the friendship between Petr and Marek, cemented by the journey over the Alps and their vigil together over Eli's disfigured corpse, had never become strained. They understood each other. Marek wanted to pour out some mead.

"No Marek, I don't drink anymore," Petr refused. "We have to stay sober. Both of us."

That surprised Marek. Of all of them Petr had been the readiest to drink and kick over the traces, and here he was talking of sobriety. The same Petr who used only to come back from the village in the small hours and once fell asleep outside when it was snowing and almost froze to death. "How come you're suddenly so tough on yourself?"

"Don't you understand?" Petr put his hands to his head. "We're public figures. We're in charge of a community that one day will rule the world. It's our community that is still having children. It's politics, Marek. Politics. We two have to do politics."

Eli hadn't done politics. Marek knew that for sure. Eli couldn't abide politics. "Eli didn't do politics." He said it aloud. "He just lived the life he had to live."

"Except that he's dead. And he's not replaceable. We can't do what he would have done. If you say the same things he said, you won't be convincing. If it had been me speaking at that chapel in Holesovice, someone might have agreed with me, but what I said wouldn't have touched a single heart. Nobody would have led me away as I led you away that time. And by the evening I would have been executed. I've often thought that he shouldn't have died that time in Dubrovnik. He shouldn't have gone in there. We warned him, after all. His holiness could still have been with us now. But as things are… we can't replace him. And you know how it goes with the legacy of prophets… it depends on whether anyone takes up their teachings. It's politics, Marek, just politics. People need rules. And hope. We have to give them both. It has to be clear who belongs where and what he can expect from it. Who lives in the right way. Neither of us has much time left, so don't ruin it all, Marek."

Politics… Nothing could have been more alien to Eli. It was a word that belonged to the civilization that had failed. That Eli had abolished. And something else took Marek aback. "Prophet, Petr? Just a prophet?" Marek looked his old friend straight in the eye, and Petr looked away. "He was more than a prophet. From the moment he was born I saw God in him. And my task is to speak about him, to convey that meeting to those who didn't have my good fortune. This is revelation, Petr, not politics. We mustn't do politics."

"But what do you think we're doing every day? We negotiate with Greeks, Czechs, Turks... and we go in fear of the day it will occur to them to raze our settlements to the ground. We organize everyday life, in Karlin and in Vinohrady, trying to make sure people don't kill each other, don't envy a herd or the birth of a child. If our settlements cease to exist, what will be left? Eli wanted to change the world. And we protect two villages. There are three others in Croatia, and one in Turkey. There aren't many of us and there are still a lot of them. But even so, Marek, I believe that we shall triumph."

Three villages in Croatia. That other evening, when the Vinohrady people started threatening Natalia, Marek had thought about them. He had seriously considered leaving. There were other followers who needed him.

"Triumph over whom?" he asked.

"Everyone. In the end it will be us that will flood the world. They... will die out."

The last word shook Marek. Eli would never have expressed himself like that. "You have understood nothing, Petr." Marek shook his head incredulously. "The only thing we can do is bear witness." Marek redoubled his efforts to get Petr on his side. On the right side. "No politics. Bearing witness is quite enough. I too believe that the light he brought will light up the whole world. Through us too. But we needn't do as much as you think for that to happen. It will come about of itself. It's is not within our power to force it to happen."

Petr saw things differently. "You're a dreamer, Marek. You live in your dreams. Reality is something else again."

But Marek did not live in dreams. He saw Petr, a man who had a duty to bear witness and instead was going astray. Nobody could go further astray than a follower of Eli who wanted to gain control of the world through the instruments of that world. Marek had a vision of the community divided into two movements, and it tormented him. But then he realized something crucial – the power of God over creation. The power that made itself felt through the miracle of birth. Man had gained control of it only seemingly and temporarily. Creation in a test-tube, manipulation of genes. None of that was working any longer, and so in the end everything would turn out all right. The people who were going in the right direction would have children.

Marek kept these thoughts to himself. He did not need to share them, and didn't feel called to pronounce such harsh judgments.

"So Petr, what are we going to tell the people tomorrow?"

"That was what I wanted to ask you. It was your idea. It was you that invited me."

It was true. Marek had decided to invite Petr when the settlers had confronted him on the way back from Litohoro. "I'm afraid that someone is bringing enmity into our community. It's Hana… she has been with us the whole time. Eli loved her. He must have known why. But she's changed. She is… so rigid. And she has that Jerzi by her side. Those two would like to dictate to the others how they should live. Eli never did that, remember? He didn't judge. I'm afraid of those judgments of hers. Think whatever you like about me and Natalia, but she is innocent. It's not her fault they want to see me as a man apart. She left her rich parents in Dubrovnik when she didn't agree with their way of life. And she has been a help to me. It is thanks to her that everything has become clearer to me. She's forced me to realize who I am. The role I have in Eli's story. It's thanks to her that I have gone through it all a second time. And up there in the shrine of the birth… that's the place where we can meet him. At the beginning it was only a sham. But I spent the night before I went to Litohoro there and I met him. Petr, you don't have to believe me, but I feel that if she hadn't arrived here, he wouldn't have come to the shrine. She came from the town where she was born just after he died. And he came back. And so…"

He had run out of words. Even so he had said more than he had actually known just a moment before.

Petr seemed to be thinking hard. It almost looked as if he might be ready to change his mind, but then he just drily remarked, "I understand Hana." He might have wavered for a moment, but now he quickly backtracked to his certainties. "Hana's worried about the future of the community. It's not enough that children are born. They have to be born into a proper order. There can be no strength without that. I understand you, Marek. I really do. I sympathize with you… but you must put the community first. You are Eli's brother. You were the closest to him, but that doesn't mean you get to have the last word on everything. You have a role of honour – the worthy role of brother, and as such we want to see you as pure – and you have to reconcile yourself to it. We need you to be a wise respected elder, if that's not offensive to you. You don't have to give it up completely. It'll be enough if your relationship is not in their faces. She could live somewhere nearby. But not like this… bringing in a bed next to yours. Anyone can see inside through the window. Everyone's talking about you. Everyone…"

He didn't finish. Rapid steps were approaching and Natalia burst in. She stood there full of energy, straight-backed, tall and out of breath. "I'm really warmed up, she was a hard case," she confided loudly. "She had a blockage all the way from the ribcage. I told her she has a retracted arse." She noticed Petr's wince. "Or should I say behind? Sorry Petr, I know you don't talk this way. I've heard you preach." She laughed.

Marek felt damp under his armpits. He didn't know himself quite what to think of her uninhibited temperament. He realized that people would imagine a rather different kind of woman by his side. And then, he was afraid of what Petr was thinking. Meanwhile Natalia sat down on the bed and pulled off her sweater. Underneath it she wore only a close-fitting T-shirt. "Will you be staying the night with us, Petr?" She regarded Petr with sparkling eyes. She was so direct and straight-talking. What she said was not just words. She patted the coverlet and added, "There's room for everyone."

Petr too must have been sweating now. It didn't escape Marek that he stiffened and shivered with arousal. It wasn't too hard to guess what was in his mind. She might have seemed available to him but she loved Marek.

"Thank you, I have a bed for the night elsewhere," said Petr in a strained voice. The heat was rising in him and he couldn't hide it.

"So, what about tomorrow then?" By sheer strength of will he tore his eyes off her and turned back to Marek.

"I'll go wash." She jumped up from the bed and stripped her teeshirt off on the way to the bathroom. They could see her smooth back.

She's provoking, thought Marek. She's playing a game with Petr's lust. But he wasn't sure. "Ultimately I think it would be best not to say anything. We'll do it as a pilgrimage to the shrine."

As he spoke, his thoughts ran back to her. "Let everyone meet with Eli in their own way."

"But what about her?" inquired Petr. He had once again become the cool, rational radical preacher. "Will she be coming too?"

"Why wouldn't she come? If she wants she'll come. I haven't asked her. Does it matter?" He felt like a small child. He hoped they would let him alone, that they would let him have his way, that Petr was going to say, "It doesn't matter."

But the opposite happened. "Yes it matters. Because she's a distraction. She attracts attention. The two of you together attract attention, away from what is right. Everybody will be watching her. You want to unite people, but she divides them. She's just too, too…" He looked for a word that would still be tolerable. "Uninhibited."

Internally Marek had to acknowledge that there was something in it, but all the same, this ought to be about Eli. Natalia had probably heard them for now she came and sat down beside him. Instead of a teeshirt she was wearing just a towel. "Petr, haven't you ever needed someone to love you?" she asked directly. "Someone to touch you, stroke you…"

Petr was literally gaping at her breasts. He couldn't take his eyes off them even when he started to speak. "Everyone needs that… sometimes. But I wouldn't make something so important of it. There are more important things. For example the rules that hold the community together. That enable it to survive. I'm surprised you don't see that, Marek."

Marek saw. He saw that he needed to find an answer. For himself if for no-one else. That Natalia was sitting here half-naked in their presence was quite a challenge. Something narrow-minded in him told him it was too much, but something else assured him that this was simply who she was. Her soul was at one with her body. Eli had often spoken of the natural. "Don't worry so much about the community," Marek said suddenly, searching for a place to start. "Or about yourself. Instead of that, consider what Eli used to say. Why would something like this bother him? Does it hurt anyone? Does it hold the world back from the new beginning? From passing through the gate?" He turned to Natalia, "There's no need for you to try and embarrass Petr, and maybe you're not even aware of it. But what I want to say is that Eli didn't sit in judgment on individuals. He only judged civilization – the one we created and just can't carry on with. It's written in the Bible too: 'And the lord saw how the wickedness of man spread in the land.' That's what bothered Eli: wickedness. That's why we are here in New Vinohrady, in New Karlin, or in Croatia in New Brno. It's so we can live outside the old civilization and hope for the birth of a new one. But which of us is closer to that, whether it's you Petr, or I, or Natalia, I can't say. It's too early for that. We are at the beginning. Perhaps even before the beginning. All we can do is wait."

Natalia was already getting dressed. She reached out over the table and lovingly touched Marek's hand. "You're a treasure, Marek."

Petr got up. Marek noticed how that loving gesture wounded him. How he lacked something similar. Petr had never looked for depth in relationships, and in the end he had remained alone. "We haven't resolved anything," he said coldly.

"I won't go up there tomorrow, if that reassures you," said Natalia.

Marek was afraid she had given in to Petr. Had she let herself be robbed of her nature? But she immediately added, "I'll go up there by myself when I want. Some other time."

Marek felt a new power welling up inside. He was relieved for many reasons that he couldn't immediately identify. He rose and caught up with Petr in front of the door. "You don't need to see everything in such a black way, Petr." He was almost close enough

41

The First Manifestation

Marek lay awake long into the night. He knew that Natalia was not asleep either. The very presence of her being, her womanhood, the heat of her body, radiated from the place on his right. He had never before so much felt himself to be a man. It was somehow only like this, in a couple, that he perceived his own self in full. Only with the imprint of his manhood in her womanhood. When he closed his eyes and concentrated on his own breathing, he held her whole shape inside his mind, dematerialized and at the same time alive.

Eli was the only other person he could think about with the same inner glow. In the same way he would always only have to shut his eyes and the sense of Eli's being would come with his breathing. Later his thoughts went back to Petr, and to Hana and the whole community. Politics. The malignant word Petr had uttered had to be exorcised.

Suddenly he felt a warm hand on his brow. "Are you still ruminating, my darling?" The coverlet undulated and Natalia appeared above him. The light from the lingering fire in the stove fell on her face. She was in her close-fitting night dress, which went just halfway down her thighs. "You mustn't overtax that wise head of yours." She bent down to him. "Empty it out." Immediately she started to rub his temples, and he really felt the tension ebbing away. He looked into her eyes and they were shining even in the darkness. There was no doubt they were shining, and there was no doubt that this was love. Unconsciously his hands tightened where her hips ended, while her palms ran across his cheeks, forehead and temples, and now even covered his ears. A wave of happiness and relaxation passed through him. He could hear himself more groaning than speaking: "I love you Natalia. I'm happy."

His thoughts turned into little clouds of white steam that were dissolving in a sea of sleep. He couldn't remember when falling asleep had brought him such a sense of relief, when it had last been such a blessing and a home-coming.

Although his sleep was deep and untroubled, he woke early. Natalia was still asleep. The great day of pilgrimage had come.

Carefully he extricated himself from the bed in the dim light, thinking about Natalia the whole time. Although he had slept for only a few hours he felt rested and full of gratitude, the preaching was planned for the afternoon, the time of day when Eli had been born, but he wanted to set off earlier, to be there alone and the first.

On the table there were flatbreads and pieces of roast meat, two apples and a herbal infusion. He couldn't work out when she had had time to prepare it, and how she could have known he was leaving so early. He got dressed and put the food in his backpack. His stick was propped by the door. When he eventually took it into his hand, the darkness outside had started to fade. He went back to the bed where she slept just one more time. He sensed her rather than saw her. Her eyes were closed and lips pressed together and she didn't move an iota; she was dwelling in her interior worlds that had to be as beautiful as she herself was. It had been the same when he had sometimes looked at the sleeping Eli, when he was small.

Farewell Natalia, he thought, as if he were taking his leave of her forever. And as quietly as he could he went out into the morning cold.

On the corner of the alley Venca joined him. The large man was shivering from the cold – he must have been waiting for a long time. They walked together through the settlement in silence. Lamps were already flickering in cowsheds and the sounds of work drifted from them.

When he emerged between the pasture and orchard, the sky was turning pink, Marek thought of neither the past nor the future. He carried in his heart the certainty of love.

The walk up the hill along the muddy, rain-eroded path was exhausting and painful for Marek. The weather was already wholly autumnal, and gusts of cold wind were wresting the first leaves from the trees. The sun had hardly come up when a light shower came down. Venca wrapped Marek in the raincoat that he brought with him in case of rain.

This weather too, like every other kind of weather, was associated with a very concrete memory. Eli had been sick. He had been coughing and feverish, a wretched hawking messiah in a human body. Petr sent everyone away, not wanting anyone to see Eli in this state. He was already playing politics even back then. Hana had been propping Eli up. It occurred to Marek now that Eli might then have woken with the same kind of thoughts that he had today, with the knowledge that she was giving him all her love and tenderness. That was why Hana was always forgiven everything. Suddenly he understood it, and knew he needed to find a way to her.

This time the bench above the eroded slope was wet, but Marek needed to sit down. Venca had a sheepskin in the backpack. He wiped the edge of the bench and put the skin on it. Marek had only just sat down when they heard the pounding of someone's feet. It was approaching from above. A skinny shepherd girl, hardly more than a child. "He was there!" she cried when she saw them. "I spoke with him! He talked to me!"

She ran right up to them, gasping for breath, and her agitation was intense. Marek was at first afraid that someone had hurt her, but she just kept on repeating, "He was there." Her eyes were very wide.

He took her arm, to calm her. "Who? Who did you see?"

"Him, it was him. Eli. He talked to me." With that she burst into tears, but not with pain.

Venca stared helplessly at Marek, waiting for a lead; he had no opinion himself. Only Marek's attention was taken up with the girl's immense excitement. Tears ran down her cheeks, forming rivulets in the dust on her face. "Where did you see him? What did he say to you? Tell us. Tell us what happened."

"I went up to the shrine early, as I sometimes do. It was raining. I wanted to shelter there just for a while." She was almost apologizing. "And he was there. He was standing behind the little bed."

Marek could hear his own heart thudding in his chest. He still didn't understand and couldn't think, but he knew it was serious.

"What did he look like? How old was he? Did he have a beard?"

"No he didn't. He was young. Almost still a boy. And those eyes of his. He looked at me with those eyes. I wasn't at all scared. Not at all."

"And his hair? What was his hair like?"

"Hair – kind of fair. And he had firm lips, in a wavy line, like his face. He was… beautiful."

Then it must have been Eli, thought Marek. The man she had seen was Eli. "So what did he say?"

"He said, 'I'm sorry, I've just come back.' And I said, 'I didn't expect anyone to be here. But why do you say sorry?' And he said, 'Because you were startled. I admit I was waiting for you here. Run down and tell everyone that I've come back.'"

It was as if Marek could hear him. Yes, he heard those words reported by the girl in Eli's voice. "And then what? What did he say then?"

"Then he repeated it. 'Tell them that I've come back. I'm not going to leave you – ever again. I'm staying here with you.'"

"And then?" Marek was hardly breathing.

"Then the light he was standing in started to fade. Until…" She gulped and nearly choked before she got out her last words. "He vanished." She almost seemed to blame herself for it.

"And what are you doing here?"

"I'm running down of course. To tell everyone. I mustn't let him down."

"To tell everyone…" It was only now that Marek was beginning to work out the implications. For a moment he wondered if he should stop her. Nothing like this had ever happened before. Marek was familiar with the New Testament; he had often thought of how Jesus had appeared to his disciples after death, and he had been sorry that Eli had not been granted that happiness. But now he had appeared to this girl? Why to her? Why not to him?

In that moment he realized that he was thinking like a politician. And he must not think like a politician. A miracle is simply a miracle. "Off you go then." He let go of the girl's slender arm. "Be happy. He must certainly have had a reason for showing himself first to you. I'll tell everyone that."

42

He revealed himself for you

"Could you please just wait a minute outside?" he said, turning to Venca in front of the shrine. He was full of expectations but also despair, for something told him that it was impossible for Eli to be there when he went in. Not that it had been possible when the girl went in, of course, but it had somehow happened all the same.

He went inside. The shrine was quiet, shadowy and… empty. It was what he was expecting but the disappointment could not have been greater. A few candles burned around the bed. Shepherds, woodcutters, and pilgrims came here and lit them. Yes, even pilgrims sometimes arrived from Croatia, Turkey and Albania… Marek bent his head and closed his eyes. Thirty-three years had gone by since Eli's death, and for that whole time Marek had been groping his way forward, waiting for a sign. For that whole time he had been asking – If you were who I believe you to be today, why did you allow yourself to be killed in Dubrovnik, so pointlessly? Why did I have to hold your body, with all the life gone out of it?

Eli's dead body, his sunken face with its traces of torment, pointed to what it was not. It pointed to loss, to the emptiness that remained after the dead.

A sign, Eli, Marek thought hard. Why didn't you give the sign to me? Why didn't your first steps after your return, if you have returned, lead to me?

After a while, however, Marek's frame of mind began to change. The space around him, which he had entered with closed eyes, started to fill with gratitude. Eli's gratitude. The unfailing flow of the water penetrated Marek's ears and the candle flames warmed his feet. It was as if he could hear the words. *This is your reward, Marek. Your place is in the light of my gratitude. Now and forever.*

He was flooded by an extraordinary happiness. Something similar to what he had felt when Natalia began to rub his temples, but this touched the whole of his life, from the first moment when he had waited in front of the clinic. Finally it made sense, only he couldn't comprehend why it was to him that Eli had been born.

Not just me, he corrected himself. Eli had been born for all. And immediately he understood why it was to the girl that he had appeared. Marek was Eli's brother and had lived his whole life with him, and if Eli had appeared to him, how would the others come to it? Marek realized that this was the only way it could have happened.

The rain came down hard this time. It drummed on the roof and water dripped down the walls. He remembered Venca, who was getting soaked outside, and called him inside right away. It wasn't long before the first settlers, thirsty for the miracle, came running up. Marek was afraid of their disappointment, but they fell on their knees before the little wooden bed, even though it was empty. The shrine began to fill up. Sara, one of the most pious women in the community, whispered: "He was your brother. Did you see him too?"

Now he knew how to reply. "I was with him all through his life. This time he came for you. He revealed himself for you."

The last to arrive were Hana and Petr with the girl to whom it had happened. By this time not everyone could fit into the shrine. Marek went out, although they tried to stop him. His resolve to find a path to Hana and understand her better came straight up against her indifferent face. It was as if she didn't even want to be here. He turned to Petr instead: "Petr…"

Petr admitted no hesitation or doubts: "It is mainly Alice who will speak!" That was her name. "She has to bear witness. First to us who are here, and then to everyone, the whole world."

Marek vainly tried to look beyond the wall of considered words for any trace of sincerity, any hint of what Petr really thought. Marek was so full of excitement and Petr's coolness baffled him. In the end he couldn't keep the lid on his joy, and burst out, "We called an assembly to look for Eli, and he came to meet us halfway. Isn't it wonderful?"

"Yes of course… Shall we take her inside? So she can describe to everyone what she saw."

"Or what she thinks she saw," remarked Hana sceptically.

"I spoke to her first. She came running down the slope. She was very agitated. She definitely wasn't making anything up. She experienced it. And that is enough for us to declare that it happened. It is a kind of reality. It's testimony of a miracle."

All scepticism, even Hana's, evaporated when Alice started to speak. Marek knew the people here. Many had given up education or careers to follow the unclear promise of the journey that Eli urged. This revelation that had been given to one of them, they took as their own. It was something like a confirmation of the rightness of their choice. It was a liberation from all uncertainties and doubts. Now their faith in Eli could finally become a religion.

Rules. They needed some. Petr had his own share of truth; even Marek realized that.

Inside the shrine was packed out. There was only a little space around the bed, where Alice was showing what she had seen. Marek, Petr and Hana stood immediately beside her, their faces turned to the rest. Under the weight of those hundreds of eyes Marek decided that the unity of the community came before everything else. He realized how the others saw him. He was the brother of the Messiah. He could not lead his own life. And he should give up everything for them. He didn't need to strive for personal happiness. Natalia's arrival could not have been a matter of chance, for she had taught him an awareness of himself, and it was partly thanks to her that he now grasped his role. Yet for all that, he would have to give her up. She… would understand that. He would arrange a place for her to live close by. It wouldn't mean that he no longer loved her or that he would want to deny his love for her. Only he would have to be content with what he had already got from life. And that was no small thing. He would never cease to be grateful to her.

43

Turn away from evil

Securities to cling to are sinking as fast as ships full of refugees from the north in the waves of the Baltic Sea. The old order is collapsing, and it is becoming obvious that it was no order at all and there is nothing to defend. It is hard enough for anyone to defend himself. The Warriors of the True Christ have gone back to murdering their fellow believers. They believe the Day of Judgment is approaching, but for the moment they do the judging themselves. The fighters of the Youth Liberation Army also want to destroy their enemy, and that means Lifelong. He defends himself bloodily and no-one can understand why he hasn't long ago escaped to Australia or Africa. He certainly could afford a comfortable life there, but evidently what he wants first and foremost is power. Ruling this ever chillier Central European territory is dearer to him than life.

The Slovaks somewhere in the east have found another reason to fight, and declared their own state. They are dying for it in mountains whose summits will now forever be covered by snow. They are dying for a piece of frozen land condemned to famine. There are shootings. For the moment it is just some streets, houses and villages that are changing into graves. No one knows why.

Such are the times in which Eli begins his prophetic journey. Once delicate girls with pistols and grenades on their belts listen to him talk and their eyes grow moist. They look after him too. He's such a charmer…

Only Eli doesn't want to be charming. Weapons on anyone's belt upset him. Yet how can he ever put a stop to all this hatred, which springs from helplessness and despair? From the fear that in reality there is nothing to fight or live for any longer? After all, it's turning out that mankind on the planet means no more than a colony of seals, a self-destructive animal species condemned to extinction. The advances of the last centuries are gone. Without global cooperation there is no technology. The war is waged with the old kinds of weapon. With what can be made easily, home-made.

"What do you say, Eli?" the young people keep challenging him. "If we lay down our arms, all they will do is exterminate us like rats. You can't want that."

Eli replies, "They'll exterminate you anyway, but there are two deaths. There's the death that ends everything, and the death that is the beginning of return, to the first hope, from which we are born."

Hope. It is a word they all need, and it's just that they don't show it. Petr is torn, and somewhere in between. He defends some of Eli's views, and is drawn to the strange sense of reconciliation that Eli's talk evokes. But on the other hand he points out the need to fight against evil. And Lifelong is evil.

Eli objects, saying that the right thing is not to allow evil into your life. This makes evil unnecessary and it starves to death. Because any kind of fighting and killing is its food.

One girl, Dana, listens more than the others. She has long brown hair, and when she plaits it into a braid she looks like a mythical avenger from the old fantasy movies. Once when Marek comes back unannounced to the attic room where he and Eli sleep, he finds the two sitting there holding hands. From the silence that ensues Marek realizes there is something more between them. It wounds him deeply inside, and he doesn't even know why. He will be wounded in that way many times to come.

But not even love for a yet unrecognized messiah can put Dana off the fight. The young people leave in pairs, or sometimes alone and very occasionally in a larger group, often at night. Dana vanishes like that too. Her father, once a university professor, has been executed on Lifelong's orders. Dana wants revenge. The pain that Eli experiences whenever she leaves is all the deeper for his awareness that he can't persuade her to abandon the path of death.

"Just wait, baby," Dana soothes him with a joke. She even turns to her comrades who are staying in the base. "Guard Eli for me – when I get back I want to find him here, my little mouse." Then she becomes serious. "It's important to know where your place is. Yours is here and mine is there. To fight against evil may be bad, but to defeat it, to tear it out by the roots, isn't so bad." Dana had been studying philosophy.

Eli disagrees. "Tear it out by the roots? But we are born with it. We can't uproot our own selves. At best we can turn away from the evil that we have in ourselves."

"Where on earth do you get all these big ideas, baby?" Dana grins, knowingly.

44

It somehow happens inside me

They have been living with the young people of the Liberation Army for months now. Time flies from day to day and there is always something going on, even if not much is really happening. Marek is finding it hard to reconcile himself to his new life without the security of the Holesovice apartment and a regular income. It makes it even harder that he has no work, and nothing to do but look out for Eli. Although that is a big task, because Eli does whatever he wants. "I want to go to that guarded district," he suddenly says, "but without weapons. It interests me. Maybe I can persuade them."

Everyone tries to talk him out of it, but he insists. "If you don't want to come, I'll go by myself," he says firmly and looks at Marek. Yes, Marek will go – he has to go. Petr hesitates, since even though he is not a frontline guerrilla he prefers the struggle. At the same time he can see that it's going nowhere. The young people are weak and isolated as fighters. There are other armed groups in the country and in Prague, but they don't cooperate and often fight each other. The dictator is a thousand times stronger.

"I'll come too," Petr decides in the end. "I have my doubts, but it interests me." He spreads a map of the city in front of them. "We have to think this out properly. Where do you want to go?"

"Think it out? What do you want to think out?" laughs Eli. "It doesn't matter one bit."

"These districts are guarded. Walled," Petr explains, trying to restrain his impatience. "We have several secret ways of getting into them, but even so it's risky."

"I've no need to fear. I'm not going there to fight."

Now Marek has to interject. "Eli, please try to understand. It makes no difference to them that you're not there to fight. They are in a war, and you can only get into these districts with a biometric code. I might get in, for example. I used to go there to sell apartments."

"You're serious? You can really get in?" says Petr, astonished, and there is a gleam in his eye. "Why didn't you say so a long time ago? We could have used that."

Marek doesn't know how to answer. This isn't his war, and in fact it isn't even his life. His only real life is Eli, and that has been keeping him here for half a year now. Marek is amazed that every day there is something to eat. The fighters always bring something back or they are supported by donors. There have been just two days, when there was a wave of raids by government patrols, when they went hungry.

So far he has not had to use the payment chip, and that is his one security. His whole life is in it, expressed by a number. The only trouble is that prices are sky-rocketing.

Eventually they decide to go to Dejvice. It's Petr's suggestion. Dejvice interests him; he's planning an action there. Eli insists they go the very next day. Marek and Petr make no headway at all trying to persuade him out of it. Eli makes a fuss, angrily putting his hands to his head. "But I just know when to go!" he cries, "I'm the only one who knows. And you... you're always doubting me. You just refuse to listen. If you won't come tomorrow, I'll go alone."

That night Marek and Eli lie down in bed side by side. Another two boys sleep in the room. One has been shot in the shoulder and is quietly groaning until the girl nurses give him an injection. Marek lies motionless on his back and Eli keeps a distance unusual for him. A deep silence lies between them. Yet Marek wants to ask something. Now he asks.

"Eli," he whispers finally, when the wounded boy is asleep. It is more than just an attempt at communication; it is a great and fundamental question. "Why are you like this?"

"Like what, Marek?" Eli is also whispering and his voice sounds uncertain.

"Like you know best about everything. Just you."

Eli rolls on his side, to look at Marek. "But I don't know anything, Marek."

"So how come you talk with such certainty. Like about Dejvice. Why do you have to go there tomorrow?"

"I don't know. Seriously. I don't know." He turns around for a moment and adds, "I don't understand it myself. All I know is that in the moment I say I have to, it just has to be that way."

"In the moment? But now you don't know?"

"I don't need to know now. We've decided now."

"But that's something I don't understand." He really doesn't understand. Where did that persuasiveness come from in Eli, especially when now he admits he doesn't know himself?

"It somehow happens inside me, Marek," Eli tries to explain. He is agitated and grabs Marek by the shoulder. "I'm sorry if I'm bad-tempered with you, bro. I want you to understand. It's like... what happens is that when you say, and I know you mean it, that we shouldn't go tomorrow, then I just know at that moment whether I have to or I don't have to. There are times I feel as though I'm... not free. I can't get rid of it. I can't do something else. It has absolute power over me, even though I'm just me. I think it's normal for people sometimes to cheat on themselves a little, isn't it? They can do something they know they shouldn't do. I envy that. It's something I just can't do. Do you understand, bro? It's just not an option for me."

The chasm that had opened between them has already disappeared. Marek can't remember Eli having ever opened up to him like that before. And he understands him. He begins to grasp his destiny, which he has anyway sensed from his birth. It is above all suffering. That is Eli's mission, and Marek longs for just one thing; somehow to diminish that suffering.

45

The Jews, obviously

Eli's unusually direct words stay with Marek even in his dreams that night. Even his awakening into a new day feels different. He is not familiar with this state of mind. Only after a moment does it come to him – it is the absence of fears. He is not thinking of what will happen tomorrow, or even of what will happen today. His mind is full of trust.

Although according to the calendar it is spring, there is snow lying in the street. It has been trampled into a hard ice crust and is black on the surface. Eli, Marek and Petr's breath turns to mist as they exhale. When they reach Karlin some of the shops look bombed out. In the next street the pavement is lined with the burned out wrecks of cars. At crossroads there are fortified towers with robot transporters.

Yet everywhere around them there is teeming life. People huddle over improvised fires where they burn pieces of furniture and tree branches and roast something to eat on iron grills. Children slide on icy piles of snow. It's a good thing Mum can't see this, Marek thinks.

They get to a footbridge over the frozen river. Only in the centre is the ice turning the darker colours of the future thaw. Holesovice can be seen in the distance. It leaves Marek cold.

"You've sure chosen your day," Petr hisses into his polo neck when a gust of wind catches them on the bridge.

The chill got into their bones, and Eli, that hunched youth with the sprouting fluff under his nose – is silent. He hurries, speeding on in pursuit of his incomprehensible mission. Petr and Marek let themselves be pulled along in his wake, Marek devotedly, Petr with curses on his lips. Petr doesn't even know himself what binds him to this boy.

On Letenska Square there is a state bistro in operation, for informers and employees of the regime. Marek uses his chip to get through the door. He buys them all soup and tea, and coming out with his tray, he draws the attention of an older dark-haired man. "Where are you taking that, my lad? Who are you feeding?"

"My brother…" Marek gestures ahead of him, "He's waiting outside."

Petr and Eli take the bowls and put them down on a concrete base, once part of a bench. As they sip the tea the dark-haired man eyes them curiously. Eventually he steps onto the pavement and comes over to them. "You'd be better staying home in this freeze," he remarks. "April's here and it's like in January." When they don't reply he continues, "You know, this hasn't just happened by accident. It suits somebody. Somebody's behind it."

Petr shrugs and answers diplomatically, "It's awfully cold, but they say it's going to get warmer next week. Haven't you heard?"

"But what I'm telling you is that somebody's behind it."

Marek glances at Eli. He is bent over his soup. He's really hungry. With any luck he'll keep quiet.

The man is desperate for a question and Petr supplies it. "Who would that be then?"

"The Jews, obviously!" the man says triumphantly. "It was them that invented that grille. They want to weaken us. Our Central European Federation. They want to take over the government."

Only now does Eli raise his head. He has a scrap of meat on the fluff under his nose. His large eyes regard the man innocently, but steadily. "Take over the government? Government is over. Only a madman would still bother to try."

The man is evidently uncertain as to whether to treat this as agreement or opposition. In the end he decides for the second. "So you'd like that would you? Anarchy? Disorder?"

Marek wants to give Eli a poke, but has no way of doing it. Eli continues. "It's not a matter of what I'd like. It's about the fact that there won't be anyone to govern. For a long time the human population has been rising all the time, but now it's going to fall fast. Children won't be born any more. In the end only people who make peace with nature will have children."

The man is shocked by Eli's words. Suddenly, from one second to the next, he is terrified, rigid with anxiety. "Well, you certainly know how to cheer a man up, for fuck's sake." He tries to recover his nerve and starts back for the bistro. "Weird boy... Have you any idea what you're saying? I've got kids. And I care what's in store for them."

46

The Cursing of the Machines

Dejvice is like a fortress. Closed blocks of houses and streets partitioned by walls. Despite this all three get inside, using a secret Liberation Army route through the cellars of houses. Petr is resentful, and shakes his head incredulously. "We could have brought weapons in this way. A lot of weapons. The boys and girls could use it as an escape route. And we're using it... Why exactly?"

Marek can't understand the point of the trip either. He will only understand several hours from now, when the three get back to Liben.

Marek knows Dejvice; he has sold a couple of apartments here. Now that the rest of the city has fallen into destitution, the calm and order here feel almost unreal. It seems impossible that the three should not be noticed. The facades of the twentieth century houses hide the chilly architecture of luxury. The houses are connected high above by closed footbridges. They might be full of everyday hustle and bustle, but there is certainly nothing going on below. At least there is no snow and the narrow bands of grass are growing green, heated from underneath. Not far away there is a sign of life, something like a club. Parked in front of it are three antiquated but today recommissioned modern aircars, and Marek wonders where their owners can fly with them, when only here are they safe. Eli heads straight for them.

It really is a club. Behind smoked glass sit the shadows of perfect people of various ages. They are trying not to know anything about the situation in other parts of the city or beyond the city in the fields. Marek waits for Eli to head inside, and prepares to use his chip, his pass to anywhere, but Eli turns to the cars and holds out a hand towards them, as if they were his audience of the day. Indeed, he seems to be in a trance, absent. And he starts to utter something like reproaches: "You cold machines! Dead! Pointless! Do you give anyone life? Do you? Human beings are born of human beings, trees of trees, but what is born from machines?"

A few people behind the glass of the cafe notice the indignant boy. They point at him, but none of them get up to come outside, and so Eli continues to speak to the cars, while Petr walks a little further on – not wanting to be associated with the lunatic. "He could at least blow it up if it bothers him so much," he mutters to himself.

Even Marek is embarrassed. But Eli's anger increases. As if those three flying cars were to blame for all the misfortune in the world, for the whole screwed up climate and the dictatorship of Lifelong: "Only death!" Eli answers his own question. "Machines give birth to death. You are accursed machines. You are the death with which we have surrounded ourselves. The death we are spreading. So much death. I see so much death. It is coming…"

Eventually Eli is completely exhausted and sits down on the heated ground. Marek and Petr take his arms and try to haul him up. "Come on, before someone notices us." Petr is impatient. "Let's not get ourselves shot just for this!"

They slowly walk away and Eli recovers himself. He seems not to remember anything. When they are a block further on, someone comes out of the club and gets into a car. The three glance back at them. It's a man and woman. The man in the car tries something and after a while gets out, annoyed. He walks around his car, inspecting it back and front, and then gets in again, tries again. But nothing happens. The aircar won't start.

47

I couldn't have saved her

When a few hours later they cross the footbridge back over the frozen river, it is a little bit warmer and the ice in the middle is breaking up. The meaning of what has happened since morning is unclear to Marek and Petr. They still suspect nothing as they walk through Karlin, but as they approach Liben, they notice that there are fewer people in the street than before. The fires where food was roasting in the morning are now only smouldering. Marek is gripped with anxiety. When they turn into the street where the Liberation Army has its base, the dust and smoke get in their eyes. The smoke is coming from… their house. On the pavement is a pile of rubble. They run up to it and see the work of destruction. Someone has blown up the front wall. A bloody leg sticks out of the rubble. "Oh my God!" cries Petr. Other body parts lie on the steps. "Fucking hell!" Petr curses.

Marek feels ill and Eli put his hands to his head. "Death," he whispers desperately. "I see so much death."

Mum's has been the only death that Marek has encountered at close quarters, and Mum spent a long time dying; she started to die at the time of the birth of Eli. That made the transition from being to non-being hard to identify. Admittedly Marek had also witnessed the death in the middle of the river, when the ice had given way beneath the vagrants, but that was death at a distance. Compared with the death that Marek will soon find on the upper floors, that death didn't seem real. On the upper floors of the house the bodies of the boys and girls have not been torn apart by the explosion. They are just dead, lying in dramatic positions expressing the impulses of their final moments: a memory of parents, childhood, anger, surprise, shock from pain, disappointment. They had joined the Liberation Army too young to have reckoned with death as something that might actually happen to them. Gradually Marek realizes that he too could have been lying here. He even has the feeling that he has split in two and a piece of him has really died.

Perhaps it is only his soul, which bends over the bodies. It will stay with him for a long time, that feeling that he is alive by mistake. But he knows it was not a mistake. Eli was behind it, with his irresistible need to leave the house.

But Eli seems to be in shock. Completely overcome. He hasn't been expecting anything like this. Something just led him away.

For a while Marek loses him. Marek himself walks through rooms, finding two and in the end three dead government soldiers and one smashed robotic probe. Robert – he had probably surprised them. Even so he lies here, a pistol gripped in his hand. It was a quick end that he chose for himself: fast, faster than fear.

Marek comes across Eli again on the third floor. He is kneeling over someone, sunk in a pain so deep that no one on the outside can reach him. What he is kneeling over is the body of a girl. Marek takes another step and recognizes her. She lies shot through the chest and to judge by the drying stains on her light green military shirt she was hit twice. She is slightly curled up, her head fallen back, and in her smooth full face there seems to remain a trace of astonishment. As if she wanted to say, "Does it end so easily? Just now, when I've found Eli? Really?" Brave Dana. She went to meet her destiny undaunted.

Eli looks questioningly at Marek. "I couldn't have saved her." It is not a question.

For the first time Eli doesn't seem good-looking to Marek. His face is a bleary mess, he's an emaciated adolescent. Marek doesn't know what to say. His throat is closing up and his lips are trembling.

"I couldn't have. I really couldn't have." The sobs start to shake him. They burst out of him like a river, like a purifying flood sweeping away everything too burdensome to be uttered.

Later when they are hurrying along unknown streets. Marek doesn't even know how they got out. That was Petr, who has pulled himself together and is taking them to friends who he says will give them shelter. When eventually they find themselves in a chilly apartment steeped in old age and smoke, Marek the real estate agent has no idea where in the city he is.

A tall old man with glasses bows painfully and leans on the table. Petr addresses him as professor, and the professor repeats incredulously, "All of them? My best students?"

His wife is younger, although also wrinkled. Her hair is dyed black and she has a disagreeable penetrating voice full of belief in her own truth. She repeats all Lifelong's crimes, but after the calamity they have just witnessed, her words are like hail drumming on his head. You can't hide from it, but it bounces straight off. Only then the woman utters another name – which in her view belongs to criminal number two – Rudolf Nekolny. That's no harmless piece of ice – it's a missile, and it penetrates Marek's head effortlessly. Because Rudolf Nekolny is Dad.

It is beyond Marek's understanding; the criminal they speak of, and the man who once sat on his bed. On Eli the name has no effect even though it is his surname: Eli Nekolny. Even at school he insisted that no one address him as that. "I am just Eli," he would say. "That's how you'll remember me. That's how I have to be."

Their hosts make up beds for them on mattresses in a cold room with a high ceiling, a dusty bookcase and yellowed walls. Then they are alone and night is falling, and the images of death return. Marek thinks of Dana. Her image is as alive as it is dead. Actually he had been jealous of her when he caught her and Eli in intimacies. He hadn't understood how it worked between them. She was quite a lot older and regarded Eli as a child, after all, but still she couldn't resist him. She had smiled at Eli with brown eyes, usually so serious. That smile… that indulgence, with which she listened to his warnings, would never be repeated.

Petr fluffs up his pillow and suddenly gasps. "Do you realize how easily we could have been there, and dead? That was such an amazing lucky break. Do you realize?"

Only Marek doesn't see it as a lucky break. He sees it as an inevitability. He rolls on his side towards Eli. "Did you know? Was that why you wanted to go to Dejvice?"

But Eli's voice is full of self-reproach. "If I had known it, I would be to blame for her death. I would have been able to save her."

"So it was just coincidence?" Marek asks, although he knows it wasn't.

Eli suddenly sounds surer. "Nothing that happens to me is coincidence. But I don't understand who decided on it. Who sent them to their death. I thought I knew how it was, how that gate at the end stands outside time, and everyone who reaches it is equal with everyone else. But until then... It's too unjust."

Something in Eli is rebellious. If his soul came from elsewhere, now it is really suffering the agony of human destiny. Dana's destiny. Why did she die so young, so pointlessly, before she had achieved anything? Her death casts doubt on absolutely everything. Eli is tasting life as it is, vainly asking after the meaning.

48

Apocalypse

They stay a few months with the professor and his wife. Sometimes Marek uses his payment chip to improve their circumstances a little. The professor sympathizes with Eli's idea of not fighting but just leaving and going elsewhere. They start to talk of leaving for the south. Many of the inhabitants of the Central European Federation have already tried it. Only the Austrians have organized militias. They are guarding the villages, valleys and passes. They fire mercilessly on the refugees.

Occasionally the professor invites colleagues round; other university professors, scientists, former academics. He introduces Eli to them as an interesting young man with strange ideas that are nonetheless sometimes worth hearing. The conversation revolves around the current crisis. The historians compare it with other crises, such as the fall of Ancient Egypt, Rome. They also bring news from the outside world, even though the regime tries to exercise strict censorship. It is only now that Marek learns that exoduses like those in Europe have been taking place in America and the Far East. He finds out that it is raining in the Sahara and that in China power has been seized by an appalling regime which is committing genocide, and a third of the population has already been wiped out. Meanwhile in Tibet, covered by eternal snow, the life of the Buddhist monasteries has been revived. India, Pakistan and Bangladesh have completely disintegrated, and Brazil has been dislocated by permanent flooding.

One of the guests is a Catholic priest, and he sees it all as the beginning of the Apocalypse. He quotes from the Bible and seems very excited, saying that the first four angels have already sounded their trumpets, and everyone must now concede that John's vision was definitely sent by God.

Someone else seeks to dampen his enthusiasm. Where, he asks, is salvation for those who believe and live in accord with the word of God? Where is the hope – the dwelling of God with men, as it is written? Who among the believers will live to see it, when the believers are dying just like all the rest? And to add to it all they are being murdered by those lunatics, the Warriors of the True Christ, their fellow believers.

At the mention of the Warriors of the True Christ the priest is indignant. "Don't drag them into it! That has nothing to do with the faith. Does the Bible incite to murder? I'll tell you one thing, though, and it's that those people are one of the angelic trumpets. Angels include the angels of destruction. And we ourselves are angels of destruction. God doesn't need to send anyone. People who have succumbed to evil are the instrument of the Apocalypse. But to answer your question: on the Day of Judgment all of the just will live. It doesn't matter when the just died, for they will all live to see it. And will be resurrected." The priest became solemn. "You know, I never thought I would live through so many great truths. That I would be a witness to God's plan. A witness to the fulfilment of his words. That I would live to see the end that was prophesied. Isn't it wonderful?"

Eli usually keeps quiet, but this time he raises his hand to show he wants to speak. And the words slip quietly from his mouth. "Life will not end so easily. Not even human life. People will live. You are right, but there will be so few of them and it will be so different a life that it can be called a renewal of life. Except," Eli shrugs almost apologetically. "I can't find the good news for those who have already died. But there must be some. I know there must be."

49
Zest for Life

There was a new kind of holiness in everything. A feeling of acceptance and gratitude. In a remote corner of Northern Greece, encircled by a green landscape and dying villages, God had finally remembered the Followers and given them a real sign. The fact that they were having children was something they had taken more as a natural condition, as a gift they had always had. And of course it was a gift that had exposed them to the rage of others, whose infertility they were unable to explain. But with the appearance of Eli to the shepherd girl they finally saw that they were not alone, and that the last had become the first.

Even Hana's face relaxed. Everyone was showing respect for her, and all the more now that it could not be doubted that she had been the lover of God himself. On the way down from the shrine she stumbled and fell to her knees in the mud, but started to laugh it off, although perhaps she laughed too long.

As they descended along the eroded slope, Marek was still in an exalted state. But then he saw the roofs of New Vinohrady and remembered that Natalia was waiting for him in the bungalow at the end of the alley. Unsuspecting, good, ready to give him everything. Just thinking of her brought a new dimension to his life, for life with her had real taste and zest, with every instant fulfilled and no need to go anywhere or look for anything. He was seized by anxiety. And regret. He would be hurting her.

He had been so ecstatic before that the burden he bore now felt all the heavier. He saw that Eli was asking another sacrifice of him. In fact, for the first time he saw it as a genuine sacrifice. And he didn't understand why he had to make it. It seemed to him that Eli ought to be satisfied with what he had already lived through for his sake.

As he tottered down the pasture, three boys overtook him. One turned around, raised his head and stuck his tongue out. A completely idiotic expression, the sudden impulse of a child's mind, which immediately passed, and the boy fled. He could have had no inkling how much truth he expressed with that foolish gesture. The world of children; the privilege of the Followers of Eli – the future chosen people.

Children had stopped being born a year after Eli died. What he had predicted was unleashed by his own death. The miracle of conception had escaped the laws of nature as they had operated up to then, for it seemed that birth could not happen without some larger assent. Eli's story, confirmed by its tragic end, had somehow infused every egg and sperm. The human species, its population so disproportionately inflated, had lost the special status it had gained in evolution. As Eli had said, the rule of man over nature was over, but hope was not dead. It appeared again in the boy's rude gesture.

"Thank you Venca." Marek turned to his protector when they found themselves on the edge of Vinohrady. "I'll walk the rest of the way by myself."

In fact it had been a tough day for him. Dusk was falling and his whole body ached. Usually Natalia would prepare a bath for him, massage his back, and rub his temples with her warm hands, but he could no longer permit that.

The bungalow door was closed and in the window there was no glimmer of the flames in the hearth. Yet surely she had to be there.

She was not there. As soon as he entered he was struck by a new kind of emptiness. The interior was somehow abandoned, desolate. It took a moment for him to grasp what it was. It was the absence of her things.

50

Emptiness

He staggered. He had to sit down on the bed. He was completely bewildered. The fear of having to hurt her had changed into the fear that in some way it had already happened. Had his thoughts somehow reached her? Had she understood and decided to go before she was asked?

At the same time he felt disappointment. She had left him, and although that helped him, he still took it as an injury. But immediately he felt admiration for her: her strength, her clairvoyance.

Only in reality all that was just groping in the dark. Hasty, blind.

After a moment he recovered himself, went over to the table and lit a candle. He used a lighter from the town. It always reminded him that the departure from civilization on which they were resolved was not completely thorough-going. They were still using inventions, industrial products... If anyone fell seriously ill they called the Greek village for transport and were happy to have the patient taken to the hospital in Litohoro. Now he was conscious of that inconsistency again.

He lit the lamp from the candle and started to walk around the room. He was looking for any kind of object she might have left behind. Any trace.

He found nothing. Only her scent. It was strongest around her pillow. He plunged his face into it and breathed it in. Immediately he realized how foolishly he was behaving. He was unappealing, old. And now he was sniffing at a pillow. She had just left him, that was all. Why would she have stayed? How could he ever have expected her to stay?

But no, Natalia would not have left him just like that. She must have had an inkling of what he was planning to do and resolved it for him. Because who knew whether in the end he would have been able to do it. She was strong. Perhaps too strong.

Yet for all that he was afraid for her. It was already dark outside and he had no idea when she had left. How had she got away from the settlement? Where was she heading? What if something happened to her?

Maybe he should run out and ask the neighbours. Someone who hadn't gone up to the shrine. But had anyone stayed behind?

Keep calm... calm, he tried to convince himself. It was enough that he had been left, without him being ridiculous as well. He shouldn't be advertising his humiliation among those for whom he was a prophet, the brother of the Messiah.

He had no option but to face his abandonment in the solitude of the bungalow. Suddenly he got up – something else occurred to him. His hip protested as he tottered into the bathroom. Her little bottles of oil and grease had stood on the old rusty wash basin. Mouthwash, disinfectant... But not a single one remained in the bathroom, and that meant that she had left in a deliberate, considered way. Before leaving she had tidied it all into that big red bag of hers.

51

Signature

This time there was too much space in the bed. The limitation that had so disturbed him while she was there was now a sad memory. His freedom to turn and toss anywhere on the bad intensified his loneliness. He realized that now it was going to be this way forever. No more life of his own. Even the boy he had been long ago had never had one of those. His destiny had been Eli, and Eli was back.

From Alice's description there could be no doubt of it. She had not described the man that just a few older Vinohradians had known in his adulthood. She had described Eli when still a boy. With his big eyes, the fluff on his cheeks and his sharp features, beautiful and at the same time ugly – it always depended on who was looking at him.

When Marek finally fell asleep, among all the conflicting feelings that tugged at him it was gratitude that won out: gratitude to Eli and to Natalia. As far as Eli was concerned, the gratitude was mixed with a certain curiosity. If he had returned, where was he now? As far as Natalia was concerned, she had known how to look after herself even before she had arrived. She hadn't come out of necessity but of her own free will, and she would still know how to look after herself.

His sleep was restless. More than once he found himself up in the shrine. Eli was there, but separated from him by a barrier of invisibility, a thin tissue behind which Eli was hidden. It ran through every place, and so Eli too could be everywhere.

In the morning the rain started. The wind could be heard driving the drops against the back wall of the bungalow. It was long after dawn, but Marek resisted waking. Before Natalia had come to live with him, the teacher's wife Sara had always brought him breakfast. Then she had stopped. It was clear that she wouldn't be coming today. Behind his closed eyelids Marek's thoughts took shape. He ought to talk to Petr before Petr went back to Karlin. Even in his half-sleep Petr's way of thinking was obvious to him. The very essence of the miracle, that wonderful message and grace, was secondary for him. Petr had never been a mystic. He was a realist. His thoughts would be directed to the future, and how to treat what had happened. How to interpret it to those who did not believe in Eli. And how to change their attitude.

Eventually Marek opened his eyes. The way it happened was that all at once he found he was looking around him. He hadn't stoked the stove the night before and the wind had blown all the warmth from the room. He needed the bathroom and he was hungry.

He had no choice. His gut forced him to get up into the raw cold. He tottered as fast as he could to the bathroom and was just entering it when his eye fell on a spot of colour where the doorframe met the wall. It was a bloodstain, the smudged print of fingers. And nothing like that had been there before. It had to have been fresh yesterday.

He thought he was going to pass out. Of all the possibilities that had whirled though his head yesterday evening, that one had never struck him. They had forced her! Attacked her! Killed her? But who? Dear God, who would have the nerve to do that – at a time when everyone had gone up to the shrine?

He had to go to the toilet. Then he went through the interior of the bungalow again, combing it with new eyes. He pulled covers off, examined the walls. He knelt down and peered under the bed. He was breathing as hard as if he had been running uphill. He was gripped by ever greater horror but found nothing whatever until – the way his mug stood on the table. A grey ceramic mug. Now he noticed that it stood at the very edge, in fact part of the bottom of the mug protruded from the table edge. An improbable position. Senseless. But did it mean something? When he looked down into the mug, he saw another red print on the inner side – this time clear, the pattern of whirls distinct, was it a message? Or a farewell kiss? It was certainly a signature.

52

We have to find out

This time there was no alternative. He was going to have to run out and raise the alarm in the community, but when he opened the door he saw that the rain was still heavy and the water was turning the alley into a stream. There was nobody anywhere to be seen. All the same, one of the bungalows or houses scattered around the vicinity could be hiding someone who knew more than the others.

He tried to think. What had really happened? How, and why? They wanted to get her away – that seemed certain. But there was no guessing whether they had only forced her to leave, or killed her. He would have given anything to know at least that much.

He put on his long shepherd's raincoat and set off to find Venca. Venca was his link with life in the community. He usually knew everything.

But this time the huge man looked helpless: "You're asking if anyone stayed behind when the others went to the shrine? I'd have to find out. I think everyone was there."

He was frowning as if with thought, but it seemed to Marek that he was not showing enough concern for Natalia herself. He was behaving as if he had lost a spade, and not as if a human life could be at stake.

"Well go and try to find out! Ask someone!" It occurred to Marek to go and see Eva. Eva and Natalia had made friends, and when Marek had run into her a few days before, she had smiled at him and called out from a distance, "You deserve her. She's a good woman."

Marek was grateful to her for that favour, when all the others had been at best suspicious of his relationship with Natalia.

Eva lived with her husband and two children on the other side of the pasture, in a farmhouse they had built themselves. Both had studied the economics of the post-crisis age at Athens University and had realized there that things couldn't go on as before. They had chosen Eli's way, but had retained their sharpness of mind and uninhibited friendliness. Eva even retained a touch of frivolity. She didn't take things too seriously, not even faith. Jerzi and Hana couldn't stand her.

Marek was already crossing the short cropped grass of the meadow. As he walked, water oozed from the earth around his boots. The rain was driving from the side, and not even the raincoat could protect him from it. His legs were getting wet, but it didn't matter. As he walked he thought about Petr. Might he have organized it? Marek thought it very unlikely. They had lived through a lot together and Petr was not a spiteful man. Hana and Jerzi on the other hand… Or one of the settlers who had come out to confront him on his return from Litohoro.

Today there was no sign of life in the yard of the part-brick and part-timbered farmhouse. Even the hens were inside, getting dry under the roof, and the dog knew Marek. He didn't even run up. Marek remembered that it was here that Natalia had gone the day before yesterday, while he had been speaking with Petr. He tried to work out what she could have been thinking back then, what had been going on in her head. He wanted to knock, but Eva had already noticed him and was opening the door. She immediately realized that something was wrong.

"Marek…"

He was out of breath; he had been walking faster than was wise at his age. And so he just gasped, "Natalia! She's gone! And there are bloodstains from her fingers."

"Oh my God!" Eva was sincerely horrified, much more sincerely than Venca. "Who could have done such a thing?"

"Indeed who? Do you have any ideas?" He came inside and sank down on the nearest chair.

The calm of a mother who had chosen this life was gone from Eva's face, to be replaced by the sharp, intent look of the onetime outstanding student. She sat down at the table and raised a hand to her forehead. "I don't know. But we'll find out. We have to find out."

"But couldn't she have just left of her own accord?" he said, and in the end he wanted it to be true. "What if the marks were just to express that it hurt her?"

"No Marek." She shook her head. "Natalia loved you. She loves you. She talked about you with such empathy. With tenderness. About how you'd sacrificed your life to your brother and completely denied yourself."

He felt deeply ashamed. He who had decided to send her away. If this hadn't happened he would have sent her away, the woman who loved him. His sight blurred, and so he didn't see anything when Eva's children burst into the room. Five-year-old Ester and ten-year-old Matej. School had been cancelled today because of the torrential rain.

"Excuse me a moment, Marek." Eva jumped up and shepherded the children away.

Meanwhile Marek wondered whether to confide in her about his resolution of yesterday. He decided not to, even though he could not rid himself of the feeling that it had played a role in the whole tragedy. "Do you think they would be capable of killing her?" he asked, when she returned.

Eva tried to think coolly, but the idea appalled her. She opened her eyes wide. "Oh, I don't think so, Marek! Our people wouldn't do a thing like that."

"But what about Norbert? He did it. He killed Katka."

"Norbert… he was crazy. He did it in the heat of the moment too. Without thinking. Even Norbert wouldn't kill anyone who was a stranger to him."

"But then, where is she? How could they force her to leave if she wanted to stay? They would have had to drag her away."

"You know what, I'll come back to your place with you. You could have overlooked something. You're not as young as you were and everyone's blind in their own home."

Marek didn't believe he had missed anything but he was grateful for Eva's concern. For her strength. Perhaps she would know what to do.

She told Matej what to do with Ester and they set off. The rain was unrelenting and the ground squelched under their feet. With the whole settlement below them, Marek kept on wondering who it could have been. Eva seemed to read his mind. "I really can't imagine that it was one of our people. It's true that some of them were bothered by you living together. They thought you ought to be holy like some priest. They're such hypocrites. But they wouldn't go that far."

"Hana. It bothered her. Terribly," he shouted into the wind and rain.

"Jerzi is a piece of shit, that's true. But he was up at the shrine. I saw him there."

53

I shall remain alone

They didn't find anything else. Eva went back to the bloodstain on the wall. She analyzed it. "It looks like a sign she left here deliberately. Traces of violence would look different. But at the same time it's clear she didn't leave of her own accord. In that case she could just have written you a note. She wouldn't have had any reason to mask the message and cause you a lot of worry. If she'd wanted to leave you she would have written to you to make it plain. So someone turned up and somehow forced her to go without telling you. He wanted her to disappear. To leave without a trace."

Marek was less sure. He was still tormented by guilt. "You know, I have to confess something to you," he decided to say it. "When I was up there yesterday, I resolved to send her away. I realized that I couldn't do anything but live right to the end for Eli. And that it's a great happiness – to live for him. Only I was sorry that I would have to hurt her. I'm afraid that she somehow sensed it, and decided to spare me that."

Eva at first just regarded Marek searchingly. The hard life on the farm and two difficult births had carved several lines in her face. One ran across her brow and another from the corner of her left eye. A fall in the barn had cost her a front tooth. All the same, she had a scholarly look. "You seriously wanted to do that?" she said, with a note of astonishment he thought was deliberate. "So it's true you think that you'll do more for Eli without a woman? But what exactly do you achieve by denying yourself? All you do is hurt a girl with a good heart."

"It's not about me, Eva," he defended himself. "They just want to see me in a particular way and I can't completely reject that role. It's simply… a sacrifice that they demand and I came to understand that I have to make that sacrifice. I shall remain alone, for the few years I have left, if it has to be this way. Only I don't want anything to have happened to her. If we can help her, we must do something. I owe it to her."

"I'd say you owe her a whole lot more than that," said Eva angrily, "but okay, I understand you. I think it's dumb, but people are dumb, and the Followers of Eli are not exceptions.

"So let's go over what we know, shall we? She wasn't planning to leave. Someone came and forced her into it. Either they persuaded her, or she knew she didn't have a chance against them. She didn't struggle with them. But she wanted you to know that she wasn't leaving voluntarily, so she left you a message in her own blood. You could take it as a proof of her love, but apart from that she probably didn't have any alternative. Cutting herself a little may have been easier than getting to a pen."

He felt his chin, unshaven for a couple of days, start to quiver. His face too was creasing up with grief and he felt embarrassed. "And so they didn't hurt her then? She's alive?"

"Thinking about it, we can't be sure." Her answer chilled him. "She's clever enough not to have put up any resistance if she saw she didn't have a chance. She may have pretended she was packing up voluntarily, so as to have a chance to leave you those signs. But that doesn't tell us anything about what they did with her later. The other possibility is that they genuinely persuaded her. But they wanted you to think that she had left you, that it was just her decision."

It came to Marek that he didn't know the most important thing, and maybe would never find out.

"We must ask," Eva decided and got up.

"Who?"

"The children."

"The children?"

"Children know a lot. They're observant. And they didn't all go up to the shrine."

That sounded sensible. The main thing was to know something. To know whether Natalia was all right. Let her leave him, let her go wherever she wanted. But just let her be alive.

"I'll have a chat with the children," Eva continued, "You should go and talk to Hana and Petr."

"If they're involved in this, they won't tell me."

"Of course they won't. But you can use your judgment, can't you? You'll know if they're hiding something."

Before long he was knocking at the door of Hana's house. Because of the rain Petr was still there. When he saw Marek he jumped up from his chair. "There you are! Finally! I was waiting for you to come." He sounded happy and sincere.

"Waiting for me? But why? You could easily have come over to my place."

"I didn't want to disturb you when you had just had an unpleasant shock."

Marek felt winded. How could Petr have known about it? "What do you mean, Petr?"

"Natalia... you know. Venca was here. I'm sorry it turned out this way."

"If he'd asked me at the beginning," Hana cut in, "I'd have told him straight off that it would end like this. But no. He had to go kidding himself he'd found love, or something."

Hana bit back some other spiteful remark she had wanted to make. The blood rushed to Marek's head. "Only she didn't leave!" He raised his voice. "As it happened I wanted to send her away. I decided it yesterday up at the shrine. For Eli's sake. For the sake of all of us. She didn't leave voluntarily either. Someone forced her. She left fingerprints in blood on the wall."

Petr looked sceptical. He definitely didn't seem to be hiding anything. He adopted a sympathetic tone. "Marek, I'm afraid I think that she was taking you for a ride. She didn't want to look like... like a girl who comes and goes. Please don't be angry that I'm saying this."

"Exactly, Marek," added Hana. Since yesterday her features had been less rigid. After a long time he could once again recognize her as the woman who had loved Eli. No, Hana could not have planned an abduction. Something like that was simply unthinkable. These two were Eli's closest friends. They were the messengers of his teaching. The witnesses of his life. Marek realized that the three of them needed to stick together. Otherwise it would be the end. Eli's message would be lost. Eli's whole life would have been in vain.

That could not be allowed to happen. They were condemned to each other forever now. That knowledge suddenly suffused Marek. He stretched out his arms, and as they were standing close to each other, he suddenly embraced them. "Petr, Hana... He has really returned. Do you understand? He has come back."

54

The sea had not changed

Now that he had renewed his confidence in himself, the disappearance of Natalia was even less comprehensible. What was behind it and what was happening to her? The mystery tormented him as he walked back through the muddy alleys to the bungalow that he knew would once again be empty. The rain had stopped and the air was full of the damp chill of autumn. In the distance he glimpsed the white crests of waves on the stormy sea. Without thinking about it, he passed his house and headed down in that direction. In places the track had been reinforced with flat worked stones. Once this had been the way to the lower part of the resort, the most expensive section, but for the inhabitants of New Vinohrady it was better to live higher up, close to the pastures and forest.

He only realized why he was going down to the sea when he got there. A wet sandy beach ran along the front under an embankment. Today the waves were reaching right into the bay. He remembered his childish desire to go the sea in the car with his parents. Back then the Mediterranean had been boiling in heat and drought. So much had changed during just one lifetime. And not only the climate. His beloved Dad had become a criminal, and Eli, who had been born with the first drops of rain, had become a grown man, who had died long ago. Except that he was still here.

A little further on the waves crashed onto a stone pier. The sea had not changed, he realized. He saw in it Eli's legacy; the image of an eternal return with which the human race could not contend.

A couple of stray dogs ran out of a disintegrating bungalow. The terrace of the restaurant was overgrown with bushes and the steps ended a metre above the ground. In the lee of the pier a few fishing boats rocked on the water. The original house above the quay was the home of Krystof. He was the real reason why Marek had come here.

Krystof was sitting in the archway under the house and cleaning an engine. Some of Eli's followers were angry with Eli for using an engine. After all, Eli had taught that technology was bad, that it was the grave of life. Only Marek knew that Eli was not the giver of commandments. He had anticipated that humankind would liberate itself from technology gradually – the new age would grow out of the old age that had not yet ended. The Vinohradians accepted the fish that Krystof caught with the help of the engine.

"Marek…" Krystof was surprised to see him. "You've come all this way? Come on in!"

That was enough for Marek. The renewal of trust. Krystof could never have abducted Natalia either. "I was just out for a walk," he excused himself. "But now that I see you, do you think Jerzi could have got someone from Vinohrady to abduct Natalia? Someone who disapproved of her living with me?"

Krystof was obviously confused. "You're the best judge of what you should do," he almost apologized. "You know it. Natalia can stay with you, no problem. I let myself be bamboozled. It was a mistake. You're still a man and you've got the right to be a man."

Marek often saw himself only as others saw him – through their thoughts and views. It made him feel like something bodiless, abstract, but his worn out body kept reminding him of its existence, and there was a contradiction there. "No Krystof, I decided to send her away. I now want to live only for Eli… now that I've lasted so long. But the trouble is that in the meantime she's disappeared. Someone has probably abducted her."

"Abducted?" Krystof gaped, his dark hair so thick and tangled that he momentarily had the air of a baffled dog. "But… nobody could do that. None of us."

"Why do you think that?"

"Because Eli wouldn't want it. You know he wouldn't want it."

"No he wouldn't. But people don't only do what Eli wanted. Not even here. Bad things can happen. We're not perfect."

"No we're not," Krystof agreed and bowed his head.

Marek started to retrace his steps. He had eaten nothing since morning and weakness was beginning to overcome him. As he reached the level of the pier, Krystof caught up with him, running. "But where is she then? What's happening to her?"

"I don't know. I just hope she's alive and isn't suffering."

"But you loved her…"

"I did."

Krystof lightly touched Marek's arm. "Then I'm very sorry. It must be terrible for you."

By the time he was tottering home through the alleys, his mind had swung several times between joy in reconciliation and despair at his loss. Eva and two small children were waiting in front of his bungalow.

"I was right," she called from a distance. "Children are observant." And as he came up to them she turned to a gap-toothed little girl. "Tell Marek what you saw."

The little girl first straightened up proudly, but then the gravity of the situation overcame her and she looked down at her feet again. "I saw… I saw a big white bird. It was sitting on the meadow behind our hives. And they led Natalia there and climbed into the bird and then they flew away."

"And you Lukas, what did you see?"

The little boy burst out, "And I saw two holding Natalia by the arms and leading her. And that bird too."

"I went there to take a look," Eva continued. "There were signs that a medium large aircar had landed."

Marek's heart was pounding. Between joy and despair shone hope. They hadn't killed her immediately, and so they probably hadn't killed her at all. Otherwise he understood less and less. "She was abducted by aircar? It couldn't have been anyone from here then."

"It sure couldn't. And she was being led by armed men. You know what Marek…" Eva leaned into Marek, so that the children wouldn't hear. "Who the hell has an aircar nowadays? She must have been mixed up in something."

55

Science will not save us

Lifelong is obsessed. They say that that at night he paces the rooms of his residence and can't sleep. And the reason? A young man, hardly twenty. A helpless lad, whose only offences are words. But powerful words. They have caused five soldiers from an assault commando to throw down their weapons when they could have neutralized him. Now they're in hiding somewhere. And even worse, this self-appointed preacher has declared that the rule of Lifelong is over, and that it's not even worth fighting him. "To fight against someone who isn't in power? Why? All you do is give him the feeling he's still in some sort of control." When these words are reported to Lifelong, they make him incandescent with rage. They anger him more than the advancing cold, famine, chaos, or hunger. Eli becomes Public Enemy Number One. Anyone found consorting with him or helping him is to be shot without mercy and without trial.

Meanwhile Eli is no longer that young lad uttering great truths with seeming innocence. His face is covered in the curls of a real beard and his forehead is heavy with the weight of the responsibility imposed on him by someone that he himself seems to know nothing about.

Marek too has changed. He no longer recalls the quiet beginnings of his life in Holesovice. He no longer relies on his chip, which is down to zero and with it the whole past. Each day brings new challenges, new dangers and revelations. The Followers of Eli – yes, that is how everyone who follows him, organizes his moves and looks after his safety can now be defined – are thirsty for every word from his mouth. They even read them from his closed lips, willing to interpret his silence as a message. Sometimes there are questions:

"Do you ever speak with God? Does he tell you what you have to do?"

"I don't talk. He doesn't tell me. It's just that I can't choose."

"Tell us what you know about God."

"Only that I don't know anything about Him."

"Will I see Him after death? Is there anything after death?"

Eli answers evasively and in hints. But some followers, among them Petr, see much more in his answers. Like the time when Eli answers, "You can already touch eternity here. You can become immortal in every moment. There is nothing to wait for. Every compassionate impulse resonates with eternity. Every pain and all suffering inheres in eternity. And every happiness that is based in love shines once and forever. What is fleeting lasts and what is lasting flies away. Moments of enlightenment are eternal and centuries of darkness vanish without a trace. A violent act is not eternal through the cruelty of the perpetrator. Cruelty shatters against eternity. Only suffering remains. The perpetrator of violence is condemned to temporality, but the victim never dies."

Petr declares that in this utterance God has spoken through Eli.

Marek doesn't often think about Eli's words. Only much later will he come to regret this, and the reason is that he thinks primarily about Eli himself: the need for him to move in time for his own safety, the fear that there is a traitor among the followers, and the worry that he should get enough to drink and not forget to eat.

"This need to be filling yourself up the whole time..." sighs Eli, when Marek again forces him to eat at least some potatoes and tomato paste. Kurt is already waiting at the door.

Kurt Andersen is a Danish astrophysicist. He is one of the Northerners who came to Prague at the very start of the cooling, in the vain belief that Central Europe would remain safe. He is stuck here now, trapped. He invested all his capacity for sacrifice in that first migration, and he is not up for another one. He would rather freeze or starve to death here than set out for the south.

Kurt has sought out Eli with the help of his good friends. He thinks Eli has vision. Kurt needs a vision so that he doesn't have to move. The pupils in his small round eyes dart from side to side. Grey curls cover his prominent forehead, which seems to bulge with curiosity. Kurt is clever, highly intelligent. He wants to convince Eli of the importance of science and knowledge. Kurt sees that the world needs a fundamental change, and things cannot go on as before. He thinks Eli could be the potential messenger of the change. But Kurt wants to change Eli's mind. "What you say about a new beginning is true, of course," he says in his faulty Czech, "but there is a need to preserve all the knowledge that we have acquired. It is our greatest wealth." And he tells Eli the story of the universe: its genesis, expansion, basic principles. And then he tells Eli the story of science and its possibilities, the immortal bodies in which we could live if only if we could all agree and get along on Earth.

Eli listens with interest. His eyes are wide and unlike Kurt's they don't dart around. When Kurt finishes, Eli gives a hardly perceptible smile. He speaks with understanding, without antagonism. "And how would you like the story of a rich man who can't bear to give up his pictures and antiques, and rather than exchange them for food prefers to live surrounded by them until he dies of starvation?"

Kurt hesitates for a moment, taking in what Eli means. "No!" he then objects. "That's not a good comparison. Science helps humankind. What about medical science for example? It helps us overcome pain. And survive. Or genetics, which allows us to sustain so many people."

"There won't be so many of us soon," Eli waves a hand, as if wanting to reassure Kurt, although what he is saying sounds so gloomy. "We'll be starting again from zero. And isn't science to blame for what is happening now? It's not that I have anything against it. It must be wonderful to discover something. It could certainly have been a path. It's just that that isn't what happened."

The way Eli talks still sounds very modest. Beside the ageing Kurt he looks like a student. But his words are disturbing for Kurt, who immediately defends himself. "What then is life for? Why do we have minds? What is the point of being human if we give up on knowledge?"

"Maybe we'll need it again some time," replies Eli, whose knowledge is of a different kind. "I've heard that together the nuclear bombs in storage on Earth could destroy all life. All of it. Isn't it better to give something up? To start again very humbly?"

Kurt disagrees. He wants to salvage at least something. He wants to hear that Eli does not condemn science, and will even admit its value as a path. "That simply can't mean that all science is bad, and we must get rid of it."

"All I'm saying is that science will not save us. It's too late for that. That's my point. Just take a look around you. The decision is already made. But I haven't come for the sake of the end. I have come for the sake of the beginning that will be born out of this end."

This time Marek is listening to both of them. He has no opinion of his own, and knows only that Eli never went to university. Everything that Eli knows and so persuasively formulates has been in him since birth. It comes to Marek that Eli is a treasure, entrusted to him. If something happened – if they caught Eli – everything with which he had been born would be lost. Every minute of Marek's life is filled with fear and love.

Kurt goes away unsatisfied. He has already decided. In the same way that he will never now move from Prague, his mind isn't going to move to the renewal that Eli proclaims. Kurt believes in science.

After his departure Eli stretches out on the bed. He lies on his back with closed eyes. For a moment Marek and he are alone in the bedroom. Marek feels a strong affection. That face is the centre of his life. He sits down by his brother on the bed and places a palm on his forehead.

56

Now you don't have to do it anymore

Fortunately there is no-one to use the nuclear arsenal against. The global world has collapsed. All that remains are territories shaken by local crises, where the enemy is hard to separate from anyone else. There is nothing to gain from using nuclear weapons but one's own annihilation, and it is said that the security systems protecting them are so complicated that today no one can penetrate them. But that doesn't mean the world is safe.

Eli foresees the road ahead, "Those who are never born will not suffer." He smiles bitterly at Marek. "That's the kind of good fortune I haven't had."

After a few weeks friends take them somewhere else. The city is divided into islands of life and zones of death. In the zones of death nothing remains of the houses but burnt-out rubble. In the islands of life people are still living, almost surprisingly well. Trade functions even here. They say that the grain is imported from Italy in exchange for heating systems and timber. All of it goes via the snowy Alpine passes guarded by the Austrians. The traders pay them to let them past.

The angel trumpets of the apocalypse. This ceasefire holds. No one would have believed that life in Europe could become so unbearable, but people carry on living.

Eli and Marek move from Vrsovice to Vysehrad. From the balcony of the luxury loft apartment you can see as far as the castle. Prague Castle, the seat of kings, then the presidency and finally the stronghold of a dictator. It is summer and there is often rain. The Vltava is high. Smoke rises from many places in the expanse of city between Vysehrad and the Castle

The whole top floor belongs to a rich Norwegian who like Kurt believes in the hope that this young man is bringing. But unlike Kurt he is under no illusions about the safety of Central Europe and is arranging a home in Africa.

Petr is here with them. It is he who negotiates and organizes the moves, and screens anyone who wants to meet with Eli. Then there is Yitzak. He is an observant Jew who has a wife and four children at home. Yitzak has come to Eli to find out whether he might not be the messiah promised to the Jews in the Bible. It's a mission he prioritizes even over his family. He has a long black beard, very silken, and seems young to be the father of four. He is always watching Eli and looks very solemn. Petr would be happy to send him away, as his doubts are irritating, but Eli restrains him, saying, "Let everyone decide for themselves."

Petr objects. "They already crucified one man when they didn't like him. And he's always writing things down. One day he'll be sitting in judgment on us."

But Yitzak isn't judgmental. He is just the victim of his own learning. Instead of simply seeing Eli, he submerges himself in books for answers.

The next-door apartment, which is owned by the same man, is often visited by rich Norwegians. They go there for the services of a high-class prostitute. Sometimes cries and moans can be heard from that apartment, and sometimes more than one gentleman visits at a time. The wall between the apartments is thin.

After around a week, someone rings the doorbell. Not three short bursts followed by a long one, which is the agreed safe signal, but just one long ring. They hide Eli in the storage space under a window and Petr goes to answer the door. Petr can be heard speaking loudly, "I don't know what anyone has told you, but we're just normal tenants here."

"Bullshit," comes a low female voice. "You don't have to come up with any stories for me. I can hear what you're saying through the wall every day."

Soon Marek, Petr and Eli are sitting on the carpet with the girl from next door. She is perfectly groomed, her outfit tastefully harmonious, and perhaps she's beautiful, but Marek's attention is drawn to her mouth. She has full but rather short lips. When she purses them you can feel the strength of her will, but at the same time they seem soft, yielding. Her whole expression circles around those lips. And now it is focused purely on Eli. "I'm Hana," she introduces herself and looks at him, but immediately she drops her eyes and her lips tighten. "I've heard people saying that you know things that nobody knows. That you were born that way."

Marek knows that this girl sleeps with rich men for money, sometimes even with two at a time. Yet now Hana is somehow embarrassed. It is Eli who is awakening this embarrassment in her, but he too is behaving differently. Awkwardly. His movements seem unnatural. "I don't know anything more about myself than they do," he shrugs.

Petr notices none of these subtle signs and takes a practical line. "I hope you're not going to betray us to the men who come to see you! Lifelong is after us."

"That's not what interests the men who come to see me," she laughs, and Marek hears a trace of coarseness in her voice.

"Do you do it just for the money, or do you enjoy it?" asks Eli, suddenly.

Hana looks puzzled, and perhaps also blushes a little. "I just want to survive this hell. I'm told you say everything is going to collapse and start again. I think so too. Or rather, I don't know if anything will start again, but everything is definitely going downhill. I just have to cope with it somehow."

"So now you don't have to do it anymore." Eli smiles that irresistible smile of his.

She puts up no resistance. She shows no surprise and makes no protest. For a moment some internal struggle is visible around her lips; her expression turns inwards and then after a moment softens. She is beautiful and her lips are modest as only a girl's lips can be, and almost in a whisper she replies, "Not now I don't."

Yitzak comes in from the next room. He is deep in thought as always and fails to register what is going on. "What do you think of Isaiah?" he asks.

Nobody answers his question, not even Eli. And surprisingly enough, that doesn't bother Yitzak, who lives in another world, in a world too full of knowledge, which makes him blind to the present moment.

It is as plain as day that Eli and Hana have fallen in love. Marek swallows hard and feels as if he's turning into stone. He is superfluous, deserted on the bank while the two of them dive together into a current that will carry them away.

The most terrible moments of Marek's life. His little brother is receding from him, turning before his eyes into a banal young man fixated on a whore. For the first time Eli seems to be talking in empty phrases. Finally the conversation turns to the apartment next door. Eli wants to go and see it. Hana agrees. Hana... it's a name that will stick deep in Marek's mind, and however much he tries to reconcile himself with her later, she will always be the woman who stole his Eli.

One day, of course, forty-four years later, the tables will be turned, and Hana will be hating the woman she believes is stealing Marek from the community of the Followers of Eli.

In the days to come the two make love in the next door apartment. They seem almost never to stop. The Messiah has come into the world in a human body, which fights its way to spiritual heights though bodily joys and needs as well. In any case, it hardly contravenes Eli's teaching of the need for humanity to go back to being a humble part of the natural order. It is just that Marek imagined that return differently... He even catches himself doubting... What if Eli isn't what they consider him to be? What if he was just an extraordinary child, who has grown into an ordinary adult?

But after a week Eli and Hana appear in the doorway and this is a new Eli. He is different in having already grown up for good, grown up into his mission and towards his own death, which in a mere eleven years will confirm all of it. He has certainly become even thinner, but his features have firmed up and his body become harder. His spirit has united with his body, and from this unity of spirit and body an undeniable leader has emerged.

Hana is also different. She is no longer so perfect, and no longer uses cosmetics, but she has become calmer and this is most obvious around her mouth, where the tension has relaxed.

"It's time to leave the city, my dear Marek," says Eli. "Events are now in motion. We must find a new beginning."

57

My suffering too will one day end

In his whole life Marek has been away from the capital only about four times. Once on an excursion with his parents, when he was very small, and three times to sell real estate. Since that time much has changed. The landscape is greener, but has a woebegone appearance. There are almost no fields anymore; now they have become pastures or marshland. The stumps of the dried out trees, victims of the drought, are overgrown with new green. There is water in all the hollows, forming stagnant lakes. A strange unease seems to hang over their surfaces. Lifelong's army guards herds of cattle. Lifelong offers protection, but only for his faithful, his people, and supplies them with goods that ordinary citizens have to buy.

Marek, Eli and Hana leave the city by private microbus. Its old driver has found himself a living in hard times: early in the morning, before dawn, people who need transport assemble at his parking place in a suburb, and when all the seats are full he sets off. At this time of day the highways are safer.

Eli is holding hands with Hana, which is also camouflage. No one is expecting a prophet in love.

All the ostentation has fallen away from Hana. She is a normal girl now, dressed naturally and perhaps even more attractive than before. Anyone who gives her a second look probably wonders what she sees in that skinny, unshaven youth, who seems to have his head in the clouds or god-knows-where.

Marek follows the two into the bus. Petr left the same way yesterday, to make all the necessary arrangements.

On the third day they are all together again in the safety of a South Bohemian farm. Eli's reputation as a prophet has gone before him. Everyone expects him to provide answers to three basic questions: What will happen to me? What will happen to the world? and What comes after death? Eli's replies are always a little different. In fact he never fulfils expectations.

Soon after their arrival Hana comes down with a fever. They take turns by her bedside, and when it's Petr's turn, Marek and Eli finally get a moment for each other. Eli knows what Marek has been thinking about all this time, and he goes straight to the point: "Don't look at me that way, Marek. I didn't come here to fulfil anyone else's wishes or notions. I don't even know how to fulfil my own. But believe me, only what should and must happen is happening."

"But do you love her? Do you really love her?" Marek asks, and he sounds indignant even though he doesn't want to.

"I love... not just her. All of you. You, my dear brother, as the first. But it's only with her that I can take a rest. At least for a moment she takes part of the burden from my shoulders."

"But why her in particular? Doesn't it bother you, what she was doing before?"

"You mean that she had sex for money? That she made a few men happy? Is that such a crime?" Eli smiles. "When I saw her, Marek, I immediately knew she was the one. She's the only one strong enough for me to be able to lean on her. In this moment, Marek, and in every other, there is so much more suffering in the world than you can even imagine. A mountain, a huge mountain of pain. And it's even worse when you start to see the separate stories in it. All the stories. Children abducted from their parents and abused, women humiliated and tortured, fathers who have to stand by helpless and watch the death of their women and children. In suffering we've come a lot further than any other animal species. And the one piece of luck, Marek, is that life is finite. And so every suffering has an end. My suffering too will one day end. It's the only thought that gives me the strength to live."

Marek once again sees his beloved brother, the one for whom he was born. He takes him by his slender wrist. "Are you truly what I've always seen in you? When the raindrops began to fall on the dust of Holesovice, I already sensed who was coming, but tell me Eli, once and for all, that I'm not wrong."

"You want certainty, Marek? From me?" Eli is puzzled. He looks at Marek as if Marek were mad. "You, who has had it inside you the whole time?"

58

They no longer do crucifixions

As summer came to an end they are still living quite well. From morning to night their hosts are bundling hay. The winter will be long, and if there isn't enough, their animals will perish.

Their hosts are not farmers. They are people from the city who bought the farm fifteen years ago, hoping it would be for them the refuge that Prague is for the Norwegians.

Marek, Petr, Eli and Hana join in the work. For security reasons they work mainly in the barns and courtyard. They pile up manure in a pit behind the barn. Nobody now would ever recognize the high-class prostitute in Hana. But not even under the burden of physical labour that is sometimes almost too much for him, does Eli forget a different burden and mission. Sometimes his listeners gather round in the evenings. These days Eli speaks less of an end and more of a new beginning, the new home that those who follow him will find in the south. "It isn't over yet. It's going to cool down even more. I don't know when the right moment will come, but I'll know it when it comes. Then we'll go."

Along the track that leads into the forest there are little shrines, the stations of an ancient Calvary – the Way of the Cross. The original statues in them were destroyed long ago, but a local woodcarver replaced them in the previous century. It is where Eli goes when he wants to be alone. Marek follows him at a distance. It is always the same, with Marek a couple of hundred metres behind Eli, who halts and stands for a long time at each station. When he finally returns, he looks distressed. "I understand him. I understand him so well," he says.

"Mightn't you actually be him?" it occurs to Marek to ask. The idea makes him happy, because if it were true everything would be so much simpler.

"That's not something I could ever say," Eli answers without hesitation.

"But you have a lot in common with him."

"Really? I haven't yet experienced even a fraction of his suffering. And anyway, times have changed. Everything. They no longer do crucifixions, for example."

"I don't think he ever had a woman." Marek tries to broach the subject that is still always on his mind. "He concentrated on his teaching."

"Don't you believe that." Eli raises his voice, evidently upset. "How could you? It's a ridiculous idea. Even if he was the son of God, he was born into a human body. And into the whole predicament of a human being in the world. That's what it's all about. He wasn't stronger and he didn't have any supernatural power. And he wasn't more resistant to temptation either. If he had just had a human form but in reality had remained God, then his sacrifice of himself would never have been real."

Later Marek reports this conversation to Petr. There is a glint in Petr's eye. "That's it! That's how we should be talking about him – as the new incarnation of Jesus."

The trouble is that when he tries it, it goes down badly. People don't even have to be Christians to regard Jesus as inviolable. They are ready to see Eli as a man with an extraordinary mission, but they are not prepared to go as far as to see themselves as direct witnesses of God's direct participation in human destiny.

At the beginning of October the first snow falls. They have hardly bailed the last straw, and harvested the last potatoes, carrots, cabbage and apples, when the landscape turns white. A dusting of snow lies sprinkled on the freshly frozen surfaces of ponds.

Suddenly there is more time. When everyone sits down by the crackling stove, it seems impossible that Prague is in ruins and the whole country on the edge of collapse.

In the end all the conversations still come back to God. The human longing to utter his name, although they have never seen Him and no one has ever spoken with Him, is stronger than the conviction of reason. In November the owner Simon's old father dies. Instead of looking for an official or a priest, they ask Eli to give an address.

59

Eternity starts during life

Snow has been falling steadily for three days together. The hosts have a hard time finding a place where the ground is not frozen, but in the end they dig a grave. A large extended family is living and working on the farm: two brothers, their women and children, the siblings of the wives and their families, and some even more distant relations. The whole project of the farm was planned and is managed by the older brother Simon. He bought it together with the forest and pastures, and they all left the city and gave up their original professions. Simon has a feeling that in the time that is coming everyone will have to fend for himself. He and his family members have weapons. The living that they make by the sweat of their brows is not one that they will give up easily.

Simon has a weakness for Eli. It was Simon that invited Eli and his party and decided to support them for as long as it would be safe for them to stay at his farm. What Simon admires about Eli is that he has a vision, just like Simon. He recognizes that Eli's vision is orientated to the future, which he cannot see for himself. As he puts it one time, "Eli sees further."

They nail planks together to make a simple coffin. Eli stands beside it and snow pours from the sky. Marek suddenly thinks that Eli might perform a miracle and raise the dead, like the man depicted in the sculptures in the nearby Way of the Cross. That would be a deed to put Eli's divine origins beyond challenge. Marek longs for a deed like that. So that everyone can see. So that no-one can doubt any more.

However Eli looks uncertain. He doesn't command the dead man to rise. He gazes at a cold body that signifies nothing but an absence. The human consciousness has vanished somewhere unknown.

Finally Eli takes a breath to speak. "Don't expect me to overcome death," he says, "We all start out inside ourselves. It is only through ourselves that we exist in the world, and then we either come together in one point, or we disappear without trace. It depends not on me but on you. A wasted life has no continuation, but a fulfilled life is eternal. You are expecting me to pray for someone who was dear to you, but his fate has already been decided." Eli speaks slowly, with pauses separating the sentences. Sometimes he seems to be waiting for the sentences. Marek realizes now that the dead man is not going to rise. Eli has no power over death, and Jesus could not have had this power either. Each individual's life is his own journey. And Marek's life is a journey at Eli's side.

Hana's life too, it seems. Hana stands here, hands hidden in her sleeves, rocking a little on her heels with her eyes fixed on Eli.

"I know what you would like from me," Eli's tone is suddenly sharper. "You want me to give you proof. Aren't I giving you enough? That's not a power I have, partly because it would already mean I was fulfilling expectations. I haven't come to fulfil expectations. I am only what I am."

After the ceremony Eli turns to Marek. They are all frozen through, and Eli has frost on his beard. He seems depressed. "To be honest I can't even see the point of prolonging life," he says. "Everything could end right now and it would make no difference. We still return to the place from which we came, so why the need to live the whole interval called life? It is so wearying."

Eli does indeed look exhausted. It's as if he is being sucked dry by the futile battle that he has waged with death. "When he was still alive," he continues after a moment, "that was when he could have become immortal. Perhaps he did. In the moments when he raised a hand to touch one of the family... there was so much feeling in it. He wrapped my hand in his several times. It wasn't an attempt to cling on. It was more like a message."

Marek is surprised. He never noticed Eli's contact with the old man. He hadn't visited him himself, and had never pressed his hand. Now he reproaches himself for it.

"It's like our Mum," Eli goes on. Today he is somehow full of grief. He hasn't spoken about Mum for years. "We were with her, after all. We could do something for her back then. Eternity starts during life, not after death."

Marek at least takes Eli's hand. It is cold and trembles. For the first time Marek is glad that Eli has Hana. Sometimes he simply has to be able to forget. People are wanting more and more from him. He is arousing expectations that are too great.

Marek tries to comfort his brother. "You can't do more than is within your power."

"But what is within my power, Marek? I don't know myself. It seems to me that I only know how to bear witness. I stand on the bank and can see which way the river is flowing. Where there is a blind creek, where there are rapids and whirlpools. But I don't know how to turn back the flow."

60

I'm not going to sleep with her anymore

The river rolls on. At the end of the winter refugees bring news that in the neighbouring region several farms have been occupied by the rebel army known as "My Homeland," one of the many armed groups that are fighting Lifelong and each other. My Homeland is composed mainly of former soldiers in Lifelong's forces. For the local population it is all one who is doing the occupying. If they are lucky, their food stores will be all that they lose. If they are unlucky they will be slaughtered.

Petr takes notice of the reports. Eli's safety is his responsibility, and he has already been thinking of moving on. Eli's rich admirer is prepared to send an aircar.

They decide to move in a week. It might have been earlier, but Hana isn't feeling well. She keeps taking to her bed and all the energy has drained from her lips. As she lies there, even that circle around her lips, earlier so full of life, has somehow slackened. Her mouth is like a half deflated ball.

It occurs to Marek that she might be pregnant. The idea is disturbing. How could Eli – if he is what Marek believes him to be – have a child? Could a human child of his remain on earth after he dies?

Marek takes a long time to summon up the courage to mention it, but he finally exploits a moment when they are together at work. "Eli, have you ever thought about the possibility of you having a child?"

Eli is startled. He straightens up and then leans on his spade. "A child?" It clearly seems unthinkable to him too. "That simply couldn't happen."

"Why not?" Marek is encouraged by the effect of his words. "Why couldn't it? It can, when you're sleeping with her."

"No, it's impossible!" Eli protests, although he is evidently not entirely sure. "It can't happen. If it happened, it would mean I didn't understand anything at all."

Now Marek realizes that for Eli too it would be a calamity. He would see it as a calamity not because he is irresponsible, but precisely because of his sense of responsibility. In any case, Marek has never thought of having a child himself, either. He has Eli, after all. And Eli has everyone. The whole of humankind. All the same, what if it happened? It's even likely, when he and Hana are always together. Maybe it has already happened. "And she's not feeling well… couldn't that be the reason?"

Eli looks at Marek with horror in his eyes. "No Marek, I don't think so. But you're right. I can't just rely on her…" He absently glances upwards. "I'll renounce it. I am not going to sleep with her anymore."

61
One Drop of Blood

The news of Natalia's abduction or flight spread fast and for a short time even overshadowed the appearance of Eli. Marek was unimpressed by the peculiar sympathy that everyone started to show him. He knew that in fact the situation suited them, and the knowledge infuriated him. He was lost in his own feelings. His self-reproach changed into grief and his grief easily grew into anger.

One thing was certain. He missed Natalia; as she really was, in her form and character. He kept recalling the unaffected way she had shared her nakedness with him. He kept remembering that wholly individual expression on her face when she pressed her lips together, and her prominent not quite even teeth when she smiled. Without them her face would just have been delicate. With them it was earthy. She was the one and only person who could be that way. It was bitterly obvious to him that only now did he realize how much he had been in love with her.

The days went by and it was ever colder. Sara was bringing him breakfast again and Venca collecting firewood for the winter. Eli was silent – one appearance had been all. And Marek could find no peace of mind. In vain he told himself that he had, after all, experienced just a few short weeks with Natalia. Their lives had touched only briefly, creating what might well be a wonderful illusion going far beyond the facts. But he could not accept that it was an illusion and instead he felt impoverished. This mode of existence – without love, without a beloved person – was a kind of deprivation.

To make matters worse, there were the questions that would not go away. What had really happened to her? Was she still alive, was she suffering?

Marek knew that this could not go on. He had to overcome it in his own mind. And the person for whom he had lived since the age of ten would have to help him with it. He would go up to the shrine of the birth.

Venca was not keen on the idea. He was just getting close to Beta, the daughter of Croatians who had recently joined the community, and he was looking for excuses: it was already too cold and Marek could catch his death.

What happened next was something else entirely. Marek was just finishing his breakfast when he heard shouts and running steps. The door flew open and someone on the threshold called out, "An aircar! An aircar's landed! She's come back to you!"

The blood rushed to his head. It was the same mortal fear he had once known in the Alps, when he thought they were about to be caught. But at least back then he had known what he was afraid of. Now he understood nothing. An aircar? Why would she come back?

He staggered out. Everyone's attention was on the pasture at the back. Yes, there it was – a huge aircar. Bigger than the biggest he had ever seen back in Prague when he was selling real estate. He wondered whether perhaps Eli... He sank to his knees. Then he started to notice the details: the first to alight were soldiers, and on the body of the car gleamed the blue star of David. The insignia of the State of Israel.

The other inhabitants of Vinohrady also realized that this was probably not Natalia. Some started to run away, and mothers looked desperately around for their children.

Then a metallic sound boomed out over the settlement and the whole plain right up to the wooded slope of the mountain. It was a voice. Speaking in Czech. "There is no reason to fear. Nothing will happen to anyone. We are a peaceful mission from the State of Israel. The Chief Rabbi Shlomo Heller wishes to speak with Marek of Prague, brother of Eli of Prague. The Chief Rabbi accompanied by members of the Rabbinical Council will now alight and invite Marek of Prague to join with them in prayer."

Everyone who had not yet fled now looked around for Marek. "Are you going there?" "Don't go!" "Hide!" "What can they want from you?"

Marek didn't have the kind of voice that could compete with amplifiers, and so he couldn't challenge the Chief Rabbi and his colleagues to come to speak to him at home. He had no choice. He had either to submit to these guests or let this strange opportunity slip away. The mere fact that they had flown all this way prompted respect. In such moments Marek's essential guide was how Eli would have behaved, and Eli had never sought to prevent people from coming to him. He had received scientists, preachers and penitent criminals. Marek set off across the meadow.

Behind him he heard uneasy voices: "Are you really going?" "Is he going?" "What if they kidnap him?"

It flashed through his mind that they might have had something to do with the disappearance of Natalia. They might have taken her away, to ask her about everything before they met him. Or they might even have sent her to him in the first place – deliberately, as part of a plan. If only that were true, in a few moments he would know she was alive and well. Of course that would mean that she had probably never really loved him, but he would accept that in return for certainty, because he genuinely loved her. It was at this moment that he really understood that fact, and it brought him a geyser of inner joy. It had been in old age, but he had still eventually found out what it was to love someone other than Eli.

The Chief Rabbi was bearded but not completely elderly. Some of the Rabbinical Council members who accompanied him were older. They all wore kippahs on their heads. Marek approached them. Meanwhile comfortable white chairs, and a long white conference table with refreshments, were being set out in front of the flying car. Shlomo came forward to meet Marek. One member of his bodyguard wanted to go with him, but he waved the man back. He met Marek in the pasture between goat droppings and cowpats. He stretched out both hands to Marek and said something in Hebrew. It sounded friendly. Another man came to join them from the table. Entirely grey, with glasses. "Don't you recognize me,

Marek?" he asked in Czech, and behind the lenses Marek saw eyes that were somehow familiar. He would probably have remembered even if the man himself had not hurried to his aid: "I'm Yitzak…"

Of course, Yitzak – that young Prague Jew who for several weeks had left his family in order to find out about Eli's teaching. Yitzak, who had been there when Eli first met Hana.

He had aged to an incredible degree. Or more precisely, it had been an incredibly long time since they had last met. Today Yitzak's expression was much less uncertain than back then. Now it was firm and self-confident.

"Yes, I recognize you."

Together they walked to the table. All the rabbis looked confident, but also curious. Marek too was confident. Face to face with this distinguished delegation he saw himself as an important mediator of Eli's legacy.

They seated him at the head of the table. Shlomo sat opposite him. The white, slightly grainy tabletop gleamed dully against the overcast sky. Everyone was polite and very adroit – Marek was hardly aware of how he found himself at the table.

Shlomo spoke and Yitzak translated. "The Jewish people has been waiting for its messiah since ancient times. We wait for him to come to take up the leadership of his nation and to transform the world. Sometimes our hopes have been too high. There have been many false messiahs and many believed them, but instead of rebirth they brought only confusion and misfortune. This is why we have had to follow, and continue to follow, vigilantly follow, the teaching of your brother Eli with the utmost caution. We are anxious not to allow ourselves to be deceived, but nor do we want to remain in thrall to our own small-mindedness and the belief that the Messiah cannot possibly have come in our lifetimes." Here Yitzak seemed for a moment to be listening so keenly to Shlomo's words that he forgot to translate. He smiled. "He asks why you think your brother was the Messiah. What has led you to believe that? I have told him about my firsthand knowledge of Eli's teaching and actions in Prague. To be honest, at the time I did not think that he could be the one that we wait for. Yet much has changed since that time, and plenty of things that he predicted have indeed happened."

"But I don't think anything," Marek shook his head. "From the beginning that was simply who he was." How could a messiah be split up into separate characteristics? How could some complicated link be theorized between messiah and man? Eli was a man and had been a man despite his mission as messiah, and that was the hardest thing about his destiny. Marek was suddenly sorry for these rabbis. How could he explain anything to them?

"We would like to know when you developed this conviction."

"I didn't think about it. The moment he was born – with the first drops of water after a decade of drought – I knew that something extraordinary had happened. And then he confirmed it in my eyes again and again."

Shlomo patiently listened as Yitzak translated back, and then left a long silence, as if Marek might decide to say something more. Only then did he start to speak himself. This time he spoke at such length that it seemed that Yitzak would never be able to remember it all. But Yitzak translated with the same calm as Shlomo had spoken. "We know a great deal about Eli's life. We know many of the things he said. He proclaimed the end of the existing order of civilization, and that has indeed happened. Of course that was not so hard to predict, and the messiah expected by the Jewish people is supposed not just to predict but to bring about a new order... I see Eli's power as lying in his ability to persuade. He managed to proclaim these ideas despite the fact that Lifelong wanted him dead, and despite the chaos and people's general reluctance to listen. Despite the fact that his voice could have been extinguished without trace. He was convincing even in the face of obstinacy, and without straining to insist. As far as I can see, he was convincing naturally, in himself. Something about his personality even had the power to stop hostility in its tracks. To change minds. The way he persuaded the Italian militias to give up violence..." (It struck Marek as incredible how much he knew about Eli.) "The Italians could simply have shot him, but they didn't," Yitzak continued. "Something like that happened many times, until Dubrovnik, but then that seems to have been an end that he went out to meet voluntarily. Before that, his survival was a series of small miracles. What do you think of that? It truly interests Shlomo Heller, Chief Rabbi of all Jews in the Holy Land. We have come to hear you. Because you were present."

Put this way, it was a question that Marek felt compelled to consider, whatever his reluctance. Yes, it had been like that. Marek's life at Eli's side had been a life of endless fear for him. He had never been sure that Eli would survive as long as he needed to. "Once he said to me – when we left the house of the Youth Liberation Army and survived because we left it – that he didn't know what was going to happen. He knew only that he had to go. He often told me that he wasn't a free agent in what he did, that mostly he had no choice, and just did the one thing that he had to do. What happened around him happened through him, but he didn't see it as his own success. Or as a victory – as we would probably see it. In just those moments he may even have felt more helpless than at any other time. The power – that seeming power that accompanied him – was born out of helplessness. He never took any credit for it, but in fact felt guilt. I know how much he suffered because of all the awful things that happen in the world and his inability to intervene. Because he didn't know how, or maybe simply couldn't prevent all the suffering. He only knew how to experience it in his heart. No-one suffered as much as he did."

Yes, that was how it had been. No one knew that better than Marek.

"By the way," Shlomo continued, and after him Yitzak, "our teaching speaks of two messiahs. The first is supposed to unite the Jewish people, and make it once more the first among the nations. In this century we have in fact become the leading world power, partly though our own capacities and partly, it seems, through the operation of many forces in a way that could not have been predicted. I don't think our scientists predicted the impact that the grille would eventually have. I mean that it would turn the desert our enemies had left us into fertile ground. Yet there can be no doubt that even so, this turn of events may be the result of the will of some purposeful force, in other words the will of the Lord – the God of All Jews. To be honest, I can't see the work of your brother Eli as a factor in all this, but what he predicted is nevertheless a situation that would correspond very precisely to the arrival of the second messiah – the one who will come to create a new balance and unity. This might mean that he himself was the first messiah. Of course in a different way than we expected, but that could happen, for the Lord chooses his own paths – unexpected paths. For this reason the rabbinical council has decided to investigate the messianic status of your brother, and the way you have been treating his legacy. What is the basis of your faith in him?"

The question reminded Marek of Professor Simonides's inquiry in Litohoro: the question of the principles of faith. "It is still too early," Marek sighed, unsure how to answer. "It all needs time, I think. But a couple of weeks ago there was a manifestation. My brother appeared to Alice, a young girl, and spoke to her. He said, 'I'm sorry, I have just returned.' He spoke to her in the form that he had at the beginning, in Prague. Nobody, not even her parents could have known what he looked like back then."

As Yitzak translated Marek's answer, Shlomo glanced at the rabbi on his right, if indeed the man was a rabbi at all. He was definitely the youngest of them and had no beard. His expression seemed very severe when he spoke. Yitzak interpreted: "Could not have known? What about photographs? Digital records?" The beardless man fumbled for some device under the table.

Marek didn't like this pragmatism. Eli had appeared to a shepherd girl. A pure soul. Guileless, and they were trying to explain it away rationally. Furthermore, Marek knew of no photographs. That time was gone. All media carriers were gone. The war had destroyed all that and Eli had anyway rejected it from the beginning. "Eli rejected technology," he almost shouted, "Didn't you know that? He saw technology as a wasted opportunity. A blind alley. As something that mankind would now have to manage without. None of his followers would have dared to photograph or record him. No one owned any electronic devices. There are no photographs and no recordings."

The man just silently held up a flat tablet and pulled it out to the size of a proper monitor. Suddenly a picture appeared on the body of the aircar. Something that Marek had never seen: a picture of Eli. Eli when they had still been in Prague. Marek was gripped by waves of emotion as other photos and video clips flashed by on the exterior of the aircar. Eli sitting in a room at the farm. Eli wading through snow in the Alps. Somewhere close he can see Hana, Petr... and then himself. It is almost... almost like another revelation. Marek's heart pounds and he covers his eyes. "How... how did you obtain them."

"We didn't want to hurt your feelings. On the contrary, as you can see from this, we always took Eli seriously. From the beginning."

"But you expressed your interest in a way that was foreign to him. That he didn't agree to, and that he would have resisted. You used technology when he didn't want to be recorded by technology. He said he wanted to be recorded only in people's memory."

"But we have recorded only fragments of his life," Shlomo tried to reassure him. "Just tiny fragments. And from those alone we can see what an unusual man he was. There can be no doubt of that. And we are certainly not claiming that your recent miracle could not have happened, that he couldn't have appeared to the girl by some other..."

There was a forbearing smile under Shlomo's beard, and Marek suddenly froze, struck by suspicion. What if it had been them? What if they had staged the miracle? Somehow manipulated Alice? Projected an image? What other technical powers might they have?

Meanwhile another two men emerged from the aircar. They were carrying plates, glasses, biscuits and bottles in a plastic chest.

"I hope you won't refuse some wine from the Holy Land. By the way, we have the impression that it was holy for Eli too. He was very interested in the messianic position of Jesus. And to some extent saw Jesus as a prefiguration of himself, even though he could not understand the connection with himself. As you rightly said, he perceived his mission spontaneously; from a kind of necessity into which he had been born as a human being."

Marek did not refuse the wine. The atmosphere was friendly, but it was becoming obvious that the whole meeting had been very precisely choreographed. Over the wine Shlomo carried on the conversation: "But you haven't yet answered me. What are the foundations of your community?" Shlomo and then Yitzak nodded towards Vinohrady. "The communities of New Vinohrady, New Karlin, Brno…"

"Does it matter?" Marek asked, with a feeling of satisfaction, because he felt he had found the answer. "Does it matter, when it is only us who are having children? Us and only us? Isn't that the reality that defines our community? Clearly distinguishes it? Isn't that sufficient proof that we are on the right path; in harmony with the plan of creation?"

The expressions on the faces of all present made it clear that it was indeed this issue that had been really worrying them. It meant that he had answered correctly.

Shlomo looked down at his wine and seemed to be thinking hard, or rather asking himself something. Then he started to talk, this time with frequent breaks so that Yitzak could translate with ease. "Yes, that is what is troubling us. And bewildering us. Why has the Lord deserted us? Why, when we are His chosen people, are children not born to us? This is why our rabbinical council came to the conclusion that we need to consider whether Eli might not be the Messiah for whom we have waited, and whether if we accepted him we might not regain the Lord's favour. But the rabbinical council also determined that it is impossible for the Messiah to be born to any but the Jewish nation. This means that for Eli to be the Messiah of all Jews, he has to have had a Jewish origin, as defined by halacha – the Jewish law. It is perfectly possible for him to have been Jewish without knowing it. The twenty-first century was a century without roots. But we have the necessary tools to ascertain this. Modern genetics can solve these questions. We have an enormous data base and can identify lines of ancestors with a probability close to certainty. And the few remaining percent we leave to faith. This much chance we can allow ourselves. You are Eli's brother, his full brother. You have the same ancestors. If you would be so kind as to let us take one drop of your blood, we will have a result before we have drunk up this wine. The genetic test we have developed can exclude Jewish origin, or confirm it with a very high probability. That is why we are here. We are asking you, Marek, for a drop of blood. We have brought our laboratory with us." At this Yitzak, like Shlomo a moment before, gestured at the aircar.

Marek was lost for words. He was only just starting to grasp the logic of their thinking: they would accept Eli so that they, as the chosen nation of the Lord, could start having children again. But it simply couldn't work that way. Eli had said, "You cannot accept me with less than your whole heart." What difference could the result of a genetic test make to that? But should he agree anyway, and give them a drop of blood so that in the end they could make Eli their own?

He already knew their methods. They had obtained photos of Eli. Against his will. They had spies among the Followers. Even if he refused to give them blood, they would find a way to acquire some. They had sent Natalia to him, after all. That especially… He had forgotten he wanted to find out something about her. "That girl," he changed the subject. "That girl who came to me. Natalia. Did you send her to me?"

Yitzak translated the question with obvious unease, but Shlomo answered clearly: "Girl? What girl? I know of no girls."

"I mean Natalia. About three weeks ago, immediately after Eli appeared, she was abducted from here in an aircar. Wasn't that your people?" His voice was shaking. Suddenly he didn't know what to wish for; whether to be told it was them and know she was safe, or that it was not them, and she had come to him of her own accord.

All five rabbis looked at each other and then exchanged a few words. Then the beardless one turned to Marek. He looked serious. "That aircar wasn't ours. But we could find out. We monitor the movement of all aircars and remaining planes here in the Mediterranean."

"So you can tell me who abducted her and where?" Suddenly he had an idea. An exchange, a trade-off. It scared him for might it not mean that he was exchanging Eli's holiness for his own interest? No, that wasn't true, he told himself. A drop of his blood was nothing sacred, and couldn't change anything. "I'll give you my blood," he decided, "if you find out for me."

This caused a great stir among the rabbis. The beardless one gave some orders and other men, probably doctors, emerged from the aircar. Yitzak turned to Marek and this time explained everything without interpreting. "In a moment you will know. And if you give Professor Stern your hand so he can take some blood, we will know too. All about your origin."

Marek nodded, even though he felt out of his depth. He had no idea where it would lead. If the Jewish people accepted Eli for the sake of a drop of blood, would they really start to have children again? It seemed to him that it couldn't work like that, but he knew nothing of God's plans.

They took his hand and after a moment he saw the unexpectedly bright liquid moving from his worn-out vein into an ampule and then the device. He leaned back, almost collapsing in the chair and sinking into himself.

Levi soon roused him from his lethargy. "That aircar landed here on the 2nd of October at 11:38. It stayed here for seventeen minutes before taking off again and flying with no interim landing to Dubrovnik in former Croatia. Since then it has been grounded. Maybe it had a breakdown. It has not been flown anywhere else."

From this communication, this incredible and baffling news, just two things stood out for Marek. The first was: seventeen minutes. That had been all the time it took for her to pack her things, cut her finger, leave him a sign and depart. The second was: Dubrovnik, the town where Eli had perished and where she herself had been born. That meant it was likely someone she knew. That meant it had some logic in her life. That meant she was almost certainly alive. They could have killed her anywhere. There was no reason why they would take her to Dubrovnik to kill her. In her birthplace, where she had... parents. Light dawned on Marek.

Meanwhile the rabbis were silent. They sat there in the cool refreshing air, suddenly oppressed. Professor Stern was waiting for the result. They were all waiting. Marek thought of Natalia. Perhaps she was happy in Dubrovnik. Suddenly Professor Stern raised his head from the instrument. It seemed that what he wanted to say was solemn, and he immediately announced it. Only this time Yitzak did not interpret it. He didn't need to. Shlomo rose and with a violent movement tore the black robe at his chest. His face was distorted with pain. The others also rose and tore their shirts, coats and robes. Tears poured down their cheeks.

"What is it? What's happening?" Marek demanded of Yitzak.

Finally Yitzak turned to him, in his face was… it was hard to say whether his expression was one of anger, regret or hatred. "Excluded!" he cried. "Jewish origin excluded!"

62

The Followers

The wretchedness keeps mounting. Not the doom that Eli shares with the whole human race, for that is always the same, but the everyday hardships, such as discomfort, cold, a shortage of food. Civil war has already gripped the whole Central European Federation, if you can still speak of such an entity at all. The borders between country and town are dissolving and existence is becoming a struggle without goals, rules and front lines. A fight of all against all.

Eli's followers are not exempt. For them too these are years of hopelessness. All the hiding and the struggle to survive seems to have consigned them to irrelevance. Lifelong isn't even looking for Eli anymore; he has more serious worries, and anyway the self-appointed prophet has faded away. Many who had been expecting the great change of which Eli often spoke turn their backs on him now. They lack proof, anything to which they can cling. In any case, according to Eli for the moment the world is still in the phase of collapse and all that can be done is to prepare for the phase of revival. It is not enough for those of little faith. They go their own way, throwing themselves into the struggle for survival in the hope that this will save them. Others accept Christianity, or sometimes Buddhism.

Marek doesn't think like that. He sees his brother, who is always the same. He sees that Eli has no power, but then he never had, and never even strives for it. Exceptional as he is, he is unexceptional in being born into helplessness, and the one who sent him, if there is any meaning in talk of such a one, stands by him no more than he stands by anyone else. Eli's only power is to announce the renewal that will come later.

Hana is still always close to Eli. Something binds her to him, and she remains faithful to him although they no longer sleep together. Only her face is starting to take on its future rigidity. Otherwise she is admirably resilient. She copes with the cold, with nights in cellars...

Petr is disappointed by the years in the shadows. He takes it all as a defeat, as the failure of his own diplomatic abilities. He stays with Eli, however, and perhaps that is because he has already sacrificed too much for Eli to leave him now. It was for his sake that he left the Youth Liberation Army and devoted several years to organizing Eli's moves, to negotiating places to sleep, checking out new arrivals... Where else would he go, in this troubled time? And who else would care? Petr stays, but sometimes his nerve fails him and he vents his frustration on Eli. "With your abilities you could have inspired tens of thousands. Hundreds of thousands. You could have been famous throughout Europe. But you had to go and renounce electronics, and we're the only people who get to hear you. This doesn't work in today's world. Today's world needs other prophets."

Eli doesn't fight back. He isn't even angry with Petr. "You are thinking only of today," he reproves him, just once. "But today will end tomorrow. And what then, Petr?" At other times he tries to reassure Petr. "Can't you see what the world is going through? The old world is devouring itself. I don't want to be involved in it. But one day we'll set out on the journey – definitely. As soon as I know the time has come, Petr, I'll go."

Women. They are always coming to Eli. Ageing women unsatisfied by life, young girls longing for love and purity, delicate and sensitive women, women who have never been understood, widowed women. They must know instinctively that Eli isn't sleeping with Hana, and has renounced that kind of love. And it is precisely this that attracts them to him. Eli treats them considerately but keeps his distance. Usually he then sends them away, giving them some mission or other – to look after someone, to announce something, to spread some idea. They fulfil his wishes because he is their God, in some real way.

Finally there are those who join Eli because they understand his message. Sebastian the philosophy graduate, a young man with blue eyes and a sharp brain, always coughing and weak, yet joyful. Alex the former owner of a Prague hotel; his family, wife and two children, perished in the ruins of their house when it was hit by the grenades of government troops. Alex is a robust man with a brilliant face, complete with a high forehead and manly features. His grief can be sensed behind them, but he had managed to suppress his anger even before he came to Eli. Indeed, he came to him for that very reason, sure that a solution must be found for everyone, not through revenge or power but through the future. Alex follows Eli because he sees hope in him. He believes that Eli has the solution.

The wider circle of those close to Eli also includes Bara, a petite tenacious girl who devotes her energies to the service of others. Originally a nurse, she looks after the sick even when she is herself in pain.

Then Ismail. Born into a Muslim family, he has a degree in law. He is an innate optimist, and irresistible with his dark lashes and eyebrows. Ismail's large family left for the south years ago, but he didn't go with them. He thought it would be unfair to leave his new homeland now that it is hit by crisis. He still prays to his Allah, and when people ask him if it really fits with faith in Eli he replies with a smile, "I don't worry about whether it fits. It has to fit, when that's just what I do."

Eli is not bothered by Ismail's faith in Allah. Eli says that gods are more human than divine. And that it doesn't matter, because Ismail is a good man and his goodness is like a sun for the others. And so Ismail's Allah is also a sun for everyone else.

Of course, love is not the only reaction Eli gets. Mentally unbalanced people, twisted by fate, and too deeply wounded (as he calls them) often come to him wanting to vent all their hatred on him. They scream their rage that he proclaims hope when here is no hope and anyone who allows himself hope is a liar, a fool, or only screwing people over. Or that he is an agent of Lifelong because he claims there is no need to fight the dictator. Or that he is the originator of all evil, and the war is his fault, or that he is a devil in human form and they ought to burn him, or at least stone him to death. Some of these unfortunates ultimately accept Eli, often in tears. Others are unmoved by the calm and kindness of his response to their hatred. They regard theirs as the only truth and can see no further than themselves and their own misfortunes. One man tries to shoot Eli and only Alex's presence of mind prevents him.

After that, Petr convinces Hana and the others that anyone who wants to talk to Eli must be thoroughly searched. Marek agrees. Although he believes that the very nature of Eli's mission means that nothing can endanger him, that doesn't mean that he can see the membrane that may be protecting him. It would be so easy to kill him. Or would bullets bounce off him?

No they would not. Marek knows that Eli is a human being. When he was little he fell and cut his head, and what flowed from the wound was blood, red and sticky. No, Eli is not a superman. If something is protecting him, it is not something that Marek can conceive of. And so Marek is keen on Petr's idea. They agree they will say nothing to Eli himself.

63

We will go south

It is March of the year 2128. Eli will soon be twenty-three, but he looks older, for he has lived and suffered whole ages. During his lifetime the desert has changed into green landscape, and then the snow has covered it.

It is March. Eli and his group are sheltering in an abandoned guesthouse on the bank of a large frozen fishpond. All around lies snow. The roofs of a town are visible on a hill on the other side of the pond. Most of its inhabitants have gone away to Brno, in the futile hope that there is still some law and order there. The people who have stayed are either resigned, or determined not to give up. They are clinging to the old times up to the last moment and getting ready for the invasion of Hungarians. Hungary has split off from the Central European Federation and is expanding west and north. The Hungarians believe in their historical mission and are shooting any Hungarians who don't.

Marek is sitting by the stove on the first floor and gazing blankly out of the window. Someone is coming along the pathway that has been trodden in the deep snow across the pond. He is hurrying and sometimes stumbles. In their rags, coats and hats everyone looks the same, and so it is only when the figure struggles up the bank and appears directly in front of the house that Marek recognizes it as Petr. This induces him to get up. In recent months movements like getting up have been becoming rarer in the house. The listlessness is caused by hunger. Marek's head swims, and he has to lean on the chair for a moment before hurrying downstairs. Petr is just pushing open the door. His face is red and his beard frosted; even Petr, always smooth-shaven in the past, has stopped shaving. Only his eyes betray his excitement – they are full of something new. "Lifelong!" he cries triumphantly. "He's fled Prague! He's flown off with his whole rabble to Australia somewhere. The government forces have fallen apart. The castle is burning. Prague is free!"

Although so many years have gone by since the end of the Liberation Army, Petr still feels part of it, and so he regards the flight of Lifelong as a victory. For Petr it is a great day; a day when he has solved something, and he expects everyone else to see it the same way. He bursts out to Eli, "Surely we should be going back to Prague now? Crowds will listen to you there now. People need symbols. I remember how Lifelong feared you. For them you will be a victor. Maybe they'll elect you to the Castle. This is your moment." That revolutionary spark is back in Petr's eyes.

Marek realizes it is big news for him too. He is thirty-two years of age, and Lifelong has been a feature of his life since his birth. There hasn't been a day that someone hasn't mentioned him. For good or ill, everything somehow related to him. But now he is gone. He has just got into his aircar and taken off. What was the point of all those years of his rule? Why didn't he leave ages ago?

For Marek the fate of Lifelong has yet another implication. Dad.

The news leaves Eli unmoved. "You want to go back?" Petr's suggestion seems to baffle him. "And I'm supposed to put myself at the head of a crowd? Don't you realize I'm afraid of crowds? The crowd is like a beast; it has a common brain and no feeling. Anyone who wants to find me can find me. I don't need to put myself at the head of anything."

Later he returns to the subject. "So you see, he wasn't lifelong, let alone immortal."

Then in the evening, by the stove, the only one in the whole house that spreads a little warmth, he speaks into the lethargic fog that has descended on all of them. "In the spring we'll go south. Towards the new beginning." They are all so dulled by hunger that the words seem to them to have been spoken by a phantom. "I would have liked to live to see it. The end of this crazy suffering, these death throes. I would have liked to see it when a little island of grass turns green in the desert, and a tree grows on a heap of ashes. I shall not live to see it, but you will. You'll take care of that tree. Plant other trees. Slowly. It will come slowly."

These words shake Marek from his torpor. "Why shouldn't you live to see it? You're twenty-three years old. You'll be alive longer than we will. Longer than me. For goodness sake, it's you that's come to plant that tree, isn't it?"

"I've come to see the old world into the grave," Eli continues in a melancholy voice. This seems a difficult moment for him. He is seeing his own death. "I'll leave behind just... a little light. Someone else will pick it up and carry it on. You Marek, you will be there." With this Eli stands up, and with an unsteady step and wrapped in a blanket he goes to Marek and embraces him. But it is no cheering hug. Eli is shaking. "I'm afraid, Marek," he whispers. "What if there's nothing afterwards? If there's nothing afterwards, I'd rather go on living."

64

Reproaches

By the end of April the roads have finally dried out and the snow has retreated to the hilltops. Petr reports that it's impossible to get through Hungary but the route across Austria is now more passable, because the Austrians from the mountains have mostly moved south themselves and are fighting there with the Italians.

The news about the route south has set off a wave of hope among Eli's followers, as if it were the road to the promised land. In the end, well-wishers even offer them some cars, plenty of money, and gold jewellery. But Eli proclaims that he will go on foot, because he has had enough of technology. Some of the followers drive animals, so as to have something to eat on the way. Eli walks with Marek and Hana in the middle of sheep, goats and cows.

Near Brno a woman with a child in her arms approaches them. The child is bleeding and its life is fading away, and the woman tries to get to Eli. They don't want to let her through, but Eli waits for her. The woman calls over to them, "Can you save my child? If you are who you say you are, will you do it? I've believed in you since I was a girl. You stayed with us for a few days. So please do it for me."

Eli is no longer that sweet child admired by everyone. Once, back in Holesovice, it only took one look for neighbours and friends to stand up for him, but a long time ago he found that his face could also arouse extreme hatred, and for some people it is like a curse. More precisely, their own curse. For this mother his face is just a disappointment. She has expected too much from him, and as they stand looking at each other, anyone who knew nothing about it would wonder how this wretched-looking youth could help anyone. Clearly he can't even help himself. He is limping, and so thin that his ragged trousers are all but falling off him.

Hana catches Eli by the hand. She wants to protect him, but Eli seems indignant. "I didn't make your child with you or create life here on earth. Half of humankind will perish in the coming years and I can do nothing but watch it. The only hope I know of is not to be born."

The woman stands there for a moment dumb-founded. Then she overcomes her pain, turns around and leaves. "So you're not what I thought," she mumbles to herself. "You are a poor thing, a poor devil."

Hana cannot stop herself and runs to her. She takes her hand. "It's not his fault. He has no power over life. He can't change it. But still he gives hope. Not now. But in the long-term."

The woman looks at Hana. "Do you have children?"

"No."

"If you did you would know that hope in the long-term is point-less. When your child is dying, you need help right now."

It is no wonder that Eli retreats into himself. He is only a shadow of what he used to be. And the reproaches come thick and fast. They assail him from all sides. "Is this what you wanted?" "So this is what you imagined it would be like?" "It's obvious that there's no God."

Even Marek never thought it would get as bad as this. The hard-est times in Holesovice now look like Paradise. Running water, food and a roof. On the run in the succession of Prague apartments they had still lived well. Professors, scientists, philosophers... they hadn't seen a messiah in Eli, but had liked to debate with him. Now people are at their lowest ebb. They call Eli names, curse him, accuse him. Or they ridicule him. Marek recalls the scenes on the Way of the Cross. Might this not be Eli's way of the cross? Not on just one day, not with fourteen stations – but much longer and harder. The days, nights and following days merge into one great wretchedness. They pass Brno and then Vienna. Eli's most loyal friends go on ahead and search for shelter for him.

At the end of the summer they reach the first Alpine lake. Once it had overflowed with wealth. Tourists had lazed about to their hearts' content, and gone on short excursions. Today gunfire can be heard. Alex reports that there is no way of walking around the lake and anyone who has tried to drive through by car has been killed. The wrecks of cars served as barricades. The Austrians guard their passes, but unlike the Hungarians they can be bribed. And there are rich people among Eli's followers. Wealth can still save lives, at least for a while.

The snow catches them in a mountain chalet at a height of 1120 metres, as an inscription above the entrance announces. This was once at the foot of a ski-run. The wife of the owner, a robust ageing Austrian woman, believes that Eli is the Messiah. It's another of the miracles that always have to happen for Eli to come through his destined pilgrimage.

By December two metres of snow lie all around them. Nobody comes up here until spring. Inside, seventeen people survive. Sebastian speaks German and translates Eli's every word. But Eli says little. All the same, in the evenings where they silently sit together, he has his dignity once again. Those who have stuck it out are again drawing support from him. With the smallest of gestures he manages to make a guesthouse cut off from a dying civilization the centre of the universe: the starting point for the future revival, the new big bang, the new beginning.

New Vinohrady, Greece 2168–2169

65
The Burden of Solitude

New Vinohrady only rarely experienced night frosts. Mostly it was wet and windy. Snow lay only on the slopes of the surrounding hills. Sore joints and the weather kept Marek at home most of the time, and there his solitude oppressed him. There was just one thought that often came back to him.

For a long time after the unceremonious departure of the rabbis he was unable to find peace. He couldn't stop thinking of their despair. It seemed absurd to him. Were they really incapable of conceding that the Messiah need not be Jewish? Incapable of it even at the moment when their nation, in their view chosen, was facing extinction? All the same, Marek was glad that it had turned out as it had. People were supposed to find the way to Eli for his sake, not because of the need to beget children. If Eli had turned out to be a Jew, and so they had been able to accept him and children had really started to be born, then Marek would have no longer understood anything at all. He went to talk about it with Jakub Halevi.

When he described what had happened, Jakob burst out laughing. He laughed so long and hard he almost got the cramps. "That's so like them," he said, his attack of mirth still making it difficult for him to speak, "those great sages of ours." And he struck his palm against his thigh.

"Don't you respect them at all?" Marek was baffled. "You're a Jew too, surely."

"Yes I am, and so what? Do you think the Jewish people is something more than just the set of all Jews who agree they are Jews? Those rabbis are living in thrall to their books and thinking up idiocies. But it doesn't mean that individual Jews can't accept Eli. Like me. And it most certainly doesn't mean that if those rabbis

223

decided something, Jews would all start having children. Between Jew and Jew there are the same differences as between person and person, Marek. Enormous differences. There's no longer any such thing as a chosen people. That's all over, and Eli knew it. Everything must start again. And to be honest, if I were God I wouldn't bet on the same horse again!" Jakub laughed again, but only a short guffaw. The subject did not upset him.

"But what about the two messiahs?" asked Marek. "Shlomo, the Chief Rabbi, said that according to your teaching there ought to be two messiahs."

"My teaching?" Jakob protested. "I belong here. It's not my teaching but theirs. Really two?" For the first time he looked surprised. "I don't know about that. I never studied it. I've never heard of that."

All the same, Marek's mind later ran back to the two messiahs. The idea chimed in with Eli's claims that he had come to see civilization to the grave and to predict its resurrection, together with his insistence that he himself would not take part in that resurrection.

More often Marek thought of Natalia. And so Dubrovnik. Her parents, he guessed. It was they who had arranged for her to be snatched.

These days Hana sometimes came to see Marek. Jerzi had gone off to Turkey to spread Eli's message, and solitude was heavy on Hana's shoulders too. Doubts too, Marek surmised. Hana was younger than he was, but had already started thinking of her own mortality, and sensing that nothing very important would now happen in her lifetime – the Followers of Eli would grow a little in numbers and the others would gradually die off, and apart from that there was only the lowing of cattle, the squawking of children and the drumming of the rain. No fanfares and ascensions. No coming down of Eli from heaven. Hana confessed to Marek that she was sceptical about the recent vision at the shrine, but she liked to reminisce about Eli, and Marek saw that for her too he was the central point of life. That was how it had been: anyone who had come close to him and started to understand his divine humanity, could never live for anything else.

Another thought kept circling in Marek's mind. It was about Dubrovnik. He felt that he should undertake a pilgrimage. The last pilgrimage of his life. Natalia had said that a shrine had been built over Eli's grave.

The trouble was that Marek was unsure if this impulse was wholly pure with regard to Eli, and if a large part of the reason for it was not the urge to find out something about Natalia. Or at least to be close to her. Marek was used to searching his conscience, and so obviously the element of contradiction was clear to him. He knew a pilgrimage with an ulterior motive would not be genuine, and so he struggled internally and at the same time longed to be already on the road.

Then someone knocked on his door but did not immediately come in as was the custom in Vinohrady. Marek waited for a moment before realizing that he needed to go and open it. He rose slowly, and when he was emerging from the kitchen, he was suddenly afraid that the visitor would give up and leave. It was because something told him that this still unknown person was supposed to be part of his life. When he finally opened the door, he knew he was right. It was Tomas, the eager young student from Litohoro. "Good morning Marek. I can speak Czech now," he said, with a barely perceptible accent.

66

Tomas

The bed that had been moved to the bungalow for Natalia was still there. Venca had been too embarrassed to ask what he should do with it, and Marek, without admitting it to himself, had continued to nurse hopes. Now he offered Tomas the bed. Natalia was not coming back.

Tomas had indeed taught himself Czech, and had also studied everything he could find about Eli's life and teaching. What he had gleaned was frequently nonsense, however, and Marek wondered where he had got it from. "No, he never in his life met Lifelong," he assured Tomas. "Lifelong didn't interest him. He urged people not to fight against him and just to ignore him."

"I'm sorry, I really did read that." Tomas scratched his head. "I knew that you couldn't believe everything, but just how much…"

Indeed, it turned out that the restored Internet was full of inventions. There were stories of miracles that had never happened, as well as attempts to expose Eli as a fraud and even a criminal.

"That's one of the reasons I'm here, Marek. We must write down his real story."

Marek felt unsure about it. It seemed to him that Eli wouldn't want that. Nothing should be added to his story as he had lived it himself. If Eli had wanted Marek to do something like that, he would have said so.

Tomas brought the idea up again the next day. In the meantime he had settled into the bungalow, unpacking books and many notebooks. "I left the computer in town." He grinned at Marek. "I've been thinking hard. You're the only person in the world who can do it. And you don't have much time. Your testimony must serve the next generations as the only correct guide to the life and teachings of Eli."

The idea had gone round and round in Marek's head all night. Just the day before he had had no inkling that the outside world was trying to catch Eli in a net, to adopt him or interpret him. Although Marek believed with Eli that this outside world would soon cease to exist, the existence of so many lies unnerved him. "What is it really like in the world now, Tomas? How many people are there? Is it known?"

Tomas's eyes brightened. He loved passing knowledge on as much as he loved acquiring it. "Eli was right. We're going back to the beginning. We're going to be inhabitants of this planet on the same terms as every other animal species. At the moment there are around four billion of us – which is two billion fewer than at the time of Eli's death, and seven billion fewer than the high point around a century ago. Only out of these four billion more than three billion are older than thirty-three. The ageing of the population is accelerating, because only one-in-five of the one-in-five children, as they call those who were born afterwards, will have any children. So after another fifty years there will only be hundreds of millions of us. Maybe only tens of millions. The big cities are already collapsing. There's nobody to look after the empty houses and the old people, and nobody to run the transport system. Until now this population shrinkage hasn't been so obvious, and it even looked as though civilization was recovering and reviving. But now this process is speeding up, though here in the north of Greece people can turn a blind eye to it."

Marek had to sit down to digest this information. He had never doubted that Eli was right but had never got his head round it in all its real consequences. "You know what, Tomas, I'll do it. I'll tell you everything about Eli. And you can write it down. And I'll give you my notes. In the last few years I've been making jottings when I remember something I might otherwise forget. I didn't have anything to write on, so I used this calendar." He handed Tomas his old battered book diary. There was a page for each day in it, and so plenty of space for writing.

In the late afternoon Marek set off for the sea. He wouldn't let Tomas go with him. "I want to be alone."

A strong wind was blowing from the sea, which was grey and churning under low clouds. Since Natalia's disappearance, Marek had been walking worse with every day that passed. The pain was concentrated in the small of his back, as if the weight of her unsolved fate were bearing down on it.

Marek was deeply affected by Tomas's report of the state of the world. When they had settled in this abandoned resort three years after Eli's death, he hadn't had any picture of the future. He had just been full of love and pain. They had somehow survived here; somehow the community had grown, and occasionally someone had come from abroad and decided to live with them. Yet it had never been clear to him how the last could become the first. Now Marek understood that they already were the first.

There was no one on the shore, no sign of Krystof or his family, and the boats were moored at the quay. All the same, he wanted to set off for the other side. He went through a ruined wall, which long ago had formed the boundary of the resort, and found himself on a small rocky outcrop that marked the end of the beach. The plan that had been ripening in him in recent months now gained a new urgency. He wanted just once more, before his life was over, to go to Eli. Once more to go to the place of unending pain. He wanted to go now, when he was beginning to understand for the first time why it had had to happen, and why his brother had gone voluntarily to certain death, even though he had broken Marek's heart by doing so. It was clear: his brother hadn't wanted mankind to have to go on waiting for the new beginning.

67

The Day of Greatest Pain

By the time he had trudged back up, it was already dark. His heavy tread and laboured breathing reminded Marek that he didn't have much time. He had to go while his legs could still carry him. Tomas would accompany him.

The lamp was on in the bungalow. For a fraction of a second it reminded him of the times when he had come back to her. Tomas sat at the table looking very grave. He had Marek's diary in front of him. "Marek, what's this?"

Marek was chilled and dull from the wind and had no taste for discussing one of his notes just now. He leaned over the table. Tomas held the diary open at the date 7th of July: the day that Eli had died. Perhaps this was connected with what Marek had been thinking about just a moment before. The page was empty. Marek had written nothing there. "I mean that," Tomas pointed. It was a dark red stain. No, it was... a finger-print. A narrow print. Made by her finger.

Marek sat down. He gazed at the stain, lost for words. He couldn't understand. Looking closer he saw that there were two prints. One blurry at the edge, where she had held the page, and the other clean, pressed deliberately and with care.

"I've heard about her. I know everything," said Tomas in sympathetic tones.

"What do you know? What have you heard? From who?"

"There are followers living everywhere. They talked about it. How you loved her and how she was abducted by an aircar. And that she left you signs. Signs in blood."

Marek had no desire to talk about it with Tomas. As far as he was concerned Tomas should keep his mind on Eli and leave Marek's life alone. Natalia was none of his business. Nor was Marek's pain and his longing for her. "Give that to me!" Marek took the diary and got to his feet. He wanted to go to Eva's place fast.

On the way he realized he had been unfair to Tomas. He should have been grateful to him for finding the print. It had to be a meaningful message, after all, and it could easily have remained unnoticed forever.

This time the dogs barked vigorously. They were loose in the yard and Marek preferred to stay outside. After a moment Eva came out. "You Marek? At this time of night? What's going on?"

Once inside, she stared at Natalia's fingerprint, just as astonished as he had been a while before. "How did you find it?"

"Tomas did, by accident."

The fate of mankind and the desire to take a journey to Eli had receded into the background. The message from Natalia, his beloved, had overtaken it all. Yet there was some link. The date, the day of Eli's death. A terrible day. "Do you think she was trying to express something with that date?"

"She knew it was the day of greatest pain for you and she marked it in her own blood. So she probably was expressing pain at having to leave you. There was no better way of doing that." Eva scrutinized the fingerprint some more. "But I also think there could be more to it," she said after a moment. "Imagine you only had a few seconds, is that what you'd do? Just leave a message about your pain? The sign on the wall was practical. It was intended to tell you she hadn't left voluntarily. So maybe with this sign in the diary she was trying to say something else. Did you two ever speak about something relating to that day?"

"Of course we talked about it. It's a day you can't not talk about. I was surprised she'd been born in the same town and just a fortnight later. We spoke about that many times."

"Dubrovnik!" Eva exclaimed suddenly. "That's it. She wanted to put you on the trail. To tell you where she is."

Marek hadn't told Eva what he had found out from the Jews. He hadn't told anyone. But with that information he realized Eva was on the right track. "You're right, Eva. You know, when those rabbis were here… they told me that the aircar that snatched her away had flown to Dubrovnik. Probably she was abducted by her rich parents."

Eva regarded Marek reproachfully, "And you kept that a secret from me? First you come and tell me all about Natalia's prints, so I'm worrying about that girl wherever I go, and then you don't even bother to tell me that she's probably alive and well."

"Forgive me, I didn't tell anyone. It was too difficult and I couldn't bear to talk about it. Now I've managed to get over it in my head."

"Get over it?" she said irritably. "Wow, it must be just great being your lover!"

Marek fell silent. Eva was right, but so was he. Whatever happened, he had to go on being Eli's brother.

"And what if that date has another meaning?" Eva brightened.

"What meaning? Apart from it being the worst date I know."

"Maybe the date on which she'll be waiting for you."

"Waiting? Where?"

"In Dubrovnik, for goodness sake!"

"Dubrovnik is a big place. I wouldn't be able to find her."

Eva's look suggested that Marek was a complete fool. "Well, there's one place you both know, isn't there?"

Marek stiffened. If only it were true… It didn't have to be true. These were just guesses.

Not even Eva was sure. "I know I could be wrong, Marek, but it's just when I look at it all, I think I know that girl quite well. I understand her. I can imagine how she thinks. I think she'd definitely try to give you signs like that. Not just to let you know her pain, but practical signs."

"But if she wanted to meet me, and if she was free to do so, then why wouldn't she just escape? Why wouldn't she come back here?"

"I've no idea, Marek. Maybe she's not as free as all that. Maybe there's no real chance of her escaping. Or maybe she didn't want to come back. May she too decided that you've got to be first and foremost you brother's brother. She just didn't want to be an obstacle in your life and so she left it to you."

68

The Journey Beckons

"No electronics," Marek warned Tomas a few days before their planned departure. "You're not going to record me and you'll only make written notes."

"I was assuming that." Tomas nodded, but didn't seem entirely reconciled to it. "Even if it's a pity," he added.

"Eli wouldn't have wanted it. He used to say that technology drowns out ideas."

"Except how will people who live in other continents, for example, ever get to hear that? They didn't have a chance to meet Eli and they have no chance to meet with you. And now they're not going to have children because of that bad luck. If they get to read your testimony and believe, they might accept Eli. Maybe it would make the dwindling of mankind easier to bear."

News of the pilgrimage that Marek intended to make was received by the inhabitants of the settlement with a respect bordering on awe. Marek had initially feared that they would try and persuade him out of it, but in the end they honoured him for the decision, and even wanted to go with him until they realized they couldn't leave their herds, houses and families. All the same, the council decided that in addition to Tomas, Venca and two strong young men would go with Marek. It was in vain that Marek protested, saying that it was going to be a spiritual pilgrimage, on which he needed peace and quiet above all.

There was little peace in Marek's mind. On the contrary, he was agitated and impatient. His longing to go back to the place where he had buried Eli was sincere, but he also yearned to see Natalia. To solve the puzzle. Would she be there? Had he understood her message? And would he manage to get there in time for the appointed date? Was it really possible they would meet again?

No it's not possible, he told himself, but it had no effect on his desire.

69

The Last Sermon

Early on the 18th of March they are ready for the journey. It is only that Marek doesn't know if his body is ready – if he will make it to Dubrovnik at all.

The inhabitants of Vinohrady are gathered on the pasture, and Petr has turned up too. Marek is expected to give a last sermon. As he surveys them all, it reminds him of another sermon, the one when she first appeared.

In the end, however, facing the Followers of Eli and the imminence of the journey, he finds himself filled to the brim with the main reason for his pilgrimage. Which is Eli. "Do not be offended at me for leaving you," he begins, although no one is offended. "It is simply something I have to do. For his sake and for yours. Recently, thanks to Tomas, I have for the first time become truly conscious of what it means when the creator withdraws the miracle of creation. And what it means for him to continue to allow it to us. Perhaps even now I haven't fully appreciated that what Eli prophesied is already happening. Soon there will be so few people on earth that it will be impossible to maintain the existing form of human civilization. The towns will be depopulated. There will be no teachers, doctors or labourers and no one to take care of old people. Eli certainly didn't want something like that to happen. He was just the only one who knew that it was going to happen. And he is no longer here for us to ask him what can and should be done. He appeared to Alice, not to me. For that reason I must go to him. I believe he will answer me. I will think about it all the time – the questions and the answers. I will be thinking of you, of everyone, and the new home that we have found here. But above all I will think of him, and of the one who was probably speaking through him. The one who is behind everything, including the miracle of creation. I thank you. Thank you."

The assembly ripples a little with surprise. They had probably been expecting a longer speech, but Marek has no more to say. He walks up to them and starts shaking their hands. When he gets to Eva their eyes meet; they both know more than the others. "May you find what you most want to find," Eva wishes him, and offers a motherly smile.

Hana and Petr are the last in line. Hana is almost apologetic: "I thought of coming with you, but somebody has to stay, don't they?"

"Of course," he reassures her, "I'm glad you're staying."

Petr is silent. Marek has known him long enough to have no doubt that he doesn't agree with his address. For Petr it isn't bad news that the cities will die. He sees it as another victory. And he doesn't need to ask any questions.

Then at last they are setting off south along the shore. Patrick, Venca's friend, goes on ahead; he will be looking for places where Marek can rest. His other contemporary Adam walks at the back with Venca. They are carrying food supplies and gold to buy and sell. The inhabitants of Vinohrady have got together a collection for the pilgrimage.

Marek has his good old boots on, and as soon as they pass the first pasture and fields and the roofs of Vinohrady disappear behind the trees, all his fears fall away. This is no longer the time of the great migration and murder. Above all – Eli is safe.

In the end it is about Tomas that he is worried. These one-in-five children have grown up coddled by anxious parents. Who wouldn't be anxious about something as rare as a new human life. Yes, human life is again a rarity, precious. This means that Tomas hasn't done much strenuous walking in his life. He has spent most of his time studying. In his pack he carries mainly notebooks, pencils, books. It's a pity that he can't take notes on the march, because it is precisely now that Marek feels like relating memories.

The fertile plateau around New Vinohrady recedes; already they are walking along the former highway, which is covered with clay and pebbles. The sea down below them reminds Marek of the long journey by foot that he made long ago, all the way from Holesovice in Prague across Austria, Italy and the whole Balkan peninsula to this place. He knows that on such long journeys you shouldn't think too much of your destination. The only thing that should exist for you is the day as it passes, the moment, this and the next step. Venca and Adam are carrying a lot of dried meat and milk, but they are relying on Eli's supporters scattered throughout Greece, and even the lukewarm supporters, who do not really believe in him, but say to themselves, "What if...?"

More than thirty years ago Marek passed this way. Back then the Followers were crushed, exhausted and uncertain as they struggled on. Instead of care for Eli Marek had been worried for the welfare of the community, and that was a role for which he hadn't felt suited. But there had been no choice. Now as he walks in the opposite direction, it is as if he has left all those worries behind. Finally free.

70

His spirit opened up a path for us

It is easy to find a place to spend the night when there are so many empty houses everywhere. Day after day, week after week, Marek becomes ever more addicted to the sense of liberation that the journey brings. The two lights by which Marek navigates shine ever more brightly in his heart. During the day they encourage him onwards when his hips and feet ache. At night it is his back that complains, so intensely that he cannot sleep. Evenings are for memories. Tomas writes down every word. Marek gets used to speaking slowly. Venca and Adama and Patrik also listen. They are young men in the prime of life, but they gaze at Marek with the eyes of children. They hang on his words.

At first Tomas wants Marek to relate his memories in the right order, but Marek can't do it. As he travels, what he remembers first is the exhausting journey to the south. In addition he sometimes recalls some remark of Eli's that had been stored somewhere at the back of his memory. In the end even Tomas acknowledges that it is best if Marek just talks of the memories as they come to him. "I'll put it into the right order myself, Marek. It doesn't matter."

Tomas often asks questions, such as how it was at all possible for them to have survived all these horrors. On the road, during the great killing, tens or even hundreds of millions of the inhabitants of the Europe of that time had perished. But Tomas is a one-in-five child. He cannot imagine anything like that.

In fact Marek doesn't understand it either. Their survival was incomprehensible. "His spirit opened up a path to us. Not just once, but again and again. You had to be lucky not just once, but a hundred times. People were dying of hunger too. They were freezing to death in the snow. Whole desperate families. That old Austrian lady believed in Eli. He was like a son to her and her only hope. She persuaded us to stay with her for a second winter. She pointed out that we were all exhausted and it would be easier. And she was right.

During the second winter we felt as if we were on a boat. Like on Noah's Ark. As if the rest of the world was already under water. Eli often said nothing at all, but he always managed to create a magical atmosphere. Everything was there in it: pain for the suffering, but also gratitude for life. And reconciliation. I remember he once said, 'It will be the same at the end: man will be alone and also with all. Consciousness of joy and pain in a single point outside time.'"

"No promise of eternal life in paradise?"

"I don't know, Tomas. Maybe he thought so... but he never tried to make it easier for anyone by talking about it. Anyone who followed him had somehow to sense it from... from who he was. Because if he was the embodiment of God himself in a human life, he was at the same time the only possible source of knowledge about himself."

"Couldn't he have said more about that?"

"I don't think that he knew any more himself. He once said, 'I am blind, deaf and dumb, like all of you.' At the time I didn't understand him, but now I think I do. He probably meant that for God to have him come as a man, he had to strip him of all that was divine. He had to blind him. All that remained in him was the awareness that it had happened. And that was what convinced me. That awareness made him a messiah. The awareness that there existed something more. Sometimes it sprang out of him without his being able to control it. For example when he predicted something and then it happened. Or when he avoided something and so saved himself without knowing it."

After long weeks of walking, avoiding towns and the partly restored highways, in April they reach Meteora in Greece. Orthodox monks are praying again for the salvation of the world up there in cells in the rocks. At one time, in the twenty-first century, the monasteries were turned into tourist attractions, but now they are once again serving their original purpose. High above the surrounding landscape, at the point of the intersection between damnation and salvation, the monks – unlike the Followers of Eli – relate to a personal God and have a whole great religion as an aid to it. Marek passed by this place thirty years ago, desperate and overwhelmed in the roles of leader and prophet, for which he did not feel born. Back then he had envied the monks' certainties. Something had even whispered to him to stay, to live out his life up there and accept Christianity. It would have simplified so much. But now Marek knows that it would not have been the right choice. The prayers of those monks are part of the end. They plead for salvation and watch the end of the world, while he is going to a holy sepulchre to see a new beginning.

They find refuge in a dilapidated hotel. They need a few days' rest to treat their blisters and relax their backs. Tomas submerges himself in his notes.

71

Do you still believe you can buy yourself life?

Through mountainous northern Greece and Albania the going is slow. Marek's boots fall apart and the new boots they find for him are not so comfortable. He prefers to go barefoot and sometimes has to lean on Vasek. He hates to be a burden, but otherwise feels well. As his goal gets nearer, his mind seems clearer.

Occasionally they pass the fortified residences of the rich. Most were built forty or fifty years ago and enabled their owners to survive, but now they are sunk in silence. Nothing moves in them.

Patrik and Adam are impatient and Marek understands them. Their girls are waiting for them at home and their young bodies are thirsty for physical love. Even Marek feels that thirst sometimes, when he thinks of Natalia.

Sometimes Marek wonders about Tomas. The young man has a brilliant mind and can understand all Eli's sayings. He also grasps the mission of the Followers of Eli and the meaning of this pilgrimage. He even claims that the pilgrimage is taking place under the sign of a special grace and that what is happening to them is as inevitable as what happened to Eli. Despite all this, Marek is not sure if he should consider him a real follower. Something is missing in Tomas and that is the sheer surrender involved in faith. That Eli was the Messiah is a matter of inexorable logic, and he is prepared to propagate this sense of the inexorable. Marek cannot see wonder in him. Or that groping in the dark. Those moments when you know something even though you don't understand.

It is the rivers that hold them up the longest. Once dried up streams have become fierce torrents prone to overflow their banks. Most of the bridges have been washed away. It often rains, sometimes for several days without stopping. Sometimes in the evenings the travellers sit by a campfire naked and hang their garments over the flames.

In the middle of May they finally reach the territory of the Federation of Maritime Nations. Not that there is much to show behind this high-sounding name. There is no functioning government.

On the second day of their journey on Federation territory they approach the barbed wire of the first Czech settlement. The surrounding fields are sown and the pastures grazed. The houses inside are modern and large. The guard doesn't want to let them in. "Why should I give a damn about you?"

Tomas tries to persuade him that Marek is a real prophet.

"I don't give a damn. He's not my prophet. I'd send all prophets to hell," the guard curses, but he lets them through.

Inside the settlement, however, they arouse active hostility. An older woman in front of a white house has an expression close to hatred on her face, and all they have done is ask her for water. "Followers of Eli? I'll set the dogs on you! My sister's daughter: they brainwashed her. They said some messiah had been born in Holesovice! Bullshit! Why would he be born in a shithole like that? There are no messiahs. There never were. And there's no God either. None of it's worth shit. And you can get the hell out of here."

They prefer not to linger, and end up sleeping two kilometres further on in an abandoned Balkan village. It is not completely deserted, for a few desiccated old men and women are eking out an existence here. They walk bent over almost at right angles, tottering on two sticks. They don't talk but at most whisper.

"Most Czechs headed here, back then," Marek explains. "The Austrians and Germans pushed down into Italy. The Germans, Danes and French into Spain. When we reached here with Eli, he had two years left to live. We had been on the road for five years. And this is where we ran into Czechs. The rich ones had already been here for some time. They had flown here in their own aircars, or hired some. When the Norwegians were buying in Prague, they were already buying down here. Houses, land, businesses. They gave us the sort of welcome we've just experienced now. They were unfriendly. Eli's message that civilization was soon going to end didn't go down well with them. They didn't want to listen. They reckoned that here they would be able to live as they had until then. Maybe even better, because they were no longer limited by laws. Anyone who was enterprising and wasn't hampered by a conscience could take what he wanted. They behaved atrociously even to the locals. They allied with the Croatian Mafia. Eli was appalled, and he wasn't going to keep his mouth shut. He was twenty-eight, and hardened by years of moving about on the run, and he already had the toughness of a man. Earlier he had been persuading people by his gentleness, but now he did it by anger. One time he broke into the banquet of some local rich man. There were guerillas all over the place, guarding it, and snipers had him in their sights. Only they didn't shoot. In Prague the man had been the owner of a chain of restaurants, and here he had invested in vineyards. The tables were groaning with food. Eli came right into the room and confronted the man and his guests. 'Haven't you learned anything from what has happened?' he said. 'Do you still believe you can buy yourself life? Only a few of us will live to see the new beginning. I won't, but you won't either.'

"And do you know what was the best that man could do? He just sat there in his chair with his shaven head, and already drunk. First he wanted to get up, but when he realized he might not manage it, he remained sitting. He looked at Eli in an almost apologetic way and said, 'Well in that case we might as well enjoy a little drink and food. Isn't that better than waiting to die off?'"

"I still don't get it," Tomas said thoughtfully. "Why Eli was rejected by the Czechs of all people, when he was Czech."

"I think it's understandable. People don't believe that a miracle could be a part of their own lives. And the closer they are to a miracle, the more they resist it. When you think about it... not even the Jews accepted Jesus, even though they considered themselves the chosen people and were waiting for a messiah. I went to school in Bohemia – not something you ever experienced – and I can tell you that everyone there knew everything. They knew how to save the world, how to do politics, and how to protect the Central European Federation. But nobody ever said that a messiah was coming and he

72

The End of his Tether

It is already June. For the past few days the sun has been scorching their heads. It still has power, although the air is not as hot as it used to be. Marek is counting the days. The 7th of July is precisely a month away. There is a good chance of them reaching the tomb on the day of the sad anniversary. Every painful step forward confirms Marek's determination to be on time. But the reasons are twofold. The second reason is the more pressing. Because Eli… will wait. While Natalia, if that was truly what she meant by her message, will be there specifically on that day. Marek must not be late, but he doesn't want to get there early either.

The landscape is greener than it was thirty-three years ago, and apart from residences and settlements encircled by walls and wires it is almost uninhabited. Most of the smaller roads are falling apart, but the ones that lead to the residences are still maintained. Yet even these protected enclaves of migrants are growing old. Those who had a messiah within reach but failed to recognize him are now full of anger. It is their curse. Marek decides to bypass New Brno and another two settlements of followers. "We'll leave it to the return journey," he assures Patrick and Adam, who have been looking forward to staying there. "I don't know if I will be coming back, but you definitely will. Then you can make stops there."

As he says this, he realizes that he isn't reckoning with a return journey. He wouldn't have the strength for it anyway. He is going back to the one for whom he was born.

At the end of June they are close. So close that they can allow themselves a rest in one place for a few days. They find oil and hardened honey in a little stone house on a slope. They chew their meat, but Tomas is still crazy with hunger. He has never known this level of hardship. He gives Adam his gold chain. "Buy some bread, butter and eggs, please."

"We could have stopped in one of our settlements," mutters Venca, and it sounds like a reproach.

Marek can see that Tomas is at the end of his tether. And he has still not told him the most important part, how Eli perished. "You know what, Venca, why don't you go to the nearest follower colony? It's only a day's travel from here. You can take Tomas with you. In fact, why don't you all go? Leave me a piece of meat. I'll beg some milk over there, where that herd of goats is grazing. That'll be enough for me."

Patrik thinks Marek is being self-sacrificing, and he won't have any of it. "I'll stay with you Marek. I won't leave you."

"I won't leave you either," Adam chimes in.

But Marek doesn't see it as sacrifice. He wants to be alone. There are only two days of travel left to Dubrovnik. Not even that. He needs to prepare himself.

Finally he persuades them. Early in the morning he watches them through a small window in a stone wall as they stumble down the slope. The long journey has left its marks on them. They left Vinohrady young and strong, and now their skin hangs off them. But soon it will be over, Marek reflects.

At last some time to himself. For three months they have been together all the time. It is pleasant in the little house. The electricity doesn't work but there is running water. Once someone survived here, but then left forever. A mouse or bat rustles in the attic. Marek breathes in the solitude, gulps it down. Later he walks over to the slope where goats are grazing and he finds an old shepherd sitting on a stone. The man looks a hundred years old, although he must certainly be younger. Marek's appearance in no way surprises him. "Czechs?" he asks. His tone is critical.

Marek nods. "Do you have any milk or cheese to spare?"

The shepherd stands up. "Come with me."

Marek follows him up the slope. There is another little stone house there. The man goes inside and comes out with a mug of milk, flatbreads and cheese for Marek. "You crazy Czechs. What's your problem?"

Marek shrugs. He could have said something about Eli, but it would have been pointless.

"Thanks. Many thanks."

The shepherd waves a hand. "If there's something they haven't got, it's like they don't have anything. Czechs want everything, but what good does it do them?"

73

"Podolsky rules in Dubrovnik"

Marek sits through the whole day. His mind is empty, but in the evening he is suddenly sad. He closes his eyes, and the sadness becomes nostalgia. Marek has been relating his memories to Tomas every evening, and so his brain has got used to the exercise of memory just at this hour. Only when Tomas was with him, his nostalgia was not so intense. Now it is very hard to bear. The tears ooze through Marek's closed lids. He is once again by Eli's cot in Holesovice. Once again he takes Eli down to the river. He hugs him at night before he sleeps. He is searching for his soul, for his strange, incomprehensible thoughts. Even at thirty he was still Marek's little brother.

When they approached Dubrovnik back then, Eli already had plenty of quarrels and recriminations behind him. He was angry at the way people refused to learn. He had been showing his bitterness and disappointment.

Dubrovnik was like a fortress. It was encircled by a new wall. Embrasures had been built above it in the rocks, too, so that no one could attack the city, as people said had happened back in the twentieth century. Landing strips had also been built up high for aircars. The richest Czechs had transferred their assets here.

Eli decided to go inside, to try to persuade them to turn away from the lives they were living. To this day Marek has never been sure if it was something Eli simply didn't have the power to do, or if it was a revolt against his own destiny. If he had felt compelled to end it, or wanted to end it. And to this day Marek has been angry with him because of it. Because Eli should not have left Marek like that. He should not have died on him.

Marek has reproached himself a thousand times for not stopping him. But could he have stopped him? All Marek's previous experience suggested that Eli could never be prevented from doing what he had to do. And so they had walked together right up to the gate above the city. And they had not been allowed in, and the guards had threatened to shoot them if they showed their faces there again. Hana had been with them, Petr too, and absolutely furious at the insanity of what Eli wanted to do. Then there had been Alex and two families. They had retreated with Eli to a safe distance and everyone had been relieved that it hadn't worked out. Except Eli had said he would go anyway, and get inside.

They had lain beside each other that night, for the last time. Marek had not slept. Neither had Eli. Marek had felt his brother's body trembling inside. At one moment their palms had touched and their fingers interlinked. "Forgive me, my dear Marek," Eli had whispered. "You're the best brother in the world."

As Marek remembers it today, the tears fall down his cheeks. It had been the last time they spoke together. Towards morning Marek had fallen asleep, and when he woke up, Eli was gone.

He has never understood how Eli managed to get into the city. Oh, his powers of persuasion. He somehow talked them into letting him through.

In the morning Marek had tried to get inside to find him, but they had just driven him away. They had even fired in the air. Everyone had then sat down a few hundred metres from the gate in a former bistro by the highway. Every so often an armoured car would drive by. After two days another such car, silver, had driven out of the gate and stopped beside them. Loud music had been coming from inside. The door had opened and two men had thrown Eli's lifeless body at their feet.

"Here's your prophet for you."

Eli had been beaten out of all recognition. They must have killed him with clubs.

Marek was to hear various reports of what had happened inside. There were supporters of Eli inside Dubrovnik too. It had been Eli's misfortune that he always got what he wanted, and that included persuading the bodyguards of a man called Podolsky – not the richest, but the most brutal powerful man in the town – to take him to their boss. Podolsky owned a palace on the ancient square. He made sure that every imaginable material pleasure was available in the town. Czechs with big money here could enjoy casinos, enslaved girls and yachts.

Nobody witnessed Eli's confrontation with Podolsky, and so stories spread. According to one, Podolsky had fallen apart and started weeping under the pressure of Eli's personality and it was his bodyguard who beat Eli to death because they couldn't bear to see it. According to another, Podolsky's fear of Eli turned into brutal hatred. He had Eli locked up and early the next day beaten to death in front of his friends. According to yet another, Eli prophesied that Podolsky would have no more children. His first son had died in an accident after getting drunk on a yacht, and Eli told Podolsky that children would no longer be born and nobody would be able to do anything about it. Apparently this so enraged Podolsky that he beat Eli to death himself, on the spot, and because he wanted it to be known, he sent the body back to the followers. That would fit with the legend that was sprayed on Eli's bloody clothes: "Podolsky rules in Dubrovnik."

74

What will become of us now?

Recriminations, love, pain, reconciliation. Marek is alone for a whole four days. And every moment of them is full of one of these emotions. And the whole time he talks with Eli. On the morning of the fourth day he strips and goes to wash in a stone basin. His own nakedness surprises him. He sees the tendons and protruding bones, the wrinkled skin in places where all the fat has gone. He submerges himself, and when he is drying off in the sun later, he feels ridiculous. Surely this is not him – it's just his earthly dwelling. But it's a dwelling with a memory. It remembers touches, wounds, blisters… and the relief that Natalia's hands brought him. A man is so wretched in his body, he thinks, but when someone touches it with love, it is like salvation. Marek is journeying to Eli, but thanks to Natalia he is no longer just his brother's brother; he is himself, with his body too. He is saved.

In the afternoon the young men return. Marek can see that even just a few days without him have done them good. Adam and Patrik have accepted Tomas as one of them, and even seem to respect him although he is a one-in-five child. The three look like a cheerful band of young men. The future lies in them.

They bring food and Marek enjoys a decent meal with them. It is the 4th of July. It will be enough if they set off the day after tomorrow.

The next day Marek relates and Tomas writes it all down – the last chapter of Eli's story. Marek is calm now. He speaks slowly, in fact dictating to Tomas. "We were afraid it would happen, but when we saw his limp body in front of us, it was as if life was over for us. All life. We took it as the death of the last hope. What would become of us now?

"The first of us to recover himself was Petr. He always knew how to think ahead. He said it could be the start of a legend. You know how it was with Jesus. Now the most important thing was to bury him. In some secret place, but so as people would still know about it. I was angry with Petr for thinking in such a calculating way. He didn't seem to us to be experiencing enough pain. But nobody had a better idea, and so we took Eli's terribly disfigured body and carried it up the hills.

"We wanted at all costs to get away from the gate of that accursed town. We went on until we were high above the sea, until we were over the skyline and Dubrovnik with its splendid medieval centre on that promontory was no longer visible. Around us there were white limestone rocks and rubble. We kept going for a while and saw a depression in the rock. Around it there was short fresh grass and purple, white and yellow flowers. That freshness told us it was the right place. We buried him there in the hollow.

"We didn't know how to mark the grave. We wondered whether we should put a cross there. Hana was against the idea. I reminded her that Eli hadn't rejected Jesus. And so we made the sign of the cross in rocks. Petr said it wasn't enough, and we needed to find a stonemason and have Eli's name carved in the rock. We spent the night about an hour's journey away in an empty granary and in the morning we went to the village to find a stonemason. When we were coming back to the grave we hoped for a miracle. We imagined that the stones would be cast aside and the grave empty, and he would be sitting there – or at least his spirit. And he would speak to us and tell us what we ought to do. We were all picturing something like that, but nobody said it out loud. Only the tomb was just as we had left it. Everything was the same. The stonemason carved what we asked him to carve. When he saw those numbers he looked at us with surprise. Yes, it had struck him too, a mere thirty years: Eli 18th May 2105 – 7th July 2135.

"We stayed nearby for another ten days and went to check on the tomb every morning. It became obvious that there would be no miracle. They all waited for me to tell them what we would do now, but I wasn't a leader or a prophet. Just his brother. I saw that it wasn't safe for the Followers of Eli in Croatia, and that it could get even worse. The Czechs who didn't believe in Eli hated us. Someone said that life was better in Greece. That the Greeks were more friendly and fewer people had gone there from the rest of Europe. So I said, and I didn't even know how I found the courage to say it, 'We'll go to Greece.'"

"And is the tomb still there?" Tomas asks after a moment. "The one we're going to?"

Marek looks Tomas in the eye: "I don't know. I haven't been there since then. It will be thirty-four years. But I've heard that the Followers have built a shrine around the site. Apparently it doesn't bother too many people and there's even a road leading to it from Dubrovnik. Natalia told me about it, but she'd never been there herself. She fled from the town five years ago and hadn't been interested in Eli back then."

"Well, I'm certainly curious," says Tomas. "And I can just imagine how it must be for you."

No, you can't imagine, thought Marek. Nobody can imagine. But he says nothing out loud.

75

I will go by myself

In the morning they set out. They see more and more fortified residences, but in most of them there are no signs of life. Maybe they are empty, or maybe their ageing childless owners are wandering about somewhere inside, hidden from the world.

Some places are beginning to look familiar to Marek and old feelings are stirring in him again. This time he thinks of how he has filled these thirty-four years and how mankind has spent them. At least the terrible time of dying has already receded and the wounds are healing. The greatest fear is no longer death, but the absence of birth, and Marek knows from Eli that not to be born is a good solution.

As night falls they creep into one of many deserted guesthouses. There are beds and mattresses here, but Marek cannot sleep. He keeps going back to that last night next to Eli; once again he lives his little brother's fear and his own helplessness. There was nothing he could do.

Then there is nothing left but to get up and go. To walk over the hill – which is far more overgrown than it had been back then – and walk up to where the rocks start. Marek is suddenly overcome with anxiety. It is a completely different kind of anxiety from the kind he would have expected. His jaw clenches and every second is tormenting. Will she be there?

And the answer comes back: No, of course she won't be. It's too unlikely.

But if she isn't there, then what? Marek knows that feeling. It will be the same as when they found the tomb just as they had left it. Nothing. A miracle that has failed to happen.

So why the whole pilgrimage then? Marek asks himself, still in the grip of anxiety. For Eli's sake, or for hers? He is unable to figure it out. It's strange, he thinks. He was with her for a mere month, but with Eli for thirty years. How could they both have equal weight?

Over the crest of the hill two paths converge. Back then Marek and the other mourners had come along the right hand path. Only a couple of hundred metres remain. Back then the place was visible from here, but the trees have thickened and grown. Finally they come out of the wood and see it… The shrine is bigger than a chapel and smaller than a church. It is built out of white stone, with a glass roof that gleams in the sunlight. That's good, thinks Marek – let Eli have light. He turns to the others. "I will go on by myself. Please wait for me."

"But what about those guys?" Venca objects.

He has a point: a little way away from the shrine there are two men sitting on a bench. For Marek's old eyes it is too far to see properly. "It doesn't matter." He waves a hand and walks on. These are the last few moments of hope, but now that Marek sees Eli's resting-place he knows it is not the last hope. There is another, an eternal hope. For Marek definitely. A place at Eli's side. A rest together. That is how it was always done in families, after all. Marek turns and takes a few steps back.

"Tomas, when I die, I want to lie here with him. Can you arrange that?"

"I think so." Tomas nods, and seems moved.

Marek does not turn back a second time. He slowly approaches the shrine. A great deal has changed. Paths lead here from all sides. Now he can see the two men properly. They look like gorillas, private bodyguards with shades, large bellies and shaven heads. What do they want here? When they see Marek, they give him no more than a glance.

He is already walking on grass. The same flowers as before are blooming here, but the shrine takes up the greater part of the sward. The door is ajar, beautifully carved – unlike the door at the Shrine of the Birth.

There are sounds coming from inside. Marek is already in the doorway. He peers inside. The sound is of weeping. But what kind of weeping? It is welling up from someone's throat like water from a burst dam. It is as hot as in a glasshouse here. The interior is simple and clean and incorporates the rocky depression in which they buried Eli. A woman sits leaning against the rock, and in her arms she holds a baby – a newborn, tiny. It is she who is weeping so bitterly.

Marek approaches her and… it is she! Barely recognizable, but still she. She has a much fuller face, swollen even more by crying. It is his Natalia. She stares up at him from below and looks neither surprised nor happy to see him. The reason for her tears must be strong enough to drown everything else.

Marek bends down to her. "Natalia, what has happened?"

She looks up at him and tries to say something. Finally she forces words out, "He spoke to me. I met him."

"Who? Who spoke to you?" Her weeping discourages Marek from telling her how happy he is.

"Eli. Just a moment ago." Finally she manages to speak coherently. She takes a deep breath. "When those two guys who guard me eventually left me alone, I went inside, and he was waiting for me."

Marek is bewildered. Why has he shown himself to her and not to him? When it is Marek that has come to see him? "I can't see him, Natalia. He's not here."

"Not now. He told me to greet you. He said you would be coming in a moment. He was so kind, so infinitely kind. He said… he said…" She bursts into tears again. Again the tears stream down her face. Natalia raises her free hand and pulls Marek down towards her. He can't bend that far, so he has to kneel. She kisses him madly on the cheeks. He is immediately wet from her tears.

"What did he say?" He presses her, and out of the corner of his eye he sees that tiny human being, who has just fallen asleep on his mother's breast.

"He said he would be the Messiah. Him." She lifts up the baby. "The second Messiah that will lead mankind back to the light. The true Messiah who will come after him."

The second Messiah? thinks Marek. So that was true?

"And he was so kind. So kind Marek. And he was smiling at me."

Marek strokes her hair. In her weeping and maternity she is so honest, so beautifully real. "And what child is this?" he wonders after a long period of thought. "Whose child is it?"

"Whose do you think? You silly fool. It's our son, of course."

There is a mist before Marek's eyes. Two powerful messages jostle to get through the gates of his mind, which suddenly seem too narrow for them. A second messiah then? His child? Not just Eli?

But then something even more powerful rises in him, something that comes not from his head, but from his inner temple, his chest.

Love. The sobbing Natalia with the child in her arms is the most beautiful sight he has ever seen. There are no words to express all that Eli's brother owes her. Not the least of it is that he is no longer just Eli's brother. That he is now first and foremost Marek.

That weeping being is irresistible; weeping beauty, the weeping salvation of the world. Now he kisses her, his lips touch her wet cheek and the tears gather in his own eyes.

But no, he must not weep. He has too much to arrange. Such as where they will live. The child needs a home. But can they get back to Vinohrady? Will her family let her go?

The child murmurs contentedly. A band of light crosses the tiny crumpled face submerged in his mother's shadow.

Then something else occurs to Marek. "What is his name?"

Natalia's eyes meet his. "This whole time, it is you that has been in me."

Footsteps sound from the entrance. Marek knows they belong to the bodyguards. Natalia glances in their direction and her expression changes. It is suddenly impatient and abstracted. Fear flickers across her face. "I've got to go now."

"Go? With them?" Marek cannot understand. "Can't we be together?"

"I'll always be with you, Marek."

76

Marek

Marek walks away from the shrine, back to his companions. Although hardly a minute has passed since his parting from Natalia, it feels to him like that last night spent with Eli, a memory of the distant past. He does not know if he will ever see her again. He does not know if he will ever see his son again. This means that the fate of humankind depends on her now, but Marek has no doubts about her. He knows that she is strong and practical, and in a strange way simple enough to be able to bring a child up to the threshold of adulthood without standing in his way. Simple enough for sainthood.

Then he realizes something else. "Marek. His name is Marek."

Also by Martin Vopěnka, from Barbican Press

The Fifth Dimension

A cosmic adventure story of big ideas and murder.

Your business is dead. It seems like a deal – leave your family behind in Prague for a year, isolate yourself in a research station in the Andes, and come home with a fortune. With a treatise on black holes for company, Jakob settles in at altitude. The air is thin. Strangers pass by on dangerous pilgrimage while his young wife and kids take life in his mind. In mountain starkness, the big questions take shape – like what happens to love inside a black hole?

'Ably translated from the original Czech by Hana Sklenkova, The Fifth Dimension is a weighty and at times challenging read, its themes nothing less than life, death, the universe and love. It's absorbing, haunting and intellectually engaging throughout, with a gut-punch denouement.'

> – James Lovegrove, *The Financial Times*

'Never less than thoroughly compelling… This alliance between dry style and colourful subject creates in the novel a glorious uncertainty which propels the reader through a narrative… Beautifully balanced – as any novel, science fictional or otherwise, should be.'

> – Dan Hartland, *Vector*

'A potent and haunting novel of black holes, solitude and the sublime, it is never less than immensely readable and absorbing.'

> – Adam Roberts